HALF IN LOVE WITH ARTFUL DEATH

▼

HALF IN LOVE WITH ARTFUL DEATH

BILL CRIDER

MINOTAUR BOOKS

A THOMAS DUNNE BOOK

NEW YORK

A THOMAS DUNNE BOOK FOR MINOTAUR BOOKS.
An imprint of St. Martin's Publishing Group.

HALF IN LOVE WITH ARTFUL DEATH. Copyright © 2014 by Bill Crider. All rights reserved. Printed in the United States of America. For information, address St. Martin's Press, 175 Fifth Avenue, New York, N.Y. 10010.

www.thomasdunnebooks.com
www.minotaurbooks.com

The Library of Congress Cataloging-in-Publication Data is available upon request.

ISBN 978-1-250-03967-5 (hardcover)
ISBN 978-1-250-03968-2 (e-book)

Minotaur books may be purchased for educational, business, or promotional use. For information on bulk purchases, please contact Macmillan Corporate and Premium Sales Department at 1-800-221-7945, extension 5442, or write specialmarkets@macmillan.com.

First Edition: August 2014

10 9 8 7 6 5 4 3 2 1

To Charles Ferguson, an Artful Guy

HALF IN
LOVE WITH
ARTFUL
DEATH

▼

Chapter 1

▼

Sheriff Dan Rhodes didn't know much about art, but he knew what he didn't like.

One thing he didn't like was having to listen to Burt Collins's complaints. It was the sheriff's job to listen to complaints, of course, or so the county commissioners insisted, but Collins got tiresome after a while. One day he'd come in to complain about the feral pigs that were rooting up his property, and the next day he'd be trying to get Rhodes to arrest Billy Joe Byron for picking something out of his trash. Billy Joe picked up things from trash all over town, and there was no law against it, but that didn't matter to Collins, who had a natural tendency to become irate at least once a day.

Today, he was irate about artists.

"They're all over town," he told Rhodes, "making a mess of everything. You need to run them out of here right now."

"They're our guests," Rhodes said. "They're bringing a lot of money into town. I'm pretty sure the hotel managers wouldn't want me to run them out. Neither would the folks who own the restaurants."

"I'm as much a citizen of this town as the people who own those restaurants," Collins said. Collins had been a track coach for the Clearview Catamounts at one time, but he'd retired as soon as he was eligible. Rhodes had heard that the track team had made immediate improvement. Collins had been slim in his coaching days, but he'd gained considerable weight since then. He didn't appear to have exercised at all since his retirement, and his face was becoming mottled as he got more worked up. Rhodes hoped he'd taken his blood pressure medication. "I'm a lot more of a citizen than those people running the hotels, those Patels. They're not even Americans."

There'd been more than one little run-in between Collins and the Patels, and the Patels thought that Collins was guilty of some vandalism at the hotels. He might very well have been the culprit, but Rhodes hadn't been able to prove it.

"You're wrong about the Patels," Rhodes said. "The Patels are citizens one and all."

Collins looked doubtful. "Well, maybe they are, if you say so, but they don't look like Americans to me. Neither do those artists, far as that goes. You seen their hair?"

Rhodes thought briefly about his own hair and the thin spot in back. He wondered if it had gotten any thinner lately.

"What's wrong with their hair?" he asked.

"There's this one woman, hers looks like a bunch of orange corkscrews sticking out of her head. I never saw the like."

For just a second Rhodes wondered if he'd slipped into a time warp and wound up back in the sixties. Wasn't that the era when folks got upset about how people's hair looked? Or was it the seventies?

"They're all over the place," Collins said. "In the park, downtown, out in the country. Running around like cockroaches."

Rhodes looked over at Hack Jensen, the dispatcher, who had his back to the sheriff and was pretending to be busy with something on his computer. Rhodes knew he was listening in and loving every minute of it, however.

"They're not running around," Rhodes said. "Mostly they're sitting still. Or standing still. They can't run around and paint."

Collins wasn't to be deterred by that argument. "Well, they might as well be running around. It's like an infestation of 'em. Besides, I don't call what they're doing painting. Painting is what you do to a house or a barn. They're just messing around."

"I don't think they'd agree with you," Rhodes said.

"You seen any of their so-called pictures?"

"Several," Rhodes said.

"Don't look like anything I ever saw. I saw one that was supposed to be cows. You seen that one?"

"I don't know for sure."

"No wonder," Collins said. "How could you know for sure? You can't, 'cause what they're calling cows looks more like blotches. Can't even tell if they got legs." He paused. "This is all that Lonnie Wallace's fault."

Lonnie Wallace was a young man who'd inherited a beauty shop and an antiques store at about the same time. He'd pretty much given up on the antiques after a short time because he'd found he couldn't run both businesses at once even if they were only a block apart. So he'd converted the front part of the store into an art gallery for local artists. That had worked out for a while, and then Eric Stewart had moved to town. He and Wallace became friends, and before long Lonnie had hired Stewart as manager of both the store and the gallery.

Stewart was something of an artist himself, and one of his ideas for generating more local interest was to hold a workshop and invite amateur artists from all over the state to attend. Stewart was teaching at some of the sessions, and Don McClaren, the art teacher at the local community college branch, was teaching the others.

"You'd better watch what you say about Lonnie," Rhodes told Collins. "He's a friend of mine. And he's done a lot for the downtown, what's left of it."

That wasn't strictly true, and Rhodes knew it, but since Lonnie had opened the art gallery, which, along with the antiques, was housed in a building that had once been a thriving hardware store, there'd been a little stirring of life in what was left of Clearview's central business district. A lot of the old buildings had fallen down or been razed, but a new senior citizens center had just opened, and a couple of the old stores had been remodeled and repurposed. A florist and a dentist had taken over a couple of the buildings, and others were home to a church and thrift store. Now and then there were even a few people on the sidewalks.

"You say you're friends with Lonnie?" Collins asked.

"That's right."

"I don't see how that can be. Don't you know he's a—"

"Stop right there," Rhodes said, interrupting him, "before you get yourself in real trouble."

Collins's mottled face got even redder in several places. "Man's got a right to say what he pleases."

"Man's got a right to suffer the consequences, too," Rhodes told him.

"Don't see how a man could be friends with a—"

"Uh-uh," Rhodes said, holding up a hand to stop him. "Don't say it."

Collins stood up. "I don't have to stay here and put up with this."

"You sure don't," Rhodes said. "In fact, it might be a good idea for you to be on your way. Might be a good idea for you to do a little thinking about things, too. Maybe change your attitude a little bit while you're at it."

"I'm not changing," Collins said. "You'll hear about this. I'm going to talk to your bosses and see if we can't do something about getting some real law in this town, somebody that'd do something about those artsy weirdos."

Weirdos. That was a term Rhodes hadn't heard in a good many years. Maybe he really had slipped into a time warp.

"Look, Mr. Collins," he said. "We have a lot more serious things to worry about around here than a few artists drawing pictures you don't like. We have people cooking meth in their car trunks in the Walmart parking lot. We have wild hogs tearing up property all over the county. We have automobile accidents and robberies. We have—"

"I didn't come to hear about how bad the crime in Blacklin County is," Collins said. "I came to get one little thing taken care of, and you say you can't do anything about it. Doesn't sound like you're doing much about all the other crimes, either, much less those hogs. I guess what it boils down to is that you can't handle your job."

"You just need to cool down and think about all the good Lonnie Wallace has done for the town," Rhodes told him. "You'll see that the artists are part of that."

"I don't think so," Collins said. "I think they're bad for the community, and so is that Lonnie Wallace and anybody else like him."

Collins turned and huffed out of the jail. Rhodes thought he could see steam coming out of Collins's ears, though that was probably only his imagination.

Hack waited until the door had closed behind Collins. Then he swiveled his chair around and said, "You'd think ever'body was over that kind of thing now."

"What kind of thing?" Rhodes asked.

"You know. Lonnie bein' gay."

"Collins is old-fashioned."

"That's about as polite a way of puttin' it as I ever heard. I'm older'n he is, and—"

"You're older'n anybody in town," said Lawton, the jailer, as he came into the office from the cellblock. He held the mop he'd been cleaning with in one hand. "You're even older'n me."

"I might be old," Hack said, giving Lawton a dirty look, "but I ain't any older'n you. Nobody's older'n you. Dirt ain't older'n you. I'm surprised they didn't find your bones on that fossil dig the sheriff got mixed up in a few years ago, right along with those mammoth bones."

Rhodes remembered the mammoth dig. It hadn't turned out well.

"If I'm still here," Lawton said, leaning the mop against the wall, "which I am, how could they find my bones?"

Rhodes knew from experience that this kind of dialogue could go on for quite a while. He leaned back in his chair to see how long it would go on this time.

"One thing's for sure," Hack said. "You ain't bony."

Lawton ran a hand over his stomach. "You got that right. Pleasingly plump is what I am."

"Call it what you want to. You're a fossil, anyway."

"You gotta remember," Lawton said, "I'm not the one talkin' about how old he is. You're the one doin' that. I was just agreein' with you. Kinda surprised you'd admit it, though. You been sparkin' that Miz McGee just like you was a whippersnapper."

"Don't you get started on Miz McGee," Hack said. "You're just jealous 'cause no woman could put up with you."

"Ha," Lawton said. "Shows how much you know about it. It's just a good thing for you that I'm your friend and not the kinda snake who'd try to steal your girlfriend."

Ms. McGee hadn't been a girl in a long time, Rhodes thought. A really long time.

"I'd like to see you try to steal her," Hack said. "She'd laugh in your face."

Rhodes had a feeling the argument was about to get to the "Oh yeah?" stage, and he was going to step in when the telephone rang. Hack gave Lawton a glare and answered.

"Sheriff's Department." He listened for a few seconds, then said, "We'll have somebody there in five minutes."

Hack hung up and turned to Rhodes. "There's some kind of fight at Lonnie's art gallery. You think Burt's mixed up in it?"

Rhodes was already out of his chair and on his way to the door.

"I'll find out," he said. "Call Andy and have him back me up."

"You might already have backup," Hack said.

"Andy's there?"

"Nope, but that was your friend Seepy Benton on the phone. He says not to worry. He has everything under control."

"Uh-oh," Rhodes said.

Chapter 2

▼

Seepy Benton didn't have everything under control.

The crowd outside the former hardware store was too large to be made up of just the artists, and Rhodes realized that some of the people from the new senior center must have come out to watch the fun, and maybe some of the other people from the somewhat revitalized downtown besides.

Most of the people weren't being unruly. Rhodes judged that at least half of them, and maybe more, were taking video of the unruly ones with their cell phones. Some of the videos would soon arrive on YouTube or Facebook or both, and shortly after that someone would see them and call the mayor or one of the commissioners, who would then call Rhodes and want to know why he was letting people take videos that hurt the reputation of the city of Clearview and all of Blacklin County.

It didn't matter how many times Rhodes told them that people had a constitutional right to take video of anything that was happening. The commissioners and the mayor held him personally responsible for any bad publicity that was generated. Rhodes could have mentioned that just about a hundred percent of the population of the rest of Texas and the entire United States didn't care what happened in Clearview and Blacklin County and that really there was no reputation to harm. Nobody would have appreciated that, however, so Rhodes never brought it up.

He got out of the county car and leaned against it while he waited for Andy to arrive. He looked over the crowd to see if he recognized anyone and saw Don McClaren, who looked more like a football coach than an art teacher, and in fact he'd played football in college with moderate success. He hadn't been quite big enough or fast enough for the pros, but he'd kept himself in good shape. He wore dark shorts and an Athletic Department T-shirt, which was what he always seemed to be wearing when Rhodes saw him. The shorts were smeared with something that looked like clay, which it probably was since McClaren was a potter, among other things.

At the edge of the group, just watching, was a short woman with gray hair fixed in a bun. Nora Fischer, Rhodes thought, his high school history teacher. She must have come out of the senior center, unless she'd taken up painting, which was always a possibility.

Rhodes also saw the woman with the orange hair, though it didn't look like it was twisted into corkscrews to him. She was in the midst of the crowd, and from the looks of it she was berating someone.

Seepy Benton, who supposedly had everything under control, was nowhere to be seen.

Rhodes heard a siren in the distance. Andy Shelby was on the way. Andy was fairly new to the department and still enthusiastic about the job, maybe a bit too enthusiastic, but this time the siren was probably a good idea. Rhodes hadn't used it, but as Andy got closer, some of the people in the center of the crowd heard the sound and began moving back. When they did, Rhodes saw Seepy Benton, who was standing on one side of Burt Collins.

Seepy was actually Dr. C. P. Benton, mathematics professor at the community college branch. The initials had given him the name by which a lot of people knew him. He'd come to Clearview to leave behind a failed romance at a community college near Houston, and to occupy his time he'd gone through the Citizens' Sheriff's Academy. Somehow he'd gotten the idea that his attendance at the academy had given him semiofficial status with the sheriff's department, and he'd appointed himself Rhodes's civilian helper. Rhodes had to admit that Benton had been helpful now and then, though he didn't admit that to Benton.

If McClaren looked like a football coach, Benton looked more like a rabbi, though today he was wearing a Western-style straw hat that looked as if he might have found it on the street and decided to keep it. Rhodes had no idea what Benton had been doing with the artists, though if Nora Fischer had taken up art, it wasn't beyond the realm of possibility that Benton had done so, too.

Standing on the other side of Collins was Eric Stewart. Benton had a grip on Burt Collins's right arm, and Stewart had a grip on the left. Collins occasionally jerked on one arm or the other, but he couldn't pull away.

Andy Shelby parked beside Rhodes, across the street from the hardware store. He cut the siren when he got out of the car, and it made a dying whine. He left the light bar flashing, and everyone on the opposite side of the street stopped shoving and jostling and stood looking over at the sheriff and the deputy.

Rhodes looked back at them, doing his best narrow-eyed Clint Eastwood impression. He didn't know if it was effective, but he'd always wanted to try it out.

"What's the beef, Sheriff?" Andy asked.

"We're about to find out," Rhodes said.

He started across the street, and Andy followed. When they got about halfway across, Seepy Benton called out, "I want to make a citizen's arrest, Sheriff."

Every time he heard the phrase "citizen's arrest," Rhodes thought of Gomer Pyle arresting Barney Fife.

"So do I, Sheriff," Stewart said. He was a tall, thin man about sixty with thick gray hair that reminded Rhodes of how his own hair was thinning.

"They're crazy, Sheriff," Collins said. "You make 'em let me go."

Rhodes looked around the crowd again. Now that they'd stopped arguing and shoving, even more people had their cell phones out and were taking video of the scene.

Rhodes looked at Andy. "How do you feel about being an Internet star?"

Andy grinned. He removed his carefully creased hat and smoothed down his hair with one hand. "You think there's a chance of one of those videos going viral?"

Rhodes envied anybody who could wear a hat. Even Seepy looked okay in a hat, but Rhodes was probably the only sheriff in Texas who didn't wear one. In a photo in the *Texas Lawman,* taken on the day nearly every sheriff in the state had gathered in Austin to visit legislators, Rhodes was one of only two sheriffs not wearing a hat. Now that his hair was getting thin in the back, a hat would provide him with some protection from the sun. It wasn't in the cards, however. Western hats made Rhodes look more like a comedian trying to do a John Wayne impression than a cowboy. Baseball caps were even worse. There was no way he was going to wear a baseball cap.

A car pulled to a stop back across the street. Rhodes half turned and saw Jennifer Loam get out. Loam had been a reporter for the *Clearview Herald* until she'd been downsized out of a job. Now she had her own news Web site, which claimed to present *A Clear View of Clearview.* She had her own video camera, not much bigger than a cell phone, and probably not much better. She'd started using it as soon as she got out of the car.

"The videos might not go viral," Rhodes told Andy with a nod toward Loam, "but that one will be on Ms. Loam's Web site within the hour."

Andy shrugged and put his hat back on.

"You wouldn't want to try to talk her out of using it, would you?" Rhodes said.

This time Andy blushed a little. Rhodes knew that he'd had his eye on Loam for a while. Romance was in the air.

"I don't think so," Andy said. "I don't want to use my authority to try to intimidate the press."

"Good answer," Rhodes said, and he turned to Seepy Benton. "What're you arresting Mr. Collins for?"

"Destruction of property," Benton said. "Malicious mischief. Or maybe vandalism. I'm not sure of the difference. We didn't learn that in the academy."

"I'm not a vandal," Collins said, trying without success to jerk his arms free. "I didn't do anything."

"It was vandalism, all right," Eric Stewart said. He was considerably taller than either Benton or Collins, and younger than either, probably no more than thirty. "We all just got back here from the morning session and found him. He defaced a lot of paintings before we got to him."

"Spray paint," Benton said. "He put it on one of the sculptures, too."

Collins looked shocked at the accusation. "Me? I didn't do that. Did anybody see me do that?"

It always helped when the culprit confessed, but that wasn't going to happen. Some witnesses wouldn't hurt.

"Anybody see Mr. Collins spray-paint on anything?" Rhodes asked.

Nobody spoke up. Rhodes waited. Finally Eric Stewart said, "No one else was inside when it happened. As I said, we were just getting back. We saw this man"—he jerked Collins's arm— "coming out of the building."

"He must've done it," Benton said. "He tossed the paint can in the trash, and it's still there. Should have his fingerprints all over it."

"That paint'll clean right off whatever it's on," Collins said. "Not that I had anything to do with it."

"It won't clean off," Stewart said. "The paintings are ruined."

"I'd say what they are is *improved,*" Collins said, "and if I'd done the spraying, I'd sure take credit for it."

He seemed to be enjoying himself. Maybe it was all the cameras. Everybody wanted to be an Internet star.

"Why were you in the building?" Rhodes asked him.

"I was looking for somebody to complain to. You wouldn't listen to me. I thought maybe I could talk sense into these people. Instead, they grabbed me."

"We went in and saw what he'd done," Stewart said. "We were lucky to catch him before he got away."

"Now just a minute," Collins said. "I wasn't trying to get away. I was right here on the sidewalk when you came back out."

"Is that right?" Rhodes asked.

Benton nodded. He looked a little sheepish, as well he should, Rhodes thought. Both Benton and Stewart released Collins's arms, and Collins shook himself before stepping away from them.

"Let me see your hands, Burt," Rhodes said.

"Huh?"

"Your hands. Palms out."

Collins put out his hands. Rhodes took each one and looked it over. No paint traces were visible. A test might reveal paint traces, but not if Burt had been wearing gloves. Where were the gloves? That was a good question. There were plenty of places to hide them in the building.

"That's all," Rhodes said. "You can go."

"It's about time," Collins said. "I'm an innocent man, and you're harassing me."

At that moment, Lonnie Wallace came running up. Lonnie had on a Western shirt, jeans, and boots, which some people might have thought of as being odd for the owner/operator of a beauty shop, but it was Lonnie's preferred attire. Rhodes could never wear boots, any more than he could wear a hat, and he envied Lonnie for being able to run in them.

"What's happened?" Lonnie asked, panting a little from his run.

"Somebody fixed up some of your artwork for you," Collins said. "Improved it, you might say." He grinned. "Wasn't me, though, and I didn't see who did it."

What happened next was a matter of some dispute later on, but in describing the video that she posted on her news site,

Jennifer Loam used the words "donnybrook" and "melee." Those seemed like heavy literary terms to Rhodes, who would have just called it a scuffle, and even though the whole thing was caught on video, it was still impossible to say exactly how it had started.

Lonnie Wallace claimed that he slipped, but Collins claimed that he'd been attacked. It was true that Collins was smirking, which might have been an instigation for a fight, but it did appear that Lonnie's foot might have caught on the curb, causing him to stumble forward. No video that Rhodes saw later showed Lonnie's feet.

Rhodes tended to think that Lonnie was telling the truth, since he knew it wasn't easy to run in boots, but several people from the senior center swore that Lonnie had deliberately jumped on Collins. The fact that they were friends of Collins might have swayed their testimony, however. Others said it was clear that Lonnie had stubbed his toe on the curb. Those witnesses were all women who had their hair done at the Beauty Shack, Lonnie's establishment, so that could have had something to do with what they claimed.

It didn't really matter which set of witnesses was correct. The result was that Lonnie fell against Collins. Or attacked him. Lonnie said he merely grabbed Collins to keep from falling down, but the next thing Rhodes knew they were rolling on the sidewalk and there was definitely some slugging and kicking going on. And shouting. Lots of shouting.

Collins's friends jumped to help him, and some of the artists tried to stop them. That was when the donnybrook or melee or brawl began, complete with pushing, chest bumping, fist swinging, and shouting. Lots of shouting.

Andy looked at Rhodes and said, "How do we stop it?"

Rhodes shrugged. It looked worse than it was, but there were already some bloody noses, and there'd be some bruises and black eyes eventually. Those who weren't involved were taking video or watching with considerable interest. Some seemed to be cheering for one side or the other.

"I'll get the bullhorn," Rhodes said.

He went across the street, fetched the bullhorn from the county car, and used it to announce the presence of law officers. No one paid him the least attention. Rhodes put the bullhorn back in the car and turned on the siren and light bar. That slowed things down for a moment, and what happened next was the biggest surprise of the day for Rhodes.

Seepy Benton emerged from the heart of the brawl and started picking off the angriest and most aggressive fighters one by one. Rhodes didn't know what Seepy was doing, exactly, but he appeared to be touching people up around their necks somehow or other. The people would then drop right where they were. They'd have hit the sidewalk if Don McClaren hadn't been right there to catch them and lower them gently down.

After Seepy had disabled three men, the fighting slowed considerably. Rhodes walked over and with Andy's help separated Lonnie and Collins, who were still going at it. Rhodes pulled Lonnie to his feet, and Andy did the same for Collins.

"I'm really sorry," Lonnie said to Collins. "I didn't mean to fall on you."

"Fall on me, my ass," Collins said. "You were trying to kill me, you little—"

"Watch yourself," Rhodes said. "You don't want to start anything again."

"Me start something?" Collins was boiling. "It wasn't my fault. It was his."

"He's apologized," Rhodes said. "You and Lonnie go stand over there out of the way. I'll talk to you in a minute. And no fighting." Without waiting for a response, Rhodes turned and looked at some of the crowd. "It would be a good idea for all of you to get back to what you were doing. We'll investigate here and find out what happened to the artwork. I'd appreciate it if you'd wait a while in the building until I can come talk to you. You can put those cameras away now, though. The excitement is over."

He hoped his last statement was true, and maybe it was. Even if it wasn't, everyone seemed to accept it. The people who'd come out of the senior center started to return to their domino games and Pilates classes. Some of them looked at their videos as they walked, and Rhodes hoped that nobody would trip and fall. The artists, still muttering, went back inside the gallery and antiques building.

Seepy Benton stayed behind, because Jennifer Loam was still there with her camera. Rhodes had a feeling he knew who the next big video star was going to be, and no one would enjoy the attention more than Seepy.

Rhodes was glad that Seepy was the momentary center of attention, as it would give him time for other things. He motioned for Andy.

"I'm going to have a chat with Lonnie and Burt," Rhodes told the deputy. "You go inside and see if you can get a better idea about the damage that Burt . . . or someone . . . did."

Andy looked over at Jennifer Loam, who was now doing a video interview with Seepy Benton.

"Don't worry about Seepy," Rhodes said. "You know he's dating Deputy Grady. He's not looking for a new romance."

"You sure about that?" Andy asked. "He looks interested to me."

"He just likes attention. Call Hack and have him send another deputy, and then check out that paint can and anything else you can find."

Andy did as he was told, but not without a couple of glances back in Seepy's direction.

Lonnie and Burt were already arguing again, so Rhodes went to calm them down. Or try to.

Chapter 3

▼

Before Rhodes could get to the two men, Don McClaren came out of the building and joined them. He got in on the argument and shoved Burt Collins away from Lonnie.

"Hold on," Rhodes said. "Let's not get that started again."

"He's being offensive and insulting," McClaren said. "I think somebody needs to teach him a lesson."

The implication was clear that McClaren would like to be the one to do the teaching, but Rhodes wasn't going to let it happen. Not right then, anyway, even though he had an idea of what Collins might have said.

"It's over," Rhodes said. "You go on back inside, Mr. McClaren."

McClaren didn't argue. He started back toward the building, but halfway to the door, he stopped, turned, and appeared about to return.

"Just go on in," Rhodes said.

McClaren glared at Collins, but that seemed to satisfy him for the moment. He nodded and went back inside.

"Now," Rhodes said, looking at Collins, "let's get this all straight. Lonnie says he fell against you by accident. He's apologized. Seems to me that ought to settle it."

"I'm really sorry," Lonnie said.

"Bull corn," Collins said. "You did it on purpose, and you aren't one bit sorry."

Lonnie looked at Rhodes. "I don't know what else I can say."

Rhodes didn't know, either. Collins had been taunting Lonnie, but that didn't mean that Lonnie had deliberately jumped him.

"Tell you what, Burt," Rhodes said. "You go on home. If you want to file charges on Lonnie, you come to the jail tomorrow and do it. Right now, I have to investigate the vandalism of the paintings and see if I can figure out what happened and who did it."

"Nobody hurt anything in there," Collins said. "Improved it, if anything. You go look. You'll see." He started to leave but stopped and turned. "You can expect me tomorrow. I'll be filing charges for assault and battery."

"You really think he'll file on me?" Lonnie asked when Collins was out of earshot.

Rhodes shrugged. "Hard to say. He'll probably get over it."

"I hope so," Lonnie said. "I guess I'd better go and see what he did to the paintings."

"He says he didn't do it."

"Ha," Lonnie said.

They started toward the door, but Jennifer Loam called out to Rhodes.

"Sheriff, could you just answer a couple of questions for me?"

Rhodes stopped. "If they're quick ones."

Jennifer came over to him, followed by Seepy, who was looking quite pleased with himself.

"It's a little trick I learned when I was training with Professor Lansdale in Nacogdoches," Seepy said. "It's all about pressure points. You don't have to use any fancy moves if you can just touch the pressure points. Not that I don't have some fancy moves. Would you like to have me demonstrate a few on camera?"

"Not right now," Jennifer said. She turned the camera on Rhodes. "Sheriff, do you have any statement to make about what happened here today?"

Rhodes had learned a lot about the Internet in the last year or so. He hadn't realized how many people in Clearview, and the whole county for that matter, looked at their computers or their phones or their tablet devices every day to check on the latest news. Now he knew, and he knew he had to be very careful about what he said because it wasn't just the citizens who checked out Loam's Web site. It was the mayor and the city council and the county commissioners, too. Loam would have the video up on the site within minutes after leaving the scene, and the commissioners would be looking at it soon afterward. Rhodes suspected that they all told their administrative assistants to check it hourly, if not even more often.

"I haven't formed an opinion yet," Rhodes said, feeling a little like a real politician. "I haven't looked over the whole scene to check out the possible vandalism."

"What about the donnybrook we just witnessed? Will there be any charges filed?"

"It was more of a little scuffle," Rhodes said, "and it's all settled now. I don't think it will go any further."

"Mr. Collins didn't seem to feel that way."

"I can't speak for him. I'll just have to wait and see."

"Would you say that Dr. Benton saved the day here?"

Rhodes nodded. "He sure helped calm things down."

"Thank you, Sheriff Rhodes," Loam said. She turned off the camera. "You're getting more noncommittal every day, Sheriff."

"I'm learning," Rhodes said. "You'll have to excuse me now. I need to check on things inside."

"I'll be right behind you," Loam said.

Seepy Benton fell into step beside Rhodes and said, "I hope you're not going to blame me for the donnybrook."

"More like a tussle," Rhodes said, "and I don't blame you even if you did rush to judgment."

"I hope your deputy bagged the paint can," Benton said. "I'm sure Collins's fingerprints are on it."

"Even if they are, he can just claim that he saw the can and picked it up out of curiosity. That won't convict him of anything."

"It would help, wouldn't it?"

"Maybe," Rhodes said.

They entered the store, which, although it wasn't air-conditioned, was cooler than the outside thanks to its high ceilings and the old electric fans with slow-turning wooden blades. The building had much better lighting than when it had been solely an antiques shop, but the old wooden floors were the same.

"Show me the damage," Rhodes told Seepy.

Seepy pointed. "Right over there."

Rhodes should have known. Everyone except for Andy Shelby was gathered along one side of the room, looking at two of the paintings. Andy, who had on a pair of nitrile rubber gloves, was poking around in a trash can, or what Rhodes supposed was a trash can. Given the surroundings, maybe it was some kind of art. Rhodes saw that Andy had already bagged the spray can and set it on a desk near the door, so he left him to his job.

Some of the art displayed on the walls and on little stands in various locations around the big room didn't look much like anything to Rhodes. He knew that art didn't need to be realistic and that his tastes, which ran more to Scrooge McDuck, were far from refined. Still, a blob was a blob. Or maybe not. Maybe if he looked at some of the tags, he'd learn differently.

He didn't get a chance, however, because Lonnie Wallace looked around and saw him. Lonnie walked over and said, "The damage is just terrible, but I can't stay to talk about it. I have to go back to the Beauty Shack. Mrs. Freeman's coming in about five minutes from now, and she's very picky. She won't let anybody do her hair but me. I'll be there if you need me. Just give me a call."

"Sure," Rhodes said. Lonnie hadn't been there when the paintings were vandalized, so he wouldn't be needed for a while. "I might need to see you later. In person."

"Come on by," Lonnie said. "You know where I'll be."

He left, and Rhodes and Seepy went over to the damaged artwork. Loam was already there, documenting everything with her camera. The woman with the orange hair was pointing at a painting and talking.

"You can see that it's ruined," she said.

She moved a little to the side so that Loam could get a closer shot. Rhodes saw that the painting, which had a lot of yellows and pinks and blues and greens and might have represented a field of flowers for all Rhodes knew, had a long diagonal gray line painted on it, from top right to bottom left.

"We might be able to clean it off," Don McClaren said, "but it will never be the same. Now this is a little different. I can clean this easily."

He showed Loam a sculpture of what appeared to Rhodes to be a small, twisted tree. The sculpture was mostly white with some green on the branches, if that was what they were. There was gray paint on the white.

"You can't clean this one," Eric Stewart said, pointing to a painting of something that looked familiar to Rhodes. It took him a second or two, but then he remembered when he'd seen something similar. It had been in an English book in high school, and it illustrated a poem he'd had to read, something about a seashell. The picture in the book was a photograph, not a painting, and it didn't have a gray slash across it.

"That one's mine," Seepy said. Loam turned her camera on him. "It's a cross-section of a chambered nautilus. All my artwork is based on the Golden Ratio."

Rhodes had heard Seepy discourse on the Golden Ratio before, but not on its relation to his artwork. Then again, Rhodes hadn't heard Seepy discourse on his artwork. On his music, yes. On his detecting abilities, of course. On his teaching skills and his martial arts abilities, naturally. But not on his art.

"The Golden Ratio is 1.618," Seepy said. "One plus the square root of five divided by two. That proportion occurs all through nature, just like in the chambered nautilus. Leonardo da Vinci used it often. The most famous example is in the sketch called the Vitruvian Man. Now, since my own field is nonabelian group theory—"

"Hold it," Rhodes said. Art was one thing he was pretty sure he didn't understand. Nonabelian group theory was something he was positive he wouldn't understand. "Stop right there. Does that theory have anything to do with what happened here?"

"Not as far as I know," Seepy said, "but I thought you might be interested in my art, since it's been defaced."

"I'm more interested in catching the defacer," Rhodes said. The best thing about Seepy's minilecture was that Jennifer Loam had moved away with her little camera and was taking video of some of the other pictures on display, the undamaged ones. Rhodes raised his voice and said, "Did anyone see who sprayed the paintings?"

The woman with the orange hair turned to Rhodes. Her hair, he decided, wasn't corkscrewed so much as tousled, but it was definitely orange. She wore no makeup, or didn't seem to, but then she didn't really need it. She was attractive enough without it, orange hair or not. She had large eyes, a wide mouth, and a husky voice. She wore jeans and a white shirt. There was a small tattoo of a butterfly on her neck.

"No, but one of mine is ruined," she said, "and I did see that man coming out of the building as we were returning."

"Returning from where?" Rhodes asked.

"We'd been at the college," Don McClaren said. "The art students have a small exhibit there, and I wanted to show everyone what the kids had been working on. Most of us went on the college bus, but a few people had their own cars."

"I was in my car," the orange-haired woman said. "I got back a little before everyone else, and I saw that man leaving. I went in and saw what he'd done. It had to be him. No one else was inside."

That didn't mean much. Collins could've sprayed the paintings, and Rhodes wouldn't have been surprised if that turned out to be the case, but the fact that he'd been in the building alone proved nothing.

"I didn't get your name," Rhodes said.

"Marilyn Bradley."

"You're not from around here, are you?"

"I'm from Derrick City. That's not far away."

It was only about thirty miles. Rhodes had driven there not long ago when looking into another matter. He hadn't seen any orange-haired women while he was there.

"Well, Ms. Bradley," he said, "there's a big back room full of antiques right through that door over there." Rhodes pointed to the door in the wall between two paintings, one of which might have been a cow skull. Or maybe not. "It might be locked, or it might not be. If it's not, someone could have been in there and left through the back door. So we don't know that Mr. Collins defaced the paintings."

"Defaced is too mild a word," she said. "Mine was ruined." She pointed. "That one."

Rhodes looked at the picture, which seemed to be of several golden-brown staircases leading nowhere other than into grayish clouds. Some of the staircases were upside down, or at least they looked that way to Rhodes. Maybe they were symbolic. They had no railings, but Rhodes supposed you really didn't need one on a staircase that was upside down and led nowhere. A dark streak crossed several of the staircases.

"You can see that it's destroyed," Marilyn said. "The judging is tomorrow, and now I won't have a chance at a ribbon. Not that a ribbon means all that much, but the recognition does. I believe I do something valuable with my creative talent, and I want others to appreciate it. Now my painting is ruined. That man has to be punished."

Rhodes was surprised at her vehemence. "We don't know for sure if Burt Collins did it," he repeated.

"I'll bet he did. Who else could it have been?"

"We'll find out," Rhodes said.

"I'm sure you will," Marilyn said. Her voice was calmer. "I've read about you in those books. I love those books."

"Books?" Rhodes said, though he was afraid he knew what she meant.

"You know," she said. "Sage Barton."

Just as Rhodes had suspected. A couple of women who'd been to a writers' workshop in a nearby town had become acquainted with Rhodes and had later written a very successful series of novels about Sage Barton, a two-gun lawman who was often involved in crimes that affected the entire nation. No one ever believed Rhodes when he explained that he and Barton had nothing at all in common and that a big-time crime in Blacklin County was more likely to be something like a missing sneeze guard at a restaurant buffet than terrorists bent on the destruction of Western democracy.

"Let me ask you something about Sage Barton," Seepy said, interrupting the conversation.

"What?" Marilyn asked.

"You know that my name is Seepy Benton, right?"

"Yes. We were introduced when the workshop began."

"I remember. I just wanted to be sure. Think about Sage Barton's initials. S. B. Then think about my initials. S. B. You don't think that's an accident, do you?"

"I . . . never thought about it," Marilyn said.

"It's worth thinking about," Seepy said.

Rhodes thought about it. Seepy's initials were C. P., which is where "Seepy" had come from, but if he wanted to believe he was the model for Sage Barton, more power to him.

Rhodes saw a county car drive up. "I believe that's Deputy Grady arriving," he said.

28

Seepy jumped as if he'd been stuck with a pin.

"I need to speak to her," Rhodes said. "I'll be right back."

"I'll go with you," Seepy said.

"I had a feeling you might," Rhodes said.

After explaining the situation to Ruth Grady, Rhodes told her that he wanted her to question Marilyn Bradley a bit more about her suspicions of Burt Collins.

"You need to question Dr. Benton, too," Rhodes added.

Ruth looked at Seepy. "Why?"

"He's the one who wanted to make a citizen's arrest of Collins. Well, he and Eric Stewart did. Question both of them."

"Hello?" Benton said. "I'm standing right here."

"Good," Rhodes said. "She can start with you. I'll be next door at the senior center."

He left Seepy and Ruth there and went to the senior center. When he entered the building, he could hear the click of dominoes in one room and the hum of conversation from another. Someone was warming something in the kitchen, pizza, maybe, or spaghetti. It must have been getting close to lunchtime.

Rhodes looked into the domino room. Nora Fischer wasn't there. She wasn't in the room where the conversations were going on, either. Some kind of book club, Rhodes thought, since everyone seemed to be holding a book. He went on back to the kitchen, where he found the former history teacher standing behind a counter at the stove.

"Pizza in the oven?" Rhodes asked.

"Yes, indeed," Nora said, turning to look at him. "How are you this morning, Danny?"

Only people who had known Rhodes when he was a lot younger still called him Danny. He didn't mind.

"I'm doing all right. Is that vegetarian pizza?"

"You mean no pepperoni and sausage? What kind of pizza would that be?"

It would be the kind of pizza that Rhodes got at home, when he got pizza at all.

"It has everything on it," Nora said, "but it's just store-bought."

That would be okay with Rhodes. Maybe he could cadge a piece later.

"I wanted to ask you about the disturbance next door," he said.

"That was fun," Nora said. "We old folks can use a little excitement every now and then."

"It wasn't so much fun for Lonnie Wallace and Burt Collins."

"Lonnie was a good student," Nora said. "He could name the three branches of government and tell you about checks and balances without missing a beat. Burt wasn't like that. He never seemed to care much."

That wasn't exactly the kind of information that Rhodes wanted. "Did you see the tussle between those two this morning?"

"I did," Nora said. "My eyesight is just fine, in case you were wondering. My phone's an old one, though, so I didn't get any pictures."

"Could you tell whether Lonnie fell, or whether he hit Burt deliberately?"

"Lonnie would never hit anyone deliberately. It's just not in his nature. I'm sure he fell. He caught his toe on the curb."

Since her version matched Lonnie's, Rhodes wanted to believe it. She was partial to Lonnie, though, so he'd have to ask a few more people.

"There are some interesting people in that crowd," Nora said. "I'm not surprised that Burt doesn't care for them. He seems angry a lot of the time."

"What about?"

"Just life in general, I guess. He and his wife don't get along, you know."

Rhodes had heard a few things, but he didn't know the whole story.

"You could ask Lonnie," Nora said. "Those beauty operators know everything that goes on in this town."

Rhodes knew that was true. He could ask Lonnie, or someone else at the beauty shop. Lonnie might have a reason to equivocate. At the moment it didn't seem like any of Rhodes's business.

"Did anyone here see Burt or anybody else go into the gallery while the artists were gone?"

"We were all inside. We didn't go out until the ruckus started." Nora turned to the oven. "I need to take the pizza out now. Would you like a piece?"

Rhodes grinned. "I thought you'd never ask."

Chapter 4

▼

A good bit of the afternoon was taken up with questioning, so Rhodes was glad he'd had the pizza, though Nora Fischer let him have only one slice.

Eventually Andy and Ruth were called away to look into a fender bender and a suspiciously damaged window screen at a vacant rental house. Rhodes finished up the questioning himself. His conclusions were that all of the art group believed they'd seen Lonnie Wallace trip and fall into Burt Collins. Most, but not all, of the people from the senior center agreed with that conclusion, but it was impossible to tell much from any of the videos that Rhodes saw. He didn't think that either Lonnie or Burt would be pressing charges, however, so he wasn't worried about what had actually happened. Not then, anyway.

Most of the artists were upset with Burt, not just because they thought he'd ruined some of their work but because he'd been bothering them. Don McClaren, Eric Stewart, and Marilyn Bradley were the most vocal.

"He's ruined things for the college," McClaren said. "We're cosponsoring this workshop with Eric, and now half the people think the whole town is nothing but rednecks. They'll never want to come back. It's a disaster."

Rhodes didn't think it was that bad, but Eric Stewart agreed with McClaren. "Nobody who came to the workshop from out of town will ever want to visit Clearview again. They think we're nothing but philistines."

"Is that the same as rednecks?" Rhodes asked.

"Exactly," Stewart said, "and it's the truth, too. Lonnie and I put good money into this workshop, and we planned to build something for the future. Nothing good will come of it now, and it's all Burt Collins's fault. Somebody should do something about him."

Marilyn Bradley agreed. "That man is terrible. He's given most of us a bad impression of your town, Sheriff. I know it's wrong to judge a town by one citizen, but that's the way it is. Besides that, he's destroyed my painting. It was one of my favorites, too. I'll never be able to duplicate it. I hope that man rots in jail."

Rhodes had to remind them that they were still living in a country where a man was innocent until proven guilty. Their unanimous conclusion was that Burt was guilty, no matter what proof there was. Or wasn't. He also had to remind them that even if Burt had damaged the paintings, he wasn't likely to do jail time unless the paintings were valuable. Otherwise, what had been done was just criminal mischief, a Class C misdemeanor that carried a fine but no jail time.

"What would it take to get him some jail time?" Marilyn asked.

By now McClaren and Stewart were standing beside her, and they wanted an answer, too.

"Damage to something worth between fifty and five hundred dollars," Rhodes said.

Marilyn was insulted. "Are you insinuating that my painting wasn't worth fifty dollars?"

"Uh," Rhodes said.

"What would some *real* jail time require?" McClaren asked.

"Damage of more than fifteen hundred dollars," Rhodes said.

"My painting was worth at least two thousand dollars," Marilyn said, "and some of the others were, too."

Rhodes didn't have any way of knowing if that was true, but Stewart said, "We could easily have them evaluated by an expert. Someone from the college, say. Someone like—"

"Me," McClaren said. "Or if you don't trust me, I can bring in an outside expert."

"I have an idea," Rhodes said.

They looked at him.

"You can go about doing some evaluating, and I'll try to catch whoever did the damage. Then we can get together and make a decision about what the charges will be."

They grumbled a while, but they agreed that was probably the best idea.

"Good," Rhodes said. "In the meantime, just carry on with your workshop as if nothing had happened."

Stewart waved a hand at the paintings. "That's impossible. What if Collins sneaks back in while we're gone and does more damage?"

"You can lock the door," Rhodes said.

"Then the public can't drop by and see our work," Marilyn said.

"That's right," McClaren said. "The whole idea of putting the exhibit here was to draw people back to this old downtown area. We wouldn't be very hospitable if we locked the doors."

Rhodes shrugged. "It's your exhibit. You can do as you please, but you should at least leave one person here to keep an eye on things."

"You're right," Stewart said. "We'll do that."

Rhodes turned to go, but Seepy Benton caught up with him before he got out the door.

"How do you like the art?" Seepy asked. "I haven't heard you comment on it."

Rhodes stopped. "Which art?"

"How about my chambered nautilus?"

"I could tell it was a seashell," Rhodes said. "Or part of one. I like being able to identify it."

"Art doesn't have to be representational. Take Marilyn's work."

Rhodes thought of several things he might have said and decided not to say any of them.

"You don't like it?" Benton said after a second or two.

"Everybody likes different things," Rhodes said. "Some people think a picture of a soup can is art."

"It can be," Benton said. "Art is supposed to make us see ordinary things like a soup can in a new way."

"It just looked like any other soup can to me," Rhodes said.

He started out the door, and this time he got to the street before Seepy caught up.

"I have some nonrepresentational art that I made with my computer," Seepy said. "Fractal art. It's a way to see the Mandelbrot Set."

"Is that anything like a play set?" Rhodes asked. "I know somebody who collects toy play sets. He has an Alamo play set that I like. He's a police chief in Pecan City. He collects toy soldiers, too."

"The Mandelbrot Set is nothing like that. It's—"

"Never mind," Rhodes said. "I have a feeling I wouldn't understand your explanation."

"Maybe not. It's complex. But that doesn't matter. Let's talk about the defaced paintings. I can help you crack the case."

"Crack the case?"

"Just a little shop talk, one lawman to another," Seepy said.

"Right. We professional lawmen talk like that all the time. How are you going to help me? By staying out of my way?"

Seepy looked hurt. "I can help by watching out to be sure Burt Collins doesn't do any more damage."

"All right. They need somebody to stay here and watch. Talk to Stewart about it. Just don't try making any more citizen's arrests until you have some proof of wrongdoing."

"Collins is probably guilty," Benton said.

"Maybe so, but you can't prove it."

"We'll see about that," Benton said, and Rhodes wasn't sure if he meant it as a threat or just a statement of fact.

"Remember," Rhodes said, "you aren't an official deputy, and I'm not asking for your help. You don't have any standing as an investigator."

"Right," Benton said, and Rhodes left it at that.

Andy Shelby was waiting at the jail when Rhodes got back.

"I put the spray can in the evidence room," Andy said. "I didn't find anything else suspicious in the gallery, and I don't think the can's going to help."

"Why not?" Rhodes asked.

"It had some smudges on it, but that's all. My guess is that whoever used it either wiped it or wore gloves."

"We'll have Ruth check it anyway," Rhodes said. "What about that auto accident you got the call about?"

"No biggie. Mrs. Calkins . . . you know her?"

"He knows her," Hack said from his desk. "Ever'body knows her and knows enough to watch out for her, too. Or should."

Mrs. Calkins was a retired teacher, like Nora Fischer, but Mrs. Calkins was more of a danger to the driving public. She had a tendency to drive slowly. Very slowly. It was a habit that sometimes led to complaints to the sheriff's department.

"Was she impeding traffic again?" Rhodes asked.

"Not until she hit the other car," Hack said.

Hack didn't like for anyone else to tell things when he was around. Even though he hadn't been on the scene, he always thought he knew the story better than anybody else, even the deputies.

"What car?" Rhodes asked.

"The one pullin' out of the parkin' place in front of the post office," Hack said.

"Is that right, Andy?" Rhodes asked.

"That's right," Hack said. "That driver doin' the backin' was at fault. You gotta look where you're goin' in this town. 'Specially with drivers like that Miz Calkins on the streets."

"Who got the ticket, Andy?" Rhodes asked, putting some emphasis on Andy's name so Hack wouldn't answer.

"Somebody named Leroy Dalton," Andy said.

Rhodes knew Dalton. He sold insurance, so he didn't have much to worry about if there was any damage to his car.

"Hack's right," Andy continued. "Dalton should've looked.

He was lucky it was Mrs. Calkins that hit him. She wasn't going over ten miles an hour."

"Ain't gone over ten miles an hour in the last twenty years," Hack said, as if Rhodes didn't know. "You got that art problem solved yet?"

"Not yet," Rhodes said.

"You see that orange-haired woman Burt talked about?"

"I saw her."

"Her hair really orange?"

"I'd say so. Andy?"

"It was," Andy said. "She's a nice-looking woman, though."

"Ginger, now, that's okay," Hack said. "Don't know about orange. That ain't natural."

"She has a tattoo," Rhodes said.

"Can't trust a woman with a tattoo," Hack said.

"Voice of experience?" Andy said.

"You implyin' that Miz McGee has a tattoo?" Hack asked.

"I wouldn't imply a thing like that," Andy said. "Does she?"

"Now you look here, you young whippersnapper—"

"The woman with the orange hair's name is Marilyn Bradley," Rhodes said. "No relation to anybody here in town. She's from Derrick City."

"Can't trust women from Derrick City," Hack said.

"Voice of experience?" Andy said.

Rhodes wondered if Andy Shelby was about to become the new version of Lawton, not that they needed a new version. Lawton did just fine on his own, at least when he was around.

"Let's not worry about Hack's love life," Rhodes said. "Or about anybody's hair color. Lonnie Wallace might have to go out of business if everybody stuck to their natural shade."

"Yeah, I guess that's so," Hack said. "You ever hear about that chimpanzee that was a famous artist?"

Rhodes was used to having odd conversations with Hack, so he wasn't too surprised by the sudden change in subject. He said he hadn't heard about the chimp.

"Happened a long time ago," Hack said, "so maybe you weren't around. Andy for sure wasn't around. Anyway, I saw somethin' about it on the computer the other day. Some fella got a chimp to paint some pictures. I don't know how. Just gave him a brush and some paint, I guess. Fella said later that the chimp ate more paint than he put on the paper. Anyway, he took the pictures and got 'em into an exhibition with a bunch of other artists. Didn't tell anybody they'd been done by a chimp, of course. Looked like somethin' kindergarteners might do with finger paints. All the art critics loved 'em."

Rhodes thought about the paintings he'd seen at the gallery. Some of them were odd, like the staircases in the sky, but they didn't look like the work of a kindergarten finger painter.

"What does that tell you?" Hack asked.

"I'm not sure," Rhodes said. "I haven't seen the chimp's work."

Andy laughed. "You maybe ought to run for higher office, Sheriff. You'd be a good politician."

"I don't think so," Rhodes said. "Maybe I ought to be an art critic. Sounds like a job I could handle if people don't hold being wrong against you."

"You want a job like that," Hack said, "you oughta consider being a weatherman."

"No, thanks. I'll just stick with being a sheriff. For the time being anyhow, and if I'm going to be a sheriff, I'd better act like one. I think I'll have a little talk with Burt Collins."

"You think he'll confess?" Hack asked.

"Not a chance," Rhodes said.

As it happened, neither Collins nor his wife was at home, so Rhodes drove on to his own house, figuring that the hullabaloo would die down soon enough and that the artists would get over the damage someone, maybe Collins, had done to the paintings and sculptures. They'd clean things up, and by the next day things would be back to normal.

Maybe it would have worked out that way if someone hadn't killed Burt Collins that night.

Chapter 5

▼

The robbery at the Pak-a-Sak happened first. The little convenience store sat at the edge of town, and it had been robbed before. One of the problems was that it was too near several uncleared lots that had plenty of trees and low-growing bushes on them to provide cover for someone running from the store. It was all too easy for someone to hide a car somewhere nearby and escape through the trees.

Rhodes had mentioned this fact to Oscar Henderson before, but Oscar always said the same thing: "It's not my property, and I can't just go in and clear it."

"You could talk to the owner," Rhodes said. "Just look at that mess."

Rhodes and Oscar were in back of the store, looking out at the trees. The light back there was none too good, and there was no robber to be seen. Rhodes looked up at the sky. It seemed to him that there weren't as many stars as there had been when he was young, but he'd never tried to count them, then or now.

Rhodes wasn't too happy about being called away from home about the robbery. He'd been watching an episode of *Justified* on DVD. The show was set in Harlan County, Kentucky, which sometimes seemed as dangerous as a war zone. Watching it made Rhodes feel pretty good about things in Blacklin County, Texas, which was practically Sunnybrook Farm by comparison.

"I've tried to talk to the owner," Oscar said. He was a short, skinny man with bandy legs. He had a little fuzz of gray hair fringing his head and somewhat more in his ears. "I can't find him. Or her. The deeds are all messed up."

"So for all you know, you could clear the land and nobody would know."

"Or I could get sued when the owner suddenly shows up. You gonna pay my legal bills if that happens?"

They'd been through this before, the last time the store was robbed, and Rhodes didn't want to continue it.

"How much did they get?" he asked.

"Wasn't a *they*. Was just one of 'em. You can ask Chris."

Chris Ferris was the clerk who'd been behind the counter when the store was robbed. Buddy Warren, one of the other deputies, was talking to him inside the store.

"I'll get Buddy's report," Rhodes said. "You have anything else to tell me?"

"It's like Chris said. Nothing unusual about the way it happened. Some guy with a stocking pulled over his face came in, showed Chris a gun, and said, 'Give me the money.'"

"What kind of gun?"

"I don't know, some funny-looking one, Chris said."

"How about the voice?"

"Growl was more like it, according to Chris. Disguising his voice, I guess. Anyhow, I've told Chris if somebody comes in and sticks him up to give 'em the money if they ask for it, so that's what he did. Then the guy ran out the door and around the side of the building. Off into the trees, like the other one did. That's it."

When Oscar mentioned the other one, Rhodes wondered if it wasn't just the same one, who'd found out that the Pak-a-Sak was easy pickings. Rhodes also remembered a few years back when someone had driven off from the store without paying for the gasoline he'd pumped into a little Ford Focus. That hadn't worked out.

"All right, then," Rhodes said. "I'll just check with Buddy, and he'll stick around to investigate some more."

"Hmph," Oscar said.

"Buddy's good at that kind of thing," Rhodes said.

"Don't matter if he is. Whoever robbed me is long gone, and he didn't leave any clues behind him. You'll never catch him."

"Don't count on that," Rhodes said.

"You never caught the last one, did you?"

"No," Rhodes said. "Not yet."

Buddy hadn't gotten anything more out of Chris, or at least nothing more that was helpful.

"He says it was just a guy," Buddy told Rhodes as they stood by Buddy's county car.

Chris was inside behind the counter, talking to Oscar. They were waiting for someone to come and take Chris's place, Chris being a little shaken by his experience and wanting to go home and recover.

"Not too tall," Buddy said, "not too short. Not fat, not skinny. Hair a little long, as best Chris could tell, what with the stocking mashing it. Made his voice all growly. Face was twisted out of shape by the stocking. Looked like something out of a horror movie. No beard or mustache. Gun was an automatic. That's all Chris could tell me."

"Did he think it could've been the same one who robbed him before?"

"That one had on a ski mask," Buddy said. "Size was about the same, but that's as much as I could get."

"You get Hack to have Duke Pearson come out and help you scour through the woods," Rhodes said. "Don't you go in there until Duke gets here, all right?"

"Sure." Buddy's hand dropped to his sidearm. "You think anybody's in there among the trees?"

"No, but you never can tell. You wait for Duke, and try not to shoot anybody."

"I haven't shot anybody yet," Buddy said, and Rhodes thought he detected a note of regret in the deputy's voice.

"That's a good record," Rhodes said. "Try to keep it."

"Sure," Buddy said. "You know me, Sheriff."

Rhodes did know him, and that was the trouble. Buddy had an itchy trigger finger if anybody ever did. So far, though, they'd been lucky.

"Give me a call if you need me," Rhodes said.

"Sure," Buddy said. "I'll just go talk to Hack and get him to send Duke."

Rhodes left him to it and got into his own car to go home. It was almost eleven thirty by that time, and Clearview was shut down for the night. Had been shut down for an hour or two. Rhodes drove by the art gallery and antiques store. It was dark and quiet. He didn't see Seepy Benton lurking about, for which he was glad.

The Beauty Shack was quiet, too, as was the old abandoned building across the street that occasionally provided a refuge for homeless people. Rhodes remembered that Burt Collins lived not too far away, so he thought he'd check on him while he was out.

Rhodes looked to his left and saw that the recycle center was dark. There hadn't been any trouble there for a while, for which Rhodes was grateful. Copper thefts continued, but not at the same rate of a year earlier. It wasn't that copper was less valuable so much as that the thieves were getting caught so often that they'd started to look in other counties for the metal. Or so Rhodes told himself.

The Collins house was two blocks straight ahead. The street reached a dead end at its front yard. It was an old house, two stories high, sitting on a pair of lots. The railroad tracks were a couple of blocks to the east, and no houses sat on the empty lots. There were blocks of empty lots behind the house, too. The only other house nearby was to the west, with its back to the Collins place.

Collins must have had a little bit of the artist in him, as his home was painted in three different colors. About a third of the house jutted out on the right side, and it was painted white. The first story of the other two-thirds was green, and the second story was pale yellow. A separate carport with a metal roof stood off to the right of the house. The wide brown lawn stretched right down to the street, and although there was no driveway, Collins's vehicles had worn a packed-dirt path to the carport. Rhodes was a little surprised to see that some lights were on inside the house, but maybe Collins liked to stay up and watch late-night TV.

Since he was out already, Rhodes figured it was as good a time as any to have a little talk with Collins about what had happened that day. The county car bumped up over what was left of the curb and onto the path to the carport. Rhodes stopped near the house and got out of the car. The night air was cool, as it should be only a month from Halloween. Rhodes noticed that a Chevy pickup and sedan were parked under the carport.

The night was quiet, like most nights in Clearview. Even on a Friday there wasn't a lot to do after dark, not in that part of town. The parking lot at Walmart would probably still be partially full, though, even at that hour.

Rhodes heard something from inside the house, maybe a TV set. The house didn't have a porch, just a couple of prefab concrete steps. Rhodes mounted them and knocked on a screen door that rattled in its frame. The noise from inside continued. It sounded like someone wailing, and Rhodes decided it wasn't coming from a TV set. He opened the screen and banged on the door. The sound inside got louder, a good enough reason to enter the premises, if the door was unlocked. It was, and Rhodes pushed it open.

The sound was more distinct now, and it was definitely wailing, along with some crying. It seemed to be coming from a room at the end of the dark narrow hallway where Rhodes found himself.

For years Rhodes had tried different ways of carrying a sidearm. As the sheriff, he almost always went around in plainclothes, and he'd always tried to conceal his weapon. Nothing he'd done had proved to be satisfactory, but lately he'd reverted to using an ankle holster with a little Kel-Tec PF-9. He'd used a Kel-Tec .32 for a while, but he'd begun to think that he might need a little more firepower. The PF-9 had a polymer body, so it was light and easy to carry. The seven 9 mm cartridges were powerful enough to stop someone even bigger than the .32s would, though Rhodes hoped he wasn't going to have to use the pistol for stopping anyone. The only problem was the awkwardness involved in getting to the pistol in the ankle holster. He was never going to get to it in a hurry, but he didn't plan to enter any quick-draw contests.

Speed wasn't the issue here. Rhodes bent over and got the pistol, just in case something else was the issue. He walked toward the sound, which had grown quieter. It was a muffled sobbing now.

The door to the room was open, and Rhodes took a quick look inside. Burt Collins lay on his stomach on the hardwood floor, not far from a coffee table. He didn't appear to be breathing. Rhodes was sure he was dead. A stocky woman wearing jeans and a man's shirt sat on a sofa, crying, her head in her hands.

"Ella?" Rhodes said.

The woman looked up. "Sheriff?"

Ella Collins was Burt's wife. Rhodes lowered the pistol, slipped it into his back pocket, and stepped into the room. "What happened?"

Ella brushed her hands across her face. Rhodes saw that it was creased with red lines.

"What are you doing here?" she asked.

"I came to see Burt," Rhodes said. "What happened?"

"I don't know." A sob caught in Ella's throat. "I came home and found Burt like this. I think he had a heart attack."

Rhodes had seen a lot of dead people, too many, and it always made him sad, even when the person was someone like Burt Collins, a cantankerous man nobody had really liked and whom very few would miss. Whatever kind of man he was, though, he'd been alive, seeing, breathing, smelling, tasting, maybe even smiling now and then. Now all that was gone.

Rhodes knelt down and looked at the back of Burt's head. The hair was matted with blood, and some bone showed through. Rhodes felt Burt's carotid artery. No pulse, but then Rhodes hadn't expected one. The flesh wasn't cold, but it wasn't warm, either. Burt had been dead for a little while, and Rhodes was pretty sure that Burt's heart had nothing to do with his condition.

"Were you here when it happened?" Rhodes asked, standing up.

"No. I was at Frances Bennett's." Ella's voice was a little steadier. "She's been recovering from surgery, and some of us have been staying with her, doing some housework and cooking. You know, just to help out. I'd come home and walked in here, and there was Burt on the floor. I haven't even called the doctor."

"I'll do it," Rhodes said. "Is there somewhere else you can sit? How about the kitchen?"

"All right." Ella stood up. Rhodes noticed that her knees were a little wobbly, and she had to put a hand down on the arm of the sofa to steady herself. "It's right across the hall."

Rhodes walked her to the kitchen and got her seated at the square oak table. Some water glasses stood upside down in a dish drainer beside the sink. Rhodes got one, filled it from the tap, and handed it to Ella. She took a swallow and sighed.

"You just stay put," Rhodes said. "I'll be right back."

He left Ella in the kitchen and went outside, where he transferred the pistol back to the ankle holster. Then he walked to the carport. He felt the hood of the sedan. It was still warm, so maybe Ella was telling the truth when she said she'd just gotten there. He went to the county car and called Hack on the radio.

"Get Buddy and tell him to leave the convenience store investigation with Duke," Rhodes said when Hack responded. "Send Buddy to Burt Collins's house."

"What's going on?" Hack asked.

"Burt's a little indisposed. Send an ambulance. And the justice of the peace."

"Justice of the peace? You sure Burt's just indisposed?"

The justice of the peace was the one who'd declare Burt dead.

"Indisposed is what I'm calling it for now," Rhodes said. "You get Buddy over here."

"Roger," Hack said.

Rhodes racked the radio and went back inside. He looked in on Ella, who sat at the table, her back straight, staring at nothing. Her arms were stretched out in front of her, both hands clasping the water glass.

"Are you all right?" Rhodes asked. Ella was the one who needed someone to sit with her now. "Is there somebody I can call to come over?"

"I can do it," Ella said. "My sister, Bonnie, lives in Thurston. Bonnie Crowley."

Thurston was a little town about twenty miles away. It would take Bonnie a while to get there, but maybe Ella would be all right until then.

She got up and went to an old wall phone fastened to the wall near the door. It was a gold color, a relic of the seventies, Rhodes thought, with a long, tangled cord.

"There will be some people coming in," Rhodes said. "Quite a few of them. You just stay in here."

"I will," Ella said. She lifted the receiver and started to dial.

Rhodes went back into the other room to look around. Nothing seemed to be disturbed or out of place, and he didn't see anything that looked as if it might have been used to hit Burt. There was a large afghan hanging over the back of the couch. Rhodes put it over the body and went back to the kitchen. Ella sat at the table, staring at something Rhodes couldn't see.

"Ella?" he said. "I hate to ask you to do this, but I need you to come back in the living room for a minute."

Ella stood up and said in a flat voice, "All right."

When they were back in the other room, she looked at the covered body. Rhodes said, "Don't look at Burt. Look around and see if there's anything missing."

It took a few seconds for Ella to focus, but when she did, she began to look around the room. Rhodes looked, too. A flat-screen TV and DVD player were in a cabinet opposite the sofa where Ella had been sitting. The only things on the coffee table were a couple of remote controls. A whatnot cabinet stood against the wall beside the TV cabinet. An end table with a lamp on it sat at one end of the sofa, and a matching table and lamp sat by the overstuffed recliner not far away.

Rhodes noticed a vacant space on top of the whatnot shelf and walked over to it. He saw a thin coating of dust on the shelf except for a square about five inches on each side. He put a finger on the spot and asked Ella what had been there.

"Oh, my," she said. "Where's Burt's head? It's gone!"

Chapter 6

▼

Rhodes didn't quite get it. "Burt's head is gone?"

"Not *his* head. Dale Earnhardt's."

"Dale Earnhardt?" Rhodes said.

"Junior," Ella said. "His daddy was Dale Earnhardt, too." She pointed to the vacant spot on the shelf. "His head was right there. Junior's was."

"NASCAR," Rhodes said, figuring it out.

"Dale and his daddy were both drivers," Ella said. "Junior still is. He's really good, but maybe not as good as his daddy. His daddy died in a big crash ten or twelve years ago. Dale Junior's granddaddy was a driver, too. Ralph."

"But it's Junior's head that's missing."

"Yes. Burt loved to watch the NASCAR races on TV, and Dale Junior was his favorite driver. I got him Dale's head for his birthday last year. Dale Junior, I mean."

"It was a bust," Rhodes said.

"No, he loved it. Said it was the best present he ever got."

As she said that, Ella looked down at Burt and started to sob again.

"The head," Rhodes said, knowing better than to call it a bust again, "was it heavy?"

Ella took a deep, shuddering breath and looked away from Burt. "Oh, yes. It was made out of some kind of metal. Not brass. The other one that looks kind of like it."

"Bronze," Rhodes said.

"That's it. Bronze. It was made special, too. There were only a thousand of them, and they were all numbered. This one had a real low number. It was supposed to be worth more if it had a low number. That's what the man who sold it to me said."

"Was it here when you left to go to Frances Bennett's?"

"I'm sure it was. It was always right there on the shelf. Burt was real proud of it. Where could it be?"

"Let's go back in the kitchen," Rhodes said. "We can look for it later."

As he got Ella seated at the table again, Rhodes heard a siren. Buddy was on the way, or maybe it was the ambulance.

"You stay here," Rhodes said. "I'll take care of things now."

Ella nodded, and Rhodes went out to see who was arriving.

A county car bounced onto the dirt path and slid to a stop beside Rhodes's. Buddy got out and said, "I got here soon as I could. Duke's still looking around at the Pak-a-Sak. What's the beef?"

"Burt Collins is dead. We're going to search the house."

Buddy undid the snap that secured his service revolver. "Let's go."

They went back inside, and Rhodes explained to Ella what they were going to do. She said she'd stay in the kitchen.

"I don't think there's anyone here," Rhodes said, "but we need to check things out to be sure."

He took his pistol from the ankle holster, and Buddy drew his revolver. They went through the house room by room, checking closets and under the beds. They didn't find anyone, and nothing looked as if it had been disturbed. They went back to the room where Burt's body lay. Rhodes returned his pistol to the ankle holster, and Buddy holstered his revolver.

"I want you to go outside and search the area," Rhodes told Buddy. "You'll be looking for a head."

Buddy looked down at the afghan-covered body. "Somebody cut off Burt's head?"

"No. It's Dale Earnhardt's head. Junior, that is, and it's not a real head. It's a bronze bust. It's missing from the house."

"You think somebody stole it?"

"I think somebody hit Burt in *his* head with it and took it away."

"Why would anybody take something like that?"

"Because," Rhodes said, "it might have fingerprints on it."

"Right," Buddy said. "Fingerprints. You really think it'll be around here somewhere?"

"No," Rhodes said, "but we have to look for it. It's dark, though, and if you don't find it nearby, I'll put somebody else on it tomorrow."

"I'll get started," Buddy said. He got his flashlight out of the car. "Here comes Wade Franklin."

Franklin was the justice of the peace. The ambulance was right behind him. It was going to be busy in the Collins house for a while.

* * *

It was after one o'clock when Rhodes left the Collins house. Burt Collins had been declared dead and taken away, and Rhodes had put crime-scene tape on the doorway to the room where Burt had been killed. Bonnie Crowley had arrived to take care of her sister. Rhodes had talked to Ella a bit about Burt. She couldn't believe that he'd been murdered and kept repeating that he must have had a stroke or a heart attack. How could he have been killed? Everybody loved Burt. Why, the man had not an enemy in the world, not even the Patels.

Nobody who died ever had an enemy in the world, not to hear the relatives tell it. In Burt's case, Rhodes knew better, but he'd talk more to Ella about it later.

Buddy was still searching for the bronze bust of Dale Earnhardt, Junior, not having found a trace of it so far, and Rhodes was ready to go home and get some sleep. Burt Collins's death could be investigated tomorrow.

Rhodes didn't get to go home, however, because as soon as he was in the county car, he got a call about donkeys on the loose.

"Out by the highway to Obert," Hack said. "Two of 'em at least. Car hits one of 'em, it's gonna be bad news. Too much speedin' on that road if you ask me."

"Donkeys are Alton Boyd's job," Rhodes said, Boyd being the county's animal control officer.

"He's on the way," Hack said. "Gonna need some help, though, and Duke's looking into a break-in at a house over in Milsby. You get the job. Or you can send Buddy."

Rhodes thought he might send Buddy, but it was likely the deputy would be needed for something else any minute.

"I'll go myself," Rhodes said.

"Folks oughta do somethin' about those donkeys," Hack said.

"Get 'em spayed and neutered. Don't cost that much, not much more'n it'd cost for a dog or a cat."

"If people had money," Rhodes said, wondering how Hack knew how much it would cost to neuter a donkey, "the donkeys wouldn't be a problem."

The county had been having donkey trouble for a few months now. It wasn't nearly as bad as the wild hog problem, but it was bad enough. Only a small part of the problem had to do with donkey reproduction, in spite of Hack's comment. Like a lot of other things lately, the problem was tied to the economy.

People bought donkeys because they were good at protecting livestock from coyotes and other critters, but sometimes the donkeys got too expensive to keep. The owners tried to get rid of them in conventional ways, but if one got taken to auction, it wouldn't sell. Rhodes had heard of times at recent auctions when a donkey had been run through the auction ring three or four times in one day without attracting a bid. Not being able to get rid of the animals by selling them, the owners turned them out or hauled them off and dumped them, which was when they became the county's problem. At the moment, Blacklin County had seven donkeys in custody, at a cost to the taxpayers of around a hundred and fifty dollars a week.

The commissioners weren't happy about the expense, and Rhodes didn't blame them, but it wasn't as if the problem were confined to Blacklin County. Rhodes had talked with a few other sheriffs around the state, and some of them were having even more trouble with donkeys than he was. He knew of one county that had fourteen donkeys penned up and eating on the taxpayer's dime.

Rhodes went looking for Buddy. He found him deep in the trees between the Collins house and the railroad tracks.

"Find any clues?" Rhodes asked.

Buddy shined his flashlight on Rhodes. "Depends on what you call clues. I've run across a bunch of beer cans, some plastic water bottles, and a few disposable diapers that got disposed of in the wrong place. No heads, though, metal or not."

"All right," Rhodes said. "You can go back on patrol. I'll have Andy look around some more tomorrow. We can't spend all night here."

The fact was that while the apparent homicide was the most important crime of the night, it wouldn't be the last problem the sheriff's office had to deal with. There would be plenty of others, like the robbery at the convenience store, car accidents on the highways, prowlers, domestic disputes, shoplifting at the Walmart, copper thieves, donkeys, and all too many other things that would come up. Rhodes didn't have enough deputies to deal with every one of them, but he'd do what he could with the resources he had.

"You going home?" Buddy asked.

"Nope," Rhodes said. "I'm going to see about some donkeys."

Rhodes drove over the railroad overpass and out by the community college, whose main campus was located in another county. The Clearview campus was where Seepy Benton and Don Mc-Claren taught. McClaren split his time between Clearview and the home campus because there wasn't enough demand for a full-time art teacher in Clearview.

Rhodes passed by the road that led to Seepy Benton's house. He was glad that Seepy wasn't involved with the donkeys, though if Seepy knew about some secret pressure points on donkeys, he might be a big help. Donkeys probably didn't have pressure points, however.

Flashing lights ahead let Rhodes know that Alton Boyd had already arrived. Rhodes pulled off the highway onto the shoulder and stopped about thirty yards behind the trailer attached to the big white pickup. He didn't want to get too close and be in the way of loading the trailer.

That was being optimistic, he knew. Loading the trailer would come only after catching the donkeys, and sometimes donkeys didn't want to be caught. At other times they didn't mind, though, and often those that didn't mind were the lucky ones. Rhodes knew of at least two donkeys that had been fairly tame and had been adopted by people whose property they'd been dumped on. The taxpayers had been lucky, too, because they were spared the expense and trouble of putting the donkeys up in county accommodations.

Alton Boyd strolled around from the front of the county pickup and said good evening to Rhodes, who could see him plainly in the headlights of the county car. Boyd wore what looked like flannel pajama bottoms, cowboy boots, and a red hoodie with the hood hanging down behind. He must have dressed in a hurry. A cheap unlit cigar jutted from the corner of Boyd's mouth. Rhodes knew the cigar was cheap because Boyd didn't believe in paying a lot for anything. He even put recapped tires on his personal car to save money.

"Where are the donkeys?" Rhodes asked.

"Just up the road a ways," Boyd said, without removing the cigar. "I got 'em run off the road and down in the ditch. I pitched out a little horse-and-mule feed for 'em, so I think they'll stay there till we're ready to get them."

A car went by them, its tires whispering on the highway. It wasn't going fast, not with all the flashing lights along the roadside. The driver probably thought there'd been an accident. Even though the driver wasn't speeding, Rhodes hoped the donkeys were where Boyd claimed they were. A low-speed collision could be almost as bad as any other kind. There wouldn't be much traffic on the highway at that time of night, which was a good thing.

"Let's go take a look at the donkeys," Rhodes said.

"Okay," Boyd said. "They're not much to look at, though."

They walked beside the trailer. Boyd had already opened the two side doors, each one leading to a separate stall in the trailer. He'd lowered the ramps as well.

Boyd was right about the donkeys. Rhodes had a good look at them as they stood in the ditch in the beams of the pickup's headlights. Both of them were scrawny and underfed. Rhodes could see their ribs.

"You gonna adopt 'em?" Boyd asked.

Like everyone else connected with the sheriff's department, Boyd knew about Rhodes's habit of adopting animals that he ran into on his cases. Just two dogs and two cats, so far, but there had been a couple of other narrow escapes, including the dog he'd managed to get Seepy Benton to take. Donkeys, however, were far too large for Rhodes even to consider. His wife, Ivy, wouldn't approve at all.

"Looks like they needed that feed you gave them," Rhodes said, ignoring Boyd's question.

"I'll get some more," Boyd said. "They'll be easier to handle if they're not so hungry."

He turned back to the truck, and Rhodes contemplated the donkeys, both of whom were contemplating him right back. One was black with a white stomach, and the other was solid gray. They were both males, or jacks, as they were called, and they didn't look friendly in spite of having been fed.

"I don't think that's going to help," Rhodes told Boyd when he returned with a scoop of feed in each hand.

"I'll give it to 'em anyway," Boyd said, talking around the cigar. "Better to try it than not to."

He put the feed on the ground some distance from the donkeys, who stopped looking at Rhodes and looked at the food. After a few seconds, they walked to it and began to eat. Boyd took the scoops back to the truck and returned with a couple of lariats. He had on a pair of leather gloves, and he handed a pair to Rhodes.

"You any good at ropin'?" Boyd asked, as Rhodes pulled on the gloves. "As I recall, me and Ruth had to rope the alligator that time. You remember that?"

Rhodes remembered the alligator. Seepy Benton had wanted to wrestle it, but Ruth and Boyd had roped its snout and tail and held it as best they could while Rhodes duct-taped its snout shut.

"I can handle a rope," Rhodes said.

"Good," Boyd said, and handed him a lariat.

Rhodes shook out a loop and held it at his side.

Boyd shook out a loop, too. "Okay. Once we get 'em roped, we can lead 'em to the trailer. If they cooperate, that is. Donkey's ain't always big on cooperation. Just the opposite, most of the time."

"What happens when we get them to the trailer?"

"Well, assuming we get 'em there, we'll try to get a halter on 'em and then get 'em into the trailer. I'll get 'em secured, and after that, no problems."

He made it sound easy, but Rhodes had a feeling it wasn't going to be quite that simple.

"You ready?" Boyd asked.

Rhodes nodded.

"Then let's move up a little closer," Boyd said. "We don't want to be too far away when we try to rope 'em."

Rhodes noted the word "try." He wasn't sure if it was aimed at him or just a general comment.

"Which one you want?" Boyd asked, taking a step forward. "Right or left?"

Since he was already on Boyd's left, Rhodes said, "Left."

"Okay. Move up again."

Both of them took a step. The donkeys looked up from the feed. Rhodes froze. Boyd took another step. Rhodes could tell that the donkeys didn't like that at all. One man with horse-and-mule feed might be okay, but two of them with ropes might be a different story.

The donkey on the right brayed, a series of sharp *eeeee*s, each one followed by a deeper and louder *haaaaaww*.

Rhodes took a step. Both donkeys looked ready to run at any second.

"What if we rope them and they run?" Rhodes asked.

"Two choices," Boyd said. "Let go or hang on."

"That's what I was afraid of."

"If you hang on," Boyd said, "it might pull you for a little way. Might be some grass burrs still around, even if it ain't the season for 'em, and you'll get scraped up pretty good."

"Just what I needed to hear," Rhodes said.

The donkey on the left shivered.

"Go for it," Boyd said.

He flipped his lasso. Rhodes tossed his loop as well. By what Rhodes considered a minor miracle, both loops settled over the donkeys' heads and slid down their necks.

Rhodes didn't have to tighten his loop. The donkey did it for him, by taking off at a lope. Rhodes elected the "hang on" option and was jerked off his feet. He hit the ground on his stomach and was dragged along over the grass and weeds in the ditch. He didn't know where Boyd was, and he didn't care. He'd hang on as long as he could and hope the jack would stop before he had to let go. It wasn't going very fast, so the damage would be small.

Rhodes bounced over a lump of earth, and the rope slid a foot or so through his hands. He was glad he had on the gloves. So far he'd managed to keep his head from banging into anything. He figured that was a point in his favor. He hoped his clothes would hold up.

Rhodes heard a loud braying from somewhere behind him, but since he couldn't see back there, he didn't know if Boyd was having a problem or if his donkey was being more cooperative than the one that was dragging Rhodes, who'd had just about enough.

He began to haul himself up the rope. The donkey must have felt the increased resistance, because it slowed down to a walk. Rhodes was able to get to his feet and haul back on the rope. The donkey was stubborn and tried to pull Rhodes down again.

This time Rhodes kept his feet and jogged along for a couple of steps. The donkey went a few yards and stopped.

Rhodes stood still for a while, keeping his grip on the rope. He saw the donkey in the darkness ahead of him. The donkey stood calmly, looking back at Rhodes.

"So," Rhodes said, "you give up?"

"Eeeee-*haaaaaww*."

"Good, because I was just about to get rough with you."

The donkey didn't bother to answer, so Rhodes gave a little tug on the rope. The donkey took a step toward him.

"That's better," Rhodes said. "You come on now."

He walked back toward the pickup with the donkey following. At first Rhodes didn't see Boyd. He and the other donkey seemed to have disappeared, but then Boyd stepped out of the trailer.

"Got mine taken care of," Boyd said when he saw Rhodes coming along the ditch. "You okay?"

"I'm a little dirty," Rhodes said, "but I'm all in one piece."

He looked down at his clothes. His shirt was covered with dirt, and so were his pants, but at least they weren't torn.

"More or less," he added.

"I'll get the donkey loaded up," Boyd said. "You gonna go with me to the feed lot?"

"I think I'll go home," Rhodes said, "if you can handle them by yourself."

"Easy enough, now," Boyd said.

"Then I'm going home."

"Have a good night."

"You, too," Rhodes said. "What's left of it."

Chapter 7

▼

Rhodes went into his backyard, but Speedo was nowhere to be seen. Probably asleep in his igloo, Rhodes thought. Smart dog.

Yancey, the little Pomeranian, wasn't asleep, or if he'd been asleep, he woke up as soon as Rhodes opened the back door. Rhodes heard doggie toenails clicking across the kitchen floor, and by the time the door had closed, Yancey was dancing around Rhodes's feet and yipping while the two of them stood on the little enclosed back porch.

"You're going to wake up Ivy," Rhodes said, but Yancey either didn't hear him or didn't care. The yipping continued.

"You're bothering Sam and Jerry," Rhodes said.

Sam and Jerry were the cats, and Rhodes knew that Yancey wasn't really bothering them. Nothing much bothered them, especially if they were sleeping, which seemed to be their chief occupation. Most of the time they stayed in the kitchen, sleeping in the warm air that vented from the bottom of the refrigerator.

Rhodes entered the kitchen. Yancey had stopped yipping, but he was still doing his little dance around Rhodes's feet.

"One of these days you're going to cause me to fall," Rhodes said, flipping on the light.

Sure enough, the cats were in their usual place, curled into circles. Sam slitted both eyes just enough to see what all the commotion was about, then closed them. Jerry didn't even bother to do that. Rhodes sneezed. He was allergic to cats, though Ivy didn't believe him when he told her so. She said that the sneezing was psychological.

Rhodes went back out on the enclosed porch and started to take off his clothes. He was just stepping out of his pants when Ivy came into the kitchen.

"The county really should pay you a clothing allowance," she said. "How bad are they this time?"

"Not too bad," Rhodes said, and they weren't, considering the condition they'd been in on other occasions.

"Were you in a fight?"

"Nope. Got dragged by a donkey."

"That's a new one," Ivy said, smiling.

Rhodes dropped his pants on the floor and took off his shirt. "I lead an exciting life."

"Glamorous, too," Ivy said.

Rhodes grinned. It had taken her a while to get used to his odd hours and to the fact that he was in danger now and then, but she'd adjusted very well eventually.

"You didn't have to get up," he said.

Ivy looked at Yancey, who was sniffing around Rhodes's discarded clothes. "Something woke me."

"I told him to be quiet," Rhodes said.

"Like that was going to work."

Rhodes laughed. "He was glad to see me."

"He was hoping you'd feed him."

"At this hour?"

"At any hour. What time is it, anyway?"

"Clock's in the kitchen," Rhodes said.

"Well, let's go have a look, then."

They went into the kitchen, and Rhodes saw that it was a little after three thirty.

"If I don't take a bath," he said, "I might get three hours of sleep."

"You're taking a bath," Ivy said.

"I thought you'd say that."

Yancey pranced into the kitchen.

"Finished with your inspection?" Rhodes asked.

Yancey gave a couple of yips and made a quick run in the direction of Sam and Jerry. Neither cat bothered even to open its eyes. It was just as well that they didn't. If they'd made any kind of move at all, Yancey would've run off and hidden under the bed for what was left of the night, and maybe part of the morning as well.

"Bath," Ivy said.

"Good idea," Rhodes said.

The next morning, Rhodes woke up at seven, a little later than usual. Yancey was sitting on the floor near the bed, staring at him.

"Didn't Ivy feed you?" Rhodes asked, getting out of bed.

Yancey yipped and ran off to the kitchen.

Rhodes went off to get ready to face the day. When he was

shaved and presentable, he went into the kitchen, where Ivy had whipped up some bacon and eggs and toast. It was turkey bacon, Rhodes knew, but it was better than no bacon at all. The eggs weren't real, either. They were something that was poured out of a little carton, but they were all right. There was no coffee. Rhodes had never liked it. At times in the past he'd had a Dr Pepper for caffeine, but for now he was avoiding his favorite soft drink.

"I should feed Speedo," Rhodes said. "I'm late, and he's hungry."

"Your eggs will get cold."

"I like cold eggs. I'll be right back."

Rhodes went out, followed by Yancey, who never missed an opportunity to pester any human or dog in the vicinity. Cats were a different story.

Speedo, a border collie, seemed glad to see both Rhodes and Yancey, but Rhodes knew he'd be even happier to see some food in his bowl. He waited a couple of minutes while Yancey chased the bigger dog around the yard, and then he filled the bowl.

"Sorry I don't have time to play today," Rhodes said as Speedo began to eat. "I have to go fight crime. And eat breakfast."

He went back into the house. Yancey came along, but it was obvious that he was disappointed that Rhodes hadn't taken the time to play with him and Speedo.

"Next time," Rhodes said.

He sat at the table and ate the eggs and bacon, which weren't really cold at all, and the toast, which was. Rhodes didn't mind. Yancey made a strategic retreat into another room, in case the cats woke up and decided to chase him, not that they ever had. Chased him, that is. They did wake up now and then, and in fact they were both awake now, watching Rhodes eat. Or watching

66

something. Their stares were hard to read. Rhodes thought that maybe their minds were usually filled with something like white noise, though maybe they were solving algebra problems. He just couldn't tell.

"Now about those donkeys," Ivy said when Rhodes had finished and taken his plate to the sink.

"Two more of them," he said. "Won't be the last ones, either. I just hope I don't have to help catch the next ones."

"There must have been more than just donkeys to keep you out so late."

"There was," Rhodes said, and he told her about Burt Collins.

"I heard about the fracas at the art gallery," Ivy said when he was finished. "Do you think that had anything to do with Burt's murder?"

Ivy worked for an insurance agent, and while her office wasn't like the Beauty Shack, she did hear things.

"Too soon to know of any connection," Rhodes said. "I'll get started on the investigation today. Maybe I'll have it solved by lunch."

"That would be nice. Was it his wife? The wife is always the first suspect when a husband dies."

"You've been watching *48 Hours* again," Rhodes said, though she did have a point.

Ivy ignored his comment. "They've had their problems. He never treated her well."

Rhodes recalled having heard something similar that morning. "How badly did he treat her?"

"I don't know. I don't know how far it went. I've just heard vague things."

"She bought him that bust he was killed with. Now it's missing."

"I'm not a psychologist," Ivy said, "but I did take an introductory course in college as an elective. You want me to tell you all the implications of that?"

"I took psychology, too, but I don't see too many implications."

Ivy shrugged. "Maybe you need to watch *48 Hours* with me sometime."

Rhodes pushed away from the table. "Might not be a bad idea. Could give me some tips on what I'm doing wrong."

Ivy came over and gave him a peck on the cheek. "You don't need any tips. You're the crime-busting champ of Blacklin County."

"Just the county?"

"It's a big county."

"Not the state?"

"I don't know about the whole state. We have two hundred and fifty-four counties, after all."

"How about the tri-county area, then?"

Ivy laughed. Rhodes had always liked her laugh. "I'll concede that you're probably the crime-busting champ of the tri-county area."

"Then I guess I should get out there and do my job," Rhodes said.

"Evildoers, beware."

"Durn tootin'," Rhodes said.

Rhodes's first stop was the jail, where he met with Andy Shelby and Ruth Grady. He assigned Andy to the area surrounding the Collins house and told Ruth to check the house and talk with the neighbors.

"And let Mrs. Collins know I'll want to talk to her later today," Rhodes added.

"What about fingerprints?" Ruth asked.

"You can check the room we found the body in. Too many people have touched everything else. Probably everything in there, too. Did you have a look at the paint can?"

"Nothing you can use on it," Ruth said. "Just some smears."

That was about what Rhodes had expected.

"Maybe I'll find a bronze head in the brush," Andy said. "Covered with clear fingerprints."

"That would be great," Rhodes said. "What are the odds?"

"Never mind," Andy said.

After the deputies left, Hack asked Rhodes if he'd looked at the latest news on Jennifer Loam's Web site.

"No," Rhodes said, "and that's not the end of that story. I don't plan to look at it."

"Jealous?" Hack said, with a look at Lawton, who was grinning.

"No," Rhodes said. "Jealous of what?"

"Of Seepy Benton," Lawton said.

"Why would I be jealous of him?"

"'Cause the video of the riot yesterday makes him look like the second coming of Bruce Lee. Or maybe of Sage Barton."

"Good," Rhodes said. "I hope everybody will get off my case about Sage Barton now."

"Kinda touchy about that, ain't you," Lawton said.

"Low T," Hack said.

"Low what?"

"Low T. Happens when a man gets to be a certain age. He gets the low T."

"One thing that it does to a man is make him touchy," Lawton said.

"Another thing is that a man gets thin spots in his hair," Hack said. "Low T can be a serious condition."

"I don't know what you're talking about," Rhodes said.

Lawton made a *tsk-tsk-tsk* sound. "Touchy, like I said. Bound to be a case of low T."

"I still don't get it," Rhodes said.

"T stands for testosterone," Hack said, "but in the TV ads, they just call it low T. You can get a checkup from your doctor, and he can tell you if you got the low T. Then you can get somethin' to take care of it."

"Side effects are kinda scary, though," Lawton said. "I think death is one of 'em."

"I'm too young to die," Rhodes said. He was used to having Lawton and Hack gang up on him, and he brushed it off. "Let's talk about the robbery last night at Oscar Henderson's store."

"Duke didn't solve it," Hack said. "He's got himself a clue, though. It's there in his report."

"Why don't you just tell me," Rhodes said. Hack always wormed the details about everything from the deputies. He couldn't stand not knowing about everything that went on.

"It's a pretty good clue," Lawton said.

Hack turned to look at Lawton.

"I'm tellin' this," Hack said.

"Go on, then," Lawton said. "Don't let me stop you."

Not much chance of that, Rhodes thought.

"He found the money," Hack said.

"The money?"

"The loot, the geetus, the simoleons."

"Where?" Rhodes asked.

"Back in the trees," Lawton said before Hack could get it in. He would've said more, but Hack stared him down.

"Thief prob'ly dropped it," Hack said when he was through looking at Lawton. "Buddy got there pretty quick, so the thief was in a hurry, I guess, and dropped the loot. He took a big risk for nothin'."

"Oscar's happy, though," Lawton said, "or he would be if he had his money."

"Evidence," Hack said. "Gotta get it printed and such."

Rhodes wondered how many people had handled that money. Fingerprints were highly overrated in most cases. The money wasn't much of a clue at all, in spite of what Hack had said.

"We'll get the money back to Oscar as soon as we can," Rhodes said. "Maybe there won't be any more robberies."

"Yeah, right," Hack said, "and maybe the wild hogs will all disappear or maybe move to Fort Worth and Dallas and take the copper thieves and meth cookers along with 'em."

"What about Burt?" Lawton asked. "We was kinda sorry to hear about him, even if he wasn't the best citizen in town."

Rhodes hadn't had to fence with them about Burt's death. Hack would've extracted all the details from Buddy when he made his report.

"That Burt's never been nothin' but trouble," Hack said, showing no sympathy for the deceased. "Even when he was a kid, he was a mean one."

"That's the truth," Lawton said. "'Member the time he beat up on Len Crosby's boy when they were in grade school?"

"Bully," Hack said. "Always was."

"Picked on the Patels, too," Lawton said. "I believe he's the one painted those devil signs on their hotel."

"Both hotels," Hack said.

"We never did prove that," Rhodes said. "Didn't have a speck of evidence."

"He used spray paint, too," Hack said, paying no attention to Rhodes. "Just like he did on those pictures at the gallery yesterday."

"There's no proof of that, either," Rhodes said.

"You're fallin' down on the job, then. You need to get you some proof. You could have those paint samples from the hotels analyzed and compare 'em with the ones from yesterday."

"That wouldn't help. Walmart must sell a dozen cans of that paint a week."

"Well, you better do somethin'," Hack said.

"What I need to do is find out who killed him."

"That'd be a real good thing for you to do, all right," Hack said.

Chapter 8

▼

It was still a little early for the judging of the paintings that Marilyn Bradley had mentioned, but that was all right. Rhodes had some questions he wanted to ask at the Beauty Shack.

He parked in front of the building. The pea gravel of the parking lot crunched under his feet when he got out of the car. He took a minute to look over the building. Lonnie Wallace had done a few things with it, including a new paint job, that had spiffed it up a bit. Lonnie had also installed a new alarm system after he'd been burglarized a few months ago. He should've done it sooner, but that crime had been solved, and the hair extensions that the thief had taken had been returned.

Rhodes went up the two concrete steps and into the building, where he was greeted by the usual indefinable smell of the place. Chemicals, hair spray, singed hair, and who knew what else. Lonnie was at the cash register running a credit card through a machine. A woman Rhodes didn't know chatted with him while he did it. Abby Tustin, whom Rhodes had met in the course of his investigation into the death of Lynn Ashton, was washing a woman's hair. Another woman, a petite brunette, was getting Polly Mercer seated under one of the big dryers. Polly, the wife of a local car dealer, had curlers in her hair.

Lonnie finished his transaction, saw his customer out the door, and walked over to Rhodes.

"Need a haircut, Sheriff?" Lonnie asked.

"Not today. I have a question for you, about Ella Collins."

"Does it have to do with Burt and what happened yesterday?"

"It does," Rhodes said.

"Is Burt filing charges on me?"

Rhodes didn't answer. He looked around. There wasn't any place where he and Lonnie could talk privately except the rest-room, and that didn't seem appropriate. So Rhodes went behind the counter where the cash register was. Lonnie followed him.

"Burt Collins won't be filing any charges," Rhodes said in a low voice. "He's dead."

Lonnie looked stunned. "Oh my God. What happened? Heart attack? Because he looked bad yesterday, you know? Like he had a blood pressure problem."

"It wasn't a heart attack," Rhodes said. "Somebody killed him."

"Oh my God," Lonnie said again. He must have liked saying it because he said it a third time. "Oh my God. Who did it?"

"I don't know yet," Rhodes told him.

Lonnie took a step backward. "You don't think I did it, do you? Because of what happened yesterday? I swear it was just an accident. I tripped on the curb. I didn't want to hurt Burt."

"I don't know if you wanted to hurt him or if you killed him,"

Rhodes said, "but everybody's a suspect right now. You have a good alibi?"

"I'm still in shock from hearing about Burt," Lonnie said, putting a hand to his forehead. "Give me a second."

Lonnie's shock appeared genuine, but Rhodes wasn't going to eliminate him as a suspect just yet. He was willing to give him a second, however.

"I'm surprised you hadn't heard about Burt already," Rhodes said after a little more than a second had passed.

Lonnie had composed himself. He looked around the shop. "Those are our first customers. They didn't know, or I'd have heard."

"Who's the new employee?"

"That's Paula Jean," Lonnie said. "She's taking Lynn's place. I'm still one person short, but I have somebody coming in later this week to talk about a job."

"I hope you find somebody," Rhodes said. "Now about that alibi."

"I was just so surprised that I couldn't think," Lonnie said. He looked a little bit relieved. "I was at a party last night with a lot of other people out at the college. Don McClaren had a reception out there for all the artists."

"All of them were there?"

"I think so. You could ask Don."

"I will," Rhodes said. "Were they all there all the time?"

"Well, that would be hard to say, but *I* was."

Rhodes wondered if Lonnie could prove it, but he decided to let it go for the moment. He'd talk to Seepy Benton about the party. Seepy was observant, some of the time. He'd know if Lonnie had been there.

"Eric was there, too," Lonnie said.

So everyone from the art gallery was there, or at least that was the case according to Lonnie, who might not be the most reliable witness. He'd want to protect Eric, and Eric would no doubt return the favor.

"I have another question for you," Rhodes said, getting to the other reason for his visit to the Beauty Shack. "It's about Ella Collins."

"What about her?"

"Someone told me that she and Burt didn't get along. You know anything about that?"

Lonnie looked thoughful. "I don't like to spread gossip."

"Beauty operators aren't lawyers," Rhodes said. "There's no confidentiality involved in the relationship."

"Well, some of our customers might not see it that way," Lonnie said, "but I guess you're right. Abby did Ella's hair. You should probably talk to her."

Abby had begun to blow-dry her client's hair. The dryer was not unlike the one that had been used to kill Lynn Ashton, and it sounded almost as loud as a jet engine to Rhodes, who stood beside Lonnie and waited until Abby turned it off. When she did, Lonnie went over and whispered something to her. She left him to finish with her customer and came over to Rhodes.

"Lonnie says you wanted to ask me about Mrs. Collins," Abby said. "He says somebody killed her husband."

"That's right," Rhodes said. "Somebody did, and I'm trying to find out who."

"You don't think it was Mrs. Collins, do you?"

Abby was as short as Paula Jean, and she had to look up at Rhodes. She seemed unhappy to be talking about Ella Collins.

"I don't know who killed him," Rhodes said. "I have to check everything out, and I've heard that Mrs. Collins and her husband didn't get along. I thought you might know something about that."

"People do talk an awful lot in beauty shops," Abby said. "I don't know why that is, but I guess it's always been like that."

Rhodes didn't know why it was, either, but maybe it had something to do with the fact that the little shops seemed so cozy and so friendly that people thought their secrets wouldn't go anywhere. Or that there really was some kind of confidentiality involved and that confiding in the person who was cutting your hair was like confessing to a priest. Or that the whine of the dryers would drown out their voices and that their secrets would never really be heard. Or maybe the smell and all those chemicals did something to the brain.

"What did Mrs. Collins say about Burt?" Rhodes asked.

Abby ducked her head. "She said he was mean to her."

"Did she give any examples?"

"Well, she couldn't sign the checks on the bank account. Burt kept all the money in his name, and he had a say in every penny she spent. She tried to save up a little now and then, but he always found out about it and took it away from her. There were a few times, two, maybe, that she couldn't afford to pay for her haircut, but she said she'd bring me the money. I wasn't sure I should trust her, but Lonnie said it would be all right. He said a woman needed a little something to boost her spirits now and then, even if it was just a haircut, and that she'd pay us. She did, too. The first time. Paid in cash. She didn't tip, but I never minded. Her husband was awful mean."

Money was the kind of thing that could lead to serious problems, all right. Burt hadn't worked for a while. He got some kind of disability pension, Rhodes believed, and he did odd jobs now and then, but there wasn't a lot of money flowing into the Collins household. Ella might have been able to get a job, but Burt wasn't the kind to want his wife to be the one bringing in the income.

"What about the second time she couldn't pay?" Rhodes asked.

"Well, that was just this week. On Tuesday. She said she'd have the money for me today, but she didn't come. I can understand why, though. I'm sure she'll be in with it when . . . when things are better for her."

Rhodes wondered if Ella would even remember about owing for the haircut.

"Did she say what happened when Burt found out about how she was squirreling money away?" Rhodes asked.

"He'd yell," Abby told him. "He yelled a lot. Once he hit her. She kind of tried to make a joke out of that, but I could tell it was serious. She said he didn't mean to hurt her. I think he did, though."

So did Rhodes. When he'd started out in law enforcement, he'd been surprised at how many people stayed in abusive relationships. They were always good at rationalization. It didn't surprise him anymore, but it still made him sad.

"Anything else?" Rhodes asked.

"No, that was all. She wasn't happy much, though, not when I saw her, anyway."

Rhodes imagined Burt yelling at Ella. He could see her snatching the bronze bust of Dale Earnhardt Junior and bashing him in the head with it. She could have hidden the head in the house, and that would explain why it hadn't been found.

"Thanks," Rhodes said. "I appreciate the help."

"I'm glad to help." Abby looked around the shop. "I wish I couldn've helped Lynn before she got killed."

Rhodes looked at the spot on the floor where Lynn Ashton's body had lain. There was no sign now that anyone had died there.

"You had no way to know that was going to happen," Rhodes said.

Abby sighed. "I guess, but I still wish I could've done something."

People always wished that. Rhodes wished it, too, but all he could do was to come along afterward and try to make things as right as he could.

"You'd better go back to your client," he said, "before Lonnie steals her."

Abby smiled. "He'd never do that. He's a good boss. Better than Sandra, even."

Sandra had been the previous owner of the Beauty Shack. She hadn't been such a good boss, Rhodes thought, taking everything into account.

"Ask him to come over here," Rhodes said, and Abby went over to Lonnie, who relinquished the client and returned to his spot behind the counter.

"Was she any help?" he asked.

"We'll see," Rhodes said. "It's too soon right now to make any assumptions."

"You know I didn't have anything to do with Burt's death, right?"

"I hope you didn't, but I don't know it," Rhodes said.

"Well, I didn't," Lonnie said. "Trust me."

Rhodes grinned. "Sure. Can I use your phone?"

"Since you trust me, I'll trust you," Lonnie said. "Phone's right there."

Most of the businesses left in Clearview still had landline telephones, and the Beauty Shack had a classic model, an old one that crouched on the countertop like a big black bullfrog. It had push-buttons, though, and not a dial, so it wasn't an antique. Beside it lay something else that was nearly as obsolete as the phone, a telephone book. It was a thin one, but it held the numbers for Blacklin and two other counties. The illustration on the cover was a photo of the Clearview downtown in the 1940s. There seemed to Rhodes to be as many cars parked along the streets in the picture as there were at Walmart these days. Probably not, however.

He found Frances Bennett's number in the book and punched it in. After a couple of rings, someone answered.

"Bennett residence. This is Doris Clements speaking."

"Hello, Doris," Rhodes said. "This is Sheriff Dan Rhodes."

"Sure it is, and I'm the Queen of the May. You should be ashamed of yourself. I'm going to report you to the phone company, and then I'm going to call the *real* sheriff."

Rhodes knew Doris slightly. She was one of the women who'd been outside the senior center yesterday.

"Doris," he said, "this really is the sheriff. I saw you at the senior center yesterday when all the excitement was going on." He thought for a second. "You were wearing a blue jacket."

"Hmpf," Doris said. "I guess you are the real sheriff. You're pretty observant."

"I'm a trained lawman."

Doris laughed. "That must be why you keep getting elected. I'm sorry I snapped at you like I did. Frances is always getting annoying phone calls when I'm here, and sometimes I get a little cranky about them. Those telemarketers ought to be strung up."

Rhodes wasn't fond of telemarketers, either, but stringing them up might be going a little too far.

"I hope I'm not being too annoying," he said, "but I need to speak to Frances if she can come to the phone."

The second he said "come to the phone," Rhodes realized how old-fashioned it made him sound. Nobody had to come to the phone anymore except in places like the Beauty Shack or the sheriff's department. Elsewhere the phone was just carried to the person being called if she didn't answer.

If Doris noticed anything odd, she didn't mention it. "Frances is right here. Hang on."

Rhodes heard Doris say, "It's the sheriff," and then Frances was on the line.

"Hello, Sheriff. What can I do for you?"

"First you can tell me how you're doing after your surgery."

"It was a knee replacement, is what it was. Since Larry passed away, I don't have anybody here to help me get around. If we'd had kids, maybe one of them could've come and stayed, but as it is, I need some help. I'm not in a lot of pain because I have pills for that, and I don't mind taking them like some folks do. If I hurt, I'll take whatever will help me. Even if I'm not hurting, though, I need help getting around and bathing and cooking and such. I'm lucky to have so many friends here in town, like Doris. They've all been really nice to me."

Well, Rhodes thought when Frances stopped to take a breath, *I asked.* "It was one of your friends I wanted to ask you about. Ella Collins."

"Oh, lordy, poor Ella. I guess you've heard about Burt. That was a real shock. Ella called and told me about it this morning. It happened while she was over here, you know, and she went home and found him. She thinks it might've been a heart attack. Burt's always had high blood pressure, you know, and I wouldn't be a bit surprised if he'd had a stroke or a heart attack or something like that. Ella said she'd try to come over tonight to help out, but I told her it would be all right if she couldn't. Doris said her sister, Margaret, could come if Ella can't. I swear, I don't know what I'd do without these good women. I just worry that if Ella had been home with Burt, she might've been able to do something to help him."

Rhodes didn't see any reason to tell Frances that Burt hadn't died of perfectly natural causes. Apparently Ella had convinced herself that he had, and she'd put Dale Earnhardt's head out of her mind. Or maybe she just hadn't wanted to tell Frances what had really happened. Frances was just the type to spread it all over town, not that everybody in town wouldn't know as soon as they looked at *A Clear View for Clearview*. It would be the big headline on the Web site today, and for days to come, probably.

"I'm sorry about Ella's loss," Rhodes said, "but I don't think there's anything she could've done to help Burt, even if she hadn't been there with you the whole time."

"I guess you're right. I needed her last night, and she was an angel of mercy. If she didn't make sure I took my pills, I might not ever get to sleep."

"I know she was a help to you," Rhodes said. "I'm glad you have friends to take care of you. I hope you're up and hopping around soon."

"That'll be the day, but I appreciate the thought. Thank you for your concern."

Rhodes hung up. If she had any idea that Rhodes had called for any reason other than to check on her, she didn't say so. She liked talking so much that she'd never even thought that he might have another reason, like checking on Ella's alibi. He was glad he hadn't had to mention that.

Rhodes looked around the Beauty Shack. No one was paying

him the least attention. Paula Jean was combing out her client's hair, and Abby was getting another client settled in front of a sink. Lonnie was greeting a client at the door. As soon as she was inside, Rhodes thanked Lonnie for the use of the phone and left.

The senior center didn't have many activities on Saturdays, so most of the cars parked along the block in front of the art gallery belonged to the artists or to the curious who'd come to see how the judging turned out.

Rhodes stood in the doorway and looked around. In the center of the gallery was a table with refreshments, some kind of punch, with crackers and cheese and vegetables set out on plates. Rhodes was not surprised to see Seepy Benton standing near the table. Benton liked to be near free food. He was talking to Jennifer Loam, who appeared to be listening intently. It was just as well that Andy Shelby wasn't there.

The room hummed with conversation. Don McClaren was showing someone one of the paintings that had a blue ribbon hanging from the frame. The painting was colorful, Rhodes had to admit that, with various shades of pink and red and blue, and some white thrown in occasionally. It didn't look like anything that Rhodes had ever seen before, and he figured that might be a point in its favor.

Eric Stewart and Marilyn Bradley were standing with Dr. King, the college dean, a tall woman with lacquered hair that Rhodes thought was an unnatural shade of black. Someday he'd ask Lonnie about that, though Lonnie might not want to tell him. If it didn't involve murder, Rhodes was willing to admit that confidentiality might be all right. Marilyn seemed quite agitated, and Rhodes wished he could hear what was being said.

Seepy caught sight of Rhodes, and he and Jennifer Loam came over to the door.

"Come on in," Seepy said. "Have some punch."

"While you're drinking it, you can tell me all about Burt Collins," Jennifer said.

"How did you find out?" Rhodes asked.

"It was easy. I'm a reporter."

"Have you told anyone else?"

"Just me," Seepy said. "She knows I can be trusted, since I'm the model for Sage Barton."

"That was an item I hadn't uncovered," Jennifer said. "Why didn't you tell me, Sheriff? It should've been obvious to me, considering the initials, but it was the martial arts moves that clinched it."

Seepy made an attempt to look modest and failed miserably. Modesty wasn't his best trait.

"I'm glad the truth is out," Rhodes said. "Now maybe people will stop asking me about that character."

"I wouldn't count on it," Jennifer said. "After all, Sage Barton is a sheriff, while Dr. Benton is a math teacher."

"And a darn good one," Seepy said. "As of today, you can add award-winning painter to that list."

"You won a prize?" Rhodes couldn't quite keep the surprise out of his voice. "I thought your painting was damaged."

"Well, not first prize, but I did get a ribbon. The judges met and decided not to let the vandalism affect their decisions. They'd judge the painting by the way it looked before the vandalism."

"I guess that's only fair," Rhodes said, "as long as they could tell what the original was."

"They'd seen them already," Seepy said. "They knew what they looked like before they were vandalized, so they could make an informed decision."

"Who were the judges?" Rhodes asked, but before Seepy could answer, Jennifer broke in.

"You're very sly, Sheriff," she said, "but you're not fooling me."

Rhodes tried to look puzzled, with about as much success as Seepy had when he'd tried to look modest. "Fooling you?"

"You know what I mean. You've managed to get the conversation well away from Burt Collins and what happened to him last night."

Rhodes started to say that he'd had plenty of help from Seepy in leading the conversation, but then they'd be right back to Sage Barton. So Rhodes tried another tack.

"I don't know what happened to him," he said.

"You know he's dead, and you know he didn't die of natural causes."

That wasn't technically true. Rhodes hadn't seen an autopsy report, so he didn't know the exact cause of death. He had what he considered a pretty good guess, but until it was official, a guess was all he had.

"Not exactly," Rhodes said.

"You're investigating his death, though. Or your deputies are. I saw two county cars at Collins's house this morning."

"We have to look at every angle," Rhodes said.

"I'll help you," Benton said. "Do you know how many hits the video of the riot yesterday has had already? Thanks to me and my martial arts skills."

"How many?" Rhodes asked, glad to change the subject.

"A lot," Benton said. "How can I help with the investigation?"

"You can tell me who the judges were, to start with."

"Don McClaren and Eric Stewart."

That made sense. McClaren was an art teacher and an artist,

and Stewart was the one who ran the gallery. He'd know at least a little bit about art.

"Now that we have that out of the way," Benton said, "do you want to give me a badge and swear me in?"

Rhodes wasn't paying much attention to Benton, as the conversation among McClaren, Stewart, Dr. King, and Marilyn Bradley had become heated. Rhodes thought it might be a good idea to see what was going on.

Before he could get to them, riot number two had begun.

Chapter 9

▼

Rhodes, of course, wouldn't have called it a riot, but Jennifer Loam did on her video account of it, so that's the way it was later viewed in the county. Rhodes had to admit that it did involve the throwing of vegetables and a good bit of yelling, though he still didn't believe that flung vegetables and some loud voices constituted a riot.

The person doing most of the yelling was Marilyn Bradley, and she was yelling at Don McClaren and Eric Stewart, both of whom backed away from her and started edging toward the doorway into the back part of the building, that one being the nearest to them.

Marilyn was right behind them, and as she passed the food table, she picked up one of the plates of vegetables. She then used the vegetables as missiles. Broccoli, cauliflower, and carrots sailed through the air.

If she'd had good aim and hit only her intended targets—that is, if McClaren and Stewart were indeed the targets—things might not have gotten out of hand. However, she also hit some of the others in the room, so they decided to join in the fun by hurling vegetables of their own. Crackers were also involved.

Rhodes thought that Dean King might have prevented Marilyn's actions before they got out of hand, but instead the dean just stood and watched in amazement. So did everyone else who wasn't throwing something, so it was up to Rhodes to put a stop to things.

By the time he got to Marilyn, Stewart and McClaren had escaped into the rear of the building, pulling the door shut behind them. Marilyn stood in front of the door, still yelling but no longer tossing vegetables. Others were, however, and Rhodes had to slap aside a couple of cauliflower florets and some broccoli on his way to her.

He snatched the platter away from Marilyn and handed it to Benton, who was following along right behind him.

"Hold that," Rhodes said.

Jennifer Loam was there, too, her little camera recording everything. Rhodes was starting to have serious doubts about the new forms of journalism.

"You want me to subdue her?" Benton asked.

Rhodes knew he meant Marilyn, but for one unworthy second he wondered what would happen if Jennifer were subdued and her camera confiscated.

"No," he said. "Move away."

Something in his tone must have gotten through to both Benton and Jennifer, and they stepped back so Rhodes could confront Marilyn.

"What's the matter with you?" Rhodes asked.

The noise behind him died down, and no more vegetables flew through the air. Quite a few of them lay on the floor, though.

"I'm upset," Marilyn said. Her body was taut, and her orange hair was even wilder than before, as if it might be reflecting her mood. "I needed to vent."

"This isn't exactly a good time or place for that," Rhodes said.

"I know," Marilyn said. Some of the tension went out of her body. "It was a mistake to let myself lose it like that."

Rhodes looked around. Everyone was watching them. Benton stood there holding the platter.

"It's okay," he told Marilyn. "Just a little error in judgment." To Benton he said, "See if you can find anything left to eat and eat it."

He turned back to Marilyn. "We can't talk here. We'll go outside."

He took her arm to be sure she went with him and guided her through the curious crowd and out to the sidewalk. He was glad Benton and Jennifer hadn't tried to follow.

"I'm sorry," Marilyn said as soon as they were out the door. "That was terrible behavior, and I let my temper get the better of me. I hope you can forgive me."

"I'm not in that business," Rhodes said. "I just try to keep the peace. You're not making it easy for me."

"I know, and I apologize. I really am sorry. I want to apologize to the judges, too."

"What got you started in the first place? Did they say something?"

"I don't want to talk about it. I've apologized to you, and I'll apologize to them. Isn't that enough?"

Rhodes thought it over. No real harm had been done, and maybe it was a private matter. He looked through the door and saw that Stewart and McClaren had come back into the gallery. They were talking to Dr. King and taking an occasional glance outside.

"All right," Rhodes said. "We'll go back inside so you can apologize."

"Do I have to do it now? I'm really embarrassed."

"You have to do it now," Rhodes said.

Marilyn stood where she was. "I can't."

"Sure you can. Let's go."

Rhodes went through the door, hoping that Marilyn would follow him. He didn't want to put his hand on her this time. She might get upset and start throwing things at him if he did.

He needn't have worried. She caught up with him and walked beside him over to where McClaren, Stewart, and Dr. King stood. Everyone else in the room was careful to ignore them except for Seepy Benton and Jennifer Loam, who made no attempt to conceal their curiosity. They stayed well away, however.

McClaren and Stewart looked a bit wary of Marilyn, but she said, "I'm very sorry for what I did. It was stupid and silly. I don't blame anyone but myself. I want to apologize."

Rhodes thought that sounded all right, but McClaren and Stewart still appeared a little bit put off by Marilyn. Finally Stewart said, "Well, then, I accept your apology. Let's just forget all about it."

Rhodes didn't think that was possible. No matter what people said, they never forgot all about it.

"I accept, too," McClaren said. "Let's see if we can get some of this mess cleaned up and carry on with the ceremony."

"Ceremony?" Rhodes said. "What ceremony?"

"The announcement of the winners," Stewart said. "The ribbons are on the paintings, but the official announcement hasn't been made."

Rhodes didn't think he'd stay around for that. What he'd come for was a word with Seepy Benton. He looked around and saw Benton talking to Loam again.

"Excuse me," Rhodes said. "I have to speak to someone."

He left McClaren and Stewart with Marilyn and went over to Benton.

"Come outside for a minute," Rhodes said, taking Benton's arm. "I need to ask you some questions."

"What about?" Jennifer asked.

"Nothing you'd be interested in," Rhodes said. "They're about to announce the winners. You'll want to get video of that."

"I'm one of the winners," Benton said.

"I won't keep you long," Rhodes told him, giving him a gentle tug on his arm. "Come on."

Benton went with him out of the building. "I really need to get back inside," he said.

"In a minute. They have to get the vegetables off the floor before the announcement. You don't need to help with that. Tell me about the reception last night."

"It was very nice. I was dressed to the nines. I even wore leather shoes."

"I didn't want a fashion report. I want to know who was there. I want to know especially about Marilyn Bradley, Eric Stewart, Lonnie Wallace, and Don McClaren."

"Why them? What's this about?"

"I'm just trying to find out if they all have alibis."

"Alibis? I thought you told Jennifer you didn't know the cause of death for sure."

"I don't. That is, I don't have an official cause of death. What I *think* happened was that somebody hit Burt in the head with a bust of Dale Earnhardt."

"Junior or Senior?"

"Does it matter?

"It does to NASCAR fans."

"Junior, then. Don't mention any of this to Jennifer Loam. Or to anyone else, for that matter."

Seepy touched his lips with his forefinger. "My lips are sealed."

"Good," Rhodes said. "Now what about the alibis?"

"Well, all the people you named were there, if that's what you mean."

"From when until when?"

"The reception started at seven, and just about everybody was there on time. You know how these things are. Everybody was gone by nine thirty or ten."

Rhodes thought about that. He'd found Burt about eleven thirty, and Burt had been dead for a while. Not long, maybe an hour, and it would be hard to establish a more exact time of death. It seemed to Rhodes that anyone who'd been at the reception could've killed him. So much for Lonnie's alibi.

"Nobody hung around to clean up?"

"Somebody from the college housecleaning staff took care of all that. The snacks were catered by the college, too, so someone would've come by to pick up what was left over."

"All right," Rhodes said. "That's what I wanted to know. You can go back in and pick up your award."

"I hope someone will record me on video."

"I'm sure it'll be on *A Clear View of Clearview* in mere minutes," Rhodes said.

"You're right. It won't be as good as the one of me subduing the rioters, though."

"You'd better get in there before they think you've left and give the award to somebody else."

"I'm already there," Benton said.

Two county cars were parked outside the Collins house when Rhodes got there. He didn't see either Ruth Grady or Andy Shelby, but he assumed that Ruth was still inside or talking with the neighbors and that Andy was searching the area. He parked his own car and was on his way in when Andy came out of the trees.

"Hey, Sheriff," Andy said.

"Find anything?" Rhodes asked.

"Just a lot of trash. I don't think anybody's been out there except kids. Most of the trash probably blew in from the street when people threw it out of their cars. Somebody was out there last night breaking twigs and such, but that was probably Buddy."

Rhodes might have made a mistake by having Buddy check things out. He could have covered up any clues, but it might not matter. Rhodes didn't really think that whoever killed Burt had gone through the trees.

Ruth Grady came outside and said, "I didn't find anything, either, and I've talked to the people in the three closest houses. None of them remembers hearing or seeing anything unusual. If a car drove up here last night, they wouldn't have thought anything of it."

"Did you check the computers?"

"They don't own a computer. They must be the last holdouts in town."

Rhodes doubted it. There were probably several other people who didn't have computers.

"It's a big house," he said. "You searched the whole thing?"

"The upstairs is mostly vacant," Ruth said. "I don't think anybody's been up there in years. No computers, no busts of Dale Earnhardt. Lots of dust bunnies, though."

"So you really didn't find anything," he said.

"That's right. I wish I had."

"It's okay." Rhodes hadn't had much hope that any big clues would be found. He'd occasionally read about some bank robber who filled out a deposit slip with his real name and left it in the bank or about a convenience store robber who dropped his wallet as he fled, but nothing like that had ever happened in Blacklin County. At least not since Rhodes had become the sheriff. Maybe some of his predecessors had been luckier.

"Did you know that Mrs. Collins isn't here?" Ruth asked.

Rhodes glanced at the carport. Both the Collins vehicles were parked there. "Where is she?"

"At the new hotel on the east side of town. Her sister was here to pick up a few things when I got here, and she let me in. She said they went to the hotel last night because Mrs. Collins couldn't stand to stay in the house. The thought of Burt dying here while she was gone was too much for her."

That was interesting. Manish Patel was the manager of the hotel, and he was the one who'd had more than one little run-in with Burt. Ella Collins might not even know about that, however, if Burt was the kind to keep secrets.

"You two can go back on patrol," Rhodes said. "There's a lot of county out there, and we can't spend all our time here. I'll go to the hotel and talk to Mrs. Collins."

He was going to talk to Manish Patel, too. It might be interesting to see what he was doing while Burt was being killed.

The new hotel was like so many others that had sprung up in small towns all across Texas in the last few years, plain but functional. If they could survive and even thrive there in places like Clearview, they could do just as well elsewhere. Rhodes had heard that more than half of the middle-sized motels and hotels in the country were owned by people of Indian descent, many of them named Patel, and while there'd been an occasional reaction against them earlier, it had died down. The only trouble in Clearview had come from Burt Collins.

As far as Rhodes was concerned the Patels were welcome. They worked hard, they stayed out of trouble, and they brought jobs and money into the community. It was true that a lot of the jobs were taken by family members, but Rhodes believed anything that stimulated the economy was welcome. Obviously Burt hadn't seen it that way, or he wouldn't have vandalized the hotels and the art exhibit.

Or maybe he hadn't done a thing at the art show. He'd acted guilty, but he hadn't admitted anything, and Rhodes reminded himself not to start making assumptions.

Rhodes counted eight cars in the parking lot. He didn't know if that was good or bad for a Saturday, not being in the hotel business himself. He parked next to a black pickup and got out.

The lobby of the hotel was small and so clean that it looked like a picture in a magazine ad. On the right was the check-in desk, and on the left were four overstuffed black leather-covered chairs arranged around a low square table. Rhodes didn't recognize the young man behind the desk, so he pulled his badge holder from his belt and walked over.

"Sheriff Dan Rhodes," he said. "I'd like to speak to Mr. Patel."

The man blinked, looked at the badge, and said, "One moment, please."

He opened a door behind the desk and stepped into what appeared to be an office, and in a couple of seconds he came back with Manish Patel.

Patel was considerably shorter than Rhodes and considerably better dressed. He wore a brown suit, white shirt, and brown tie. He had abundant black hair and a thick black mustache. His eyes were as black as his hair.

"Good morning, Sheriff," he said. He put a hand on the man's shoulder. "This is my cousin Jack. He has come here from Houston to work in the hotel and learn about the business. I have told him what a fine town Clearview is and how he will be very happy here."

"Pleased to meet you," Rhodes said to Jack. "I hope your cousin is right about how happy you'll be here."

"I'm sure he is," he said, and moved back to his position behind the desk.

"You have not come for a social visit, I suppose," Patel said.

"No, not exactly," Rhodes said. "Is there somewhere that we can talk?"

"Most certainly. Come."

Patel walked to the end of the counter and opened the gate that allowed Rhodes to go behind it.

"We will go into my office," Patel said, and Rhodes followed him in.

The office was small and just as neat as the lobby. The top of the black desk was bare except for a computer monitor. There were framed photographs on the wall that weren't of anywhere Rhodes had ever been or was ever likely to be. They showed buildings with domes, towers with staircases circling the outside, dancers in colorful saris.

Patel closed the door. "Gujarat. Where my parents come from. I have never been there, but I like to think that someday I will travel to see it."

Burt Collins thought of the Patels as immigrants, but Rhodes remembered that Manish had been born in Dallas. Manish's wife, Sunny, was from Houston.

"After you get rich in the hotel business, maybe you can go there," Rhodes said.

"That is the plan," Patel said. "Please. Have a seat."

Rhodes sat in a straight-backed chair with a seat covered in what appeared to be the same black leather as that on the chairs in the lobby. Patel went behind his desk and sat in his office chair.

"I have had no problems here," Patel said when he was settled. "No one has skipped on a bill. No one has tried to rob me."

"I know," Rhodes said. "This is about something else. Or someone else. Burt Collins."

"Ah, the late Mr. Collins. I am sorry that he is dead, but I cannot say I liked the man. We have had no visits from him recently, for which I am grateful." He paused. "His wife, however, is visiting us at this very moment, as you probably know. Along with her sister. That is how I know Mr. Collins is dead. I heard about it late last night when Mrs. Collins and her sister checked in. Mrs. Collins seems like a nice woman, much too nice to have been married to someone like Mr. Collins."

"He spray-painted your walls," Rhodes said.

"Yes, and not the back walls, either. The ones facing the highway. As I told you at the time, and I will say it again now, not to insult Mr. Collins's intelligence and his memory, but I was surprised that he even knew what an insult 'wog' could be."

There had been worse words than that, as Rhodes recalled. "That wasn't all he wrote on the wall."

"No, indeed, but it was a part of it. I did not wish the man ill, but I cannot say that his death fills me with great sorrow. I am a fan of *A Clear View for Clearview,* so I know that there are others he has irritated almost as much as me. The artists visiting Clearview, for example, some of whom are staying in this hotel."

It seemed to Rhodes that everyone in the county, or at least those who had a computer, took a daily look or two or three at Jennifer Loam's Web site. He hoped it was generating some good ad revenue for her.

"Did Mrs. Collins tell you how Burt died?"

"She said it was a heart attack, or maybe a stroke."

Rhodes wondered if Mrs. Collins thought that repeating that story often enough would make it true. He also wondered if Patel knew more about Burt's death than he was letting on.

"It was nothing like that," Rhodes said. "Someone killed him."

Patel's eyes widened. "Are you sure?"

Rhodes had been asked that question more than once under similar circumstances. It was as if people believed the county sheriff would tell them a lie or be mistaken about something as serious as murder.

"I'm sure," Rhodes said. "You said you were here when Mrs. Collins and her sister came in. Were you working?"

"I was. I often work late hours."

Rhodes knew that was true. Patel and his whole family had worked hard to make the hotel a success. The clock meant nothing to them.

"Had you been out last night?"

Patel tensed. "Sheriff, I hope you are not thinking I had anything to do with Mr. Collins's death."

"You and Burt have a history," Rhodes said. "I'm sure you're in the clear, but I have to ask."

Patel relaxed a bit. "I understand. I assure you that I never left the premises last night. You can ask any member of my family."

Rhodes had more or less expected that answer. The Patels were a close-knit group, and they would say Patel had been there even if he hadn't.

"What happened between me and Mr. Collins was months ago," Patel said. "I have forgotten it. He apologized, and I believe he paid a fine. I was satisfied."

Rhodes didn't believe it. Patel's earlier words about Collins had made it clear that Patel hadn't forgotten anything. Rhodes didn't think Patel was satisfied, either, but maybe he was just being polite. Now wasn't the time to press the issue.

Rhodes stood up. "I'm glad to hear it. I have to speak with Mrs. Collins now. Do you know her room number?"

Patel rose, too. "No, but Jack can tell you. I hope you find the one who killed Mr. Collins."

"I always get my man," Rhodes said.

"Or woman," Patel said, "as the case may be."

"True," Rhodes said.

Chapter 10

▼

The room looked like any hotel room anywhere. Two double beds, a landscape painting on the wall opposite the door, a flat-screen TV set on the dresser, a small desk, a night table with a lamp and clock radio sitting on top, and a desk chair. Not exactly suited for receiving visitors.

Rhodes stood just inside the door, and the sisters looked at him as if expecting him to say something profound. He wished he could think of something, but he couldn't. So he just said, "We need to talk about Burt."

"He was a son of a bitch," Bonnie said.

Rhodes looked at her. She was stocky, like her sister, but she wore her hair longer and appeared to be a few years younger.

"Please, Bonnie," Ella said. "Don't talk about Burt like that."

"It's about time somebody did. You've spent thirty years of your life defending him, and you know better than anybody what he was like. Even now when he's dead, he's still got you in a mess.

You can't even get to what little money he has in the bank. You should've left him a long time ago."

Rhodes found himself liking Bonnie. She didn't try to hide her feelings.

"He was so tight," Bonnie said, more to Rhodes than to Ella, "that if he had a penny, it'd have his fingerprints mashed into Abe Lincoln's face. He didn't give Ella a dime without quizzing her about how she'd spend it."

Rhodes remembered what Abby had told him about Ella's not being able to pay for having her hair done. Burt probably hadn't put much stock in a woman getting her hair done at a beauty shop, not when she had a sink and some soap to wash it with at home.

"Tighter than the bark on a tree," Bonnie said, "and mean besides. Did I mention that he was a son of a bitch?"

"I believe you did," Rhodes said.

"He was good to me," Ella said. "I know you don't believe it, but he was. In his own way."

"Baloney," Bonnie said. Rhodes had a feeling she would've used a stronger word if he hadn't been there. "He treated you like dirt, and I know he hit you more than once. I wouldn't blame you a bit if you'd killed him." Bonnie paused and looked at Rhodes. "Not that she did."

"He died of a heart attack," Ella said. "Or a stroke. Something like that."

"Tell her, Sheriff," Bonnie said. "She won't listen to me."

Rhodes nodded. "Somebody killed him, Mrs. Collins. I believe somebody hit him with that bronze head that's gone missing, and that's what killed him, not a stroke or a heart attack or anything like that. You have to accept it."

Ella started to sob and sat in the desk chair. Bonnie stood behind her and patted her shoulder.

"He's right, Ella," Bonnie said. "You can't keep denying it. Somebody killed Burt. Good riddance to bad rubbish, if you ask me."

Ella sobbed harder. Rhodes kept quiet.

After about half a minute, Ella got control of herself. "Who would have done a thing like that? Everybody loved Burt."

"Not everybody," Rhodes said, wondering if Ella could possibly be as oblivious to the obvious as she seemed. "He made some enemies around town. You must remember the trouble he had with the people who run this hotel."

"He said he was sorry about that. He didn't like the idea of foreigners coming here and taking our jobs, but he was sorry about painting the walls here."

"The Patels are from Houston," Rhodes said, thinking that Houston was like a foreign country to some people in Blacklin County. "They're all U.S. citizens."

"Burt never believed that. He said they came from India."

"A generation ago, maybe, but everybody working here was born in this country."

"If you say so."

Rhodes recalled that Burt had said the same thing only the day before. Neither he nor Ella was going to be confused by the facts.

"Was there anybody else that Burt had problems with?" Rhodes asked.

"No, nobody. Everybody liked him."

"I didn't," Bonnie said. "I have to tell you the truth, Ella, I'm not sorry he's gone."

Ella started to sob again. Bonnie looked at Rhodes. "I was in Thurston when he died, in case you're wondering."

"I know," Rhodes said. "I was at the house when Ella called you."

"She might've called my cell phone. I could've been lurking right outside."

"I'll check with your husband."

"You do that. Elbert Crowley. We live about a block off the street that runs in front of Hod Barrett's store. Hod doesn't much like you, did you know that?"

"I know that," Rhodes said. "He's not the only one."

"Hod says he's never voted for you and never will. That's all right. Elbert likes you. I think I do, too. You check with Elbert about me."

"I will. Will you and Ella be all right?"

Ella was still sobbing, but very quietly.

"Of course we will. I'm going to check out of here and take her by the funeral home. She needs to make the arrangements."

"Good idea," Rhodes said.

He said good-bye and left. He wanted to visit the funeral home, too, and he thought it would be a good idea to get there before the sisters did.

Rhodes pulled in behind Ballinger's Funeral Home and parked on the small paved lot. The funeral home had once been a mansion with tennis courts and a swimming pool on its grounds. Those were gone now, and the brick outbuilding that had been the servants' quarters was the office. It was also where Clyde Ballinger, the owner of the funeral home and its director, who was a bachelor, lived in the upstairs half.

"Come on in," Ballinger called when Rhodes knocked on his door.

Rhodes went inside and looked around. The office had changed a bit over the last few years, especially the top of Ballinger's desk, which used to be partially covered at all times by old paperback books, the kind that Ballinger liked to say weren't being written anymore. Their colorful and politically incorrect covers had been part of their appeal, but not to Ballinger, who was interested mainly in their contents. He still liked to read them, but now the only thing on his desk was some kind of tablet computer. He'd started out with a Kindle, Rhodes recalled, but that had been replaced.

"I thought you'd be dropping by, Sheriff," Ballinger said. "Dr. White's autopsy report is right here."

He opened a desk drawer and pulled out a folder, which he handed to Rhodes.

"Take a seat," Ballinger said. "Look it over. Then we'll get the personal effects. They're in the locker in the main building."

Rhodes sat down and flipped through the report. It confirmed that Burt's death had resulted from a blow to the head and mentioned that there were no defensive wounds. Burt hadn't been expecting anybody to pound in the back of his head. No mention of any residue on Burt's hands, either. If he'd been using spray paint, none of it had clung to him.

"You know who did it yet?" Ballinger asked when Rhodes was finished reading.

"Not yet," Rhodes said.

"Just a matter of time, though, right?"

"I hope so."

Ballinger patted his tablet. "If the boys from the Eight-Seven were on the case, they'd have it wrapped up in no time."

One of Ballinger's favorite writers was Ed McBain, who'd written a long series of books about the detectives of the 87th Precinct in a city a lot like New York. Ballinger loved to tell Rhodes what great crime-solvers the members of the Eight-Seven were. He didn't mean to imply that Rhodes and his deputies were inferior, or so he claimed.

"I don't have quite the manpower and facilities of the Eight-Seven," Rhodes said.

"They didn't have any more facilities than you do, back when they started. It was mostly grinding it out." Ballinger patted his tablet again. "You know the trouble with these things?"

"No," Rhodes said. "I don't own one."

"Well, you should, but here's the trouble. Even if you had one, you couldn't get all Ed McBain's books about the Eight-Seven for it. He wrote fifty or sixty of them, and they don't have near that many for sale."

"I thought you'd read all of them."

"Nope. There are still a few I need. I've about given up on garage sales, though. They don't turn up there anymore. I'll just have to wait till they get them into electronic format, I guess. I hope it'll be soon." He stood up. "You want to get those personal effects?"

"Sure," Rhodes said. "Let's go."

The back room of the funeral home was small and had probably been some kind of mudroom back in the old days. It was just fine now for holding two men, a locker, and not much else. Rhodes got the personal effects from the locker. They were sealed in a bag, but there was a list of them printed out: shirt, socks, pants, underwear, wallet, shoes, belt, keys, and thirty-seven cents in change.

"No cell phone," Rhodes said. He'd learned a lot about the value of cell phones in criminal cases over the last few years.

"I didn't know Burt very well," Ballinger said, "but if there was one man in town who didn't have a cell phone, it would be Burt."

Rhodes supposed that was true. No computer, no cell phone. Burt didn't care much for the twenty-first century. He probably hadn't cared much for the twentieth, either, considering the way he treated his wife.

"I'll take all this with me," Rhodes said. "Thanks for your help."

"Always happy to help the forces of the law. Will you be at the funeral?"

"Maybe. Depends on a lot of things. I'll decide after the arrangements have been made."

"Mrs. Collins is coming around later this morning. With her sister."

"I've met her sister," Rhodes said. "You'll like her."

"I like everybody," Ballinger said, and Rhodes almost believed him.

Rhodes went by the jail to file the autopsy report and to put Collins's possessions in the evidence locker. He'd have Ruth Grady go over them later.

Hack and Lawton looked ready for conversation as soon as Rhodes walked in, but he didn't give them a chance to get started. He wanted to log in the evidence and file the report before they got started on him.

When Rhodes was finished, he leaned back in his chair to relax for a second. That was all the opening Hack needed.

"Got a call from Miz Harbison this mornin'. You know Miz Harbison?"

Rhodes knew her, but Lawton didn't give him a chance to answer. He jumped right into the conversation. "She's a widow-woman lives down outside of town close to the old grain elevator. Lives by herself."

Hack wasn't about to let Lawton take over the conversation. "You know how it is with women livin' by themselves. They get a little nervous, and what she called about was a man who came bangin' on her door this mornin'."

"Told her his car broke down," Lawton said, earning himself one of Hack's patented glares.

"I'm the one took the call," Hack said.

Lawton just grinned, and Hack gave up glaring at him after a few seconds.

"Anyway," Hack said, "the man came up to her house and right up on the porch and started to bang on the door."

"You told that part already," Lawton said.

"I know I did, but you keep interruptin' me. If you'd let me tell it straight out, I wouldn't have to repeat things."

"Sorry 'bout that," Lawton said, but Rhodes could tell he wasn't sorry in the least.

"All right," Hack said, "where was I?"

"Man was banging on the door," Rhodes said before Lawton could.

"Yeah, and he was hittin' it pretty hard, Miz Harbison said. It was a brand-new door. She'd just got it the other day from Elmer at the hardware store out on the highway, and he'd sent somebody to install it. Good solid door, but she didn't want it banged up."

"She didn't open it, though," Lawton said.

Hack didn't even bother to look at him that time. He just sat and waited. When Lawton didn't offer anything more, Hack said, "She called out and asked him what he wanted. That's when he told her his car had broke down and could he use her phone."

"She didn't believe him," Lawton said.

Hack turned in his chair. Lawton clamped his mouth shut, and Hack turned back to Rhodes.

"She asked him if he had a cell phone," Hack said, "and he told her he wasn't gettin' any bars. No service out there. She didn't believe that, either. Her phone worked, so he must be lyin'."

"She has a cell phone?" Rhodes said.

"Nope. Just a landline, but it worked, so she figured his phone should work, too. She told him she was goin' for her shotgun, and she did. When she came back to the door, the man was gone, and she found out he'd punched a hole in her door."

Hack stopped.

"Brand-new door," Lawton said, and Hack didn't challenge him.

Rhodes knew they'd set him up for a big ending, but he didn't know what it could be. As usual, they were several steps ahead of him. They obviously wanted him to ask something, so he said, "Did you send out a deputy?"

"Sent Andy," Hack said. "He'd just left the Collins place, so he wasn't but a few miles away."

"Did he find the man?"

"Yeah," Hack said. "He was hikin' back toward town and lookin' plumb miserable. Andy asked him where he was headed, and he said back to town. Said his daddy had worked at the old grain elevator long time ago, when it was still operatin', and he wanted to take a look at it. Then his car conked out on him."

"Was that the truth?"

"Guess so. Andy called Cal Autry and told him to send a tow truck out to get the car and give the fella a ride into town."

"What about the door?"

"Andy asked him about that. The man said he didn't hurt the door. Just tapped on it with his bare knuckles."

"Andy checked, I hope."

"Sure he did. He knows how to treat a complaint."

"Found the hole, too," Lawton said.

Hack started to spin around in his chair, but Rhodes held up a hand to stop him.

"How big was the hole?" Rhodes asked.

"Pretty small," Hack said. "Real small, in fact."

"It was the peephole," Lawton said.

Hack stood up. Rhodes thought he might attack Lawton, who'd committed the biggest sin of all. He'd stolen the punch line. Hack didn't move for a second. Then he sighed and sat back down.

"It was the peephole," he said, as if Lawton hadn't spoken. "Miz Harbison hadn't noticed it before, and not ever havin' had one or seen one, she didn't even know it was there. Andy set her straight and showed her how it worked. She thinks it's a wonderful thing. 'What'll they think of next?' is what she said to Andy. She said she was sorry if she scared the man off, too. She didn't want to turn away anybody in trouble. The shotgun was just to make sure he didn't molest her."

"A woman livin' alone can't be too careful," Lawton said. "That's what Andy told her."

"I hope he didn't encourage her to shoot people," Rhodes said.

Andy was young and still learning the job. He had a tendency to overreact from time to time.

"Nope," Hack said. "He told her to be really picky about who she shot."

"That's a relief."

"Andy said he knew you'd appreciate how tactful he was. You found out who killed Burt yet?"

"Not yet," Rhodes said.

"Then why're you sittin' around listenin' to us?"

"Sometimes I ask myself the same thing," Rhodes said. He stood up. "I'll be at my courthouse office if you need me, and I'm turning off my cell phone. Don't tell anybody else where I am, and don't call me on the office phone unless it's a real emergency."

"Like if an asteroid is about to hit the earth and wipe out ever'body and ever'thing?" Hack asked.

"Yes," Rhodes said. "Like that."

"It wouldn't wipe out *ever'thing*," Lawton said. "The cockroaches would still be here."

"Not even the cockroaches could live through an asteroid hit," Hack said.

"I bet they could, and even if they couldn't, *somethin'* could. Like germs and such as that."

"Germs don't count," Hack said.

Before Lawton could object, Rhodes was out the door. He figured he'd escaped just in time to miss the fisticuffs.

Chapter 11

▼

When Rhodes wanted to think things over, he generally went to his office in the courthouse. That was about the only time he went there, so nobody ever thought of looking for him when he was mulling things over. He liked the solemnity of the old building, with its wide corridors, high ceilings, and marble floors. The hallways were usually deserted on Saturdays, when the offices were closed and court wasn't in session. Probably only one or two people, if that many, were in the building besides Rhodes. Rhodes liked that, too.

The only door that was open was on the side of the building. It was down a short concrete staircase, and it opened into the basement. Rhodes wondered if it was a good idea to leave even one door open, but he supposed that if anyone wanted in badly enough, it would be easy to break a window anywhere on the ground floor in back of the building and get in that way. The burglar alarm system hadn't been updated in a long time.

He went into the basement, where only a few of the lights were on, just enough to allow him to see. He walked down the hallway, the squeak of his rubber-soled shoes echoing off the walls. In the not too distant past, Rhodes had always stopped and bought a Dr Pepper when he came to the courthouse, but he was still boycotting Dr Pepper. He hadn't yet been able to bring himself to switch to one of its imitators, so he wasn't drinking soft drinks. He'd lost a couple of pounds, and Ivy attributed it to the healthful diet she was trying to get him to stick to. Rhodes thought it was the lack of Dr Pepper that was doing it, but he didn't mention that.

He usually had himself a package of orange cheese crackers from the vending machine, too, but those were good only if eaten while drinking a Dr Pepper, so he didn't buy any cheese crackers, either. Maybe that accounted for some of the weight loss, though not much since Rhodes didn't come to the courthouse often.

He looked at one of the big round clocks on the hallway wall. It was a little past lunchtime, but it wouldn't be the first time he'd skipped lunch. In fact, as many lunches as he'd skipped, he thought he should have dropped a lot more than a couple of pounds. It didn't seem to work like that, however, and he thought the Dairy Queen Blizzards that he occasionally enjoyed might be a part of the problem.

Thinking about the Blizzards, Rhodes decided he'd walk up the wide stairs instead of taking the elevator. Maybe the exercise could help him work off some calories.

When he got to the second floor, he turned and looked down the hall toward his office. Someone was standing outside his door. The hall was too dark for Rhodes to see who it was, but he didn't bother to reach for the PF-9 in the ankle holster. He didn't think anybody would be lurking there to kill him, but it occurred to him that they really should consider locking that basement door.

He took a few steps forward and saw that he was right about having nothing to be afraid of. The lurker didn't pose him any physical danger, though he couldn't say she was completely harmless.

"Hey, Sheriff," Jennifer Loam said. "I thought you might show up eventually."

"I've been busy," Rhodes said. "You could've looked for me at the jail."

"I wanted to talk to you in private. Not that I have anything against those nice men who work at the jail, but it's hard to have a private conversation there."

Truer words were never spoken, Rhodes thought.

"What if I hadn't shown up?" Rhodes asked. "You might have been waiting here all day."

"I haven't been here long. I know you like to come over here now and then. If you hadn't, then I'd have gone and talked to someone else."

It wasn't the first time she had tracked him down in the courthouse, but it was the first time she'd gotten there ahead of him. Rhodes thought she knew his habits too well, but he couldn't think of anywhere else to go when he needed privacy. Not that he was getting what he'd come for. He could suggest that she go on and talk to someone else right now, but he didn't think it would do him any good.

He unlocked the office, pushed the door open, and invited her in.

"I hope the furniture's not dusty," he said when they'd entered and he'd turned on the lights.

"I don't mind if it is," Jennifer said. "I won't take up much of your time. I just want to find out about Burt Collins. I know he was murdered."

Rhodes gave her credit. She didn't scold him for avoiding the topic earlier that morning.

"What else do you know?" he asked.

"Not much. I haven't tried to talk to his wife. No matter what you might think of me, I do try to avoid bothering family members when something like this happens."

"Something like what?"

"Like a murder. I know that Burt Collins died from a blow to the head, but that's all I've found out."

Rhodes wondered if she went to the Beauty Shack or to the funeral home for her information, not that it really mattered. It could be that she'd talked to Andy Shelby, but Rhodes wasn't going to ask her. He didn't tell his deputies not to talk to the press.

"Then you know as much as I do," he said.

"You haven't made an arrest?"

"I think you'd know about it if I had."

"True. So you haven't. Any suspects?"

"Not that I can talk about. I don't want to tip them off."

"By 'them' do you mean there might be more than one person involved?"

Rhodes grinned. "I mean there might be more than one suspect. That's really all I can tell you right now. The reason I came over here was to think things over and see what I could come up with."

"And I'm interrupting you," Jennifer said.

"I figure you'll leave eventually."

"I will, but I'd like to have some kind of solid information to put on the Web site. People want to know about this kind of thing."

"You can just say that the sheriff's department is investigating and that an arrest is expected shortly."

"How many times have you read something like that?" Jennifer asked.

"Dozens," Rhodes said. "Hundreds. It's a classic."

"That's why I'm not using it. My Web site isn't going for the same old thing." She paused. "You know that one of your deputies and I have been seeing each other?"

"So I've been told."

"I want you to know that I'd never ask him for information that wasn't supposed to be public."

That was a good sign for the relationship. "He might not tell you if you asked."

Jennifer smiled. "I'll bet he would."

She was probably right.

"Then I appreciate it that you won't ask him," Rhodes said.

"You're welcome. Now, are you sure you don't have anything more you can tell me?"

"I'm sure, but you'll be the first to know when we make an arrest."

"I'll hold you to that," Jennifer said, "but now I'll leave you alone so you can do your thinking."

Rhodes stood up, but Jennifer said she could see herself out. When she was gone, Rhodes sat back down and tried to get his thoughts in order.

As far as he could determine, nobody involved with Burt Collins had a solid alibi for the time of his death except possibly Ella Collins. Frances Bennett had vouched for the fact that Ella was with her, so Ella could be moved down to the bottom of the list of suspects.

Who were the suspects, anyway? Eric Stewart and Don McClaren each had a reason to be upset with Burt, but was it enough reason to kill him?

Rhodes had to grin at the thought. One thing he'd learned was that it didn't take much of a reason. Murder was a serious matter, but hardly anybody ever thought of it like that until it was far too late. A quick spurt of anger was all it took to drive some people to an impulsive action that they'd regret for the rest of their lives, whether they were punished for it or not.

It seemed to Rhodes that something like that must have been what happened in Burt's house the previous night. Someone said or did something, and the bust of Dale Earnhardt Junior was smashed against Burt's head. Whoever had done it didn't panic. He'd taken the head with him, or her, and disposed of it later, leaving Rhodes with no fingerprints and no murder weapon.

Marilyn Bradley had been even more upset than McClaren and Stewart, but she was from out of town. She didn't know Burt or where he lived.

Lonnie Wallace had tried to knock Burt down, or had fallen into him by accident, and that encounter hadn't ended well. Lonnie was also involved with the art gallery, so he had reason to be unhappy that the exhibit was ruined. Was that motive enough?

Rhodes had to remind himself that he hadn't proved that Burt had marked the paintings and sculpture. It was true that Burt had a history of using spray paint for vandalism, but that didn't mean he'd done it again. It was suggestive, but it wasn't proof.

Manish Patel had plenty of reason to dislike Burt, but the spray-painting of the hotel walls had been months ago, and Patel seemed to be over it. As far as Rhodes knew, there hadn't been any further trouble between the two men. That didn't mean that Patel hadn't held a grudge. He could be covering it up.

Who else? That seemed to cover things, and it certainly gave Rhodes plenty of suspects. He wished he could narrow it down, but as far as he could see nobody other than Ella had a good alibi. He'd have to talk to all of them.

He thought about Ella. Something that Frances Bennett had said had bothered him a bit. He'd have to ask her about it, and it might mean that Ella didn't have an alibi, either, except one that she'd made up.

Talking to people was usually the way an investigation went. Rhodes would poke around a little and ask questions and poke around some more. He'd come up with an answer sooner or later. It was usually the right one if he took his time. He didn't have the kind of crime-solving weapons that showed up on television, so he had to do things the old-fashioned way. If he had a medical examiner who could miraculously give him a time of death with just a cursory glance at a body or produce a DNA analysis in under a day, he'd buy himself a pair of sunglasses and come up with some snappy comments to make for Jennifer Loam's camera.

Unfortunately, Rhodes didn't have those things, not even the sunglasses. He'd had several pairs of sunglasses in the past, but he kept losing them. He figured there was a lesson in that, though he wasn't sure what it was.

Rhodes was still mulling things over when the phone rang. It was the old-fashioned kind, like the one in the Beauty Shack, with a loud, old-fashioned ring. It sat on the side of the desk, and the ring made Rhodes jump just a little.

He picked the receiver up, put it to his ear, and said, "Let me guess. An asteroid is headed for earth and it's going to hit right in the middle of Clearview."

"How'd you know it was me?" Hack asked.

"Nobody else ever calls here. Tell me about the asteroid."

"This ain't that kind of emergency."

"What kind is it?"

"It's a Seepy Benton emergency."

"Uh-oh."

"Yeah, I knew that's what you'd say. He was mighty mysterious about the emergency. Wouldn't tell me what was going on."

Hack sounded a bit huffy. He always wanted to have the lowdown on everything.

"What did he say, then?" Rhodes asked.

"He said to tell you to come back to the art gallery right now."

That didn't sound to Rhodes like an emergency on the scale of an asteroid hitting the city, but he didn't think he should ignore it, either.

"He said it has something to do with Burt," Hack added.

"I'm on my way," Rhodes said.

The art gallery was open to the public for the day, and Rhodes saw that several townspeople were inside, taking a look at the artwork and having punch and snacks. Rhodes could use a snack himself, as it appeared that he wasn't going to get to slip away for a Blizzard.

Seepy Benton was waiting just outside the door. He was usually quite calm, but Rhodes saw that he was shifting his weight from foot to foot as if nervous.

"What's the problem?" Rhodes asked as he walked up to him.

Benton looked around to be sure no one was nearby. "You said something about a bust of Dale Earnhardt Junior, didn't you?"

"I did. What about it?"

"I think I found it."

"Where?"

"I'll show you," Seepy said. "Come on."

Rhodes followed him inside the building. Don McClaren and Eric Stewart were talking to the visitors and pointing out the paintings. Marilyn Bradley was still there, and she was talking to two women and pointing to her painting. The women seemed to be sympathizing with her about the dark streak across it.

"This way," Seepy said, leading Rhodes past the snacks without giving him time to stop and grab one. They passed some sculptures on pedestals and went to the doorway that led out of the gallery and into the antiques store.

The things in the store had always seemed to Rhodes more like a collection of junk than anything else. Where others saw treasures, he saw shelves of moldy books, old lamps, old furniture, shelves of glassware and china, old clothes, old toys, glass showcases that held jewelry and fishing lures and similar small items, a few boxes of old records, several boxes of VHS tapes, and many other assorted items like horseshoes, barbed wire, and jars. Rhodes supposed that someone interested in other people's cast-offs could spend a lot of time browsing. He wasn't interested.

Among all that stuff sat a big overstuffed armchair. The light in that part of the building was poor. It hadn't been improved in fifty years or so, and the air smelled musty. A floor lamp stood beside the chair. The previous owner of the store, Jeff Tyler, had liked to sit there and read or listen to music while he waited for a customer to show up. He'd lived in a little apartment in back. Lonnie Wallace had inherited the store from Tyler, and Eric Stewart lived in the apartment now. It was one of the perks that went with managing the store.

"I was going to the restroom," Seepy said as they passed a shelf of figurines holding musical instruments.

"Thanks for sharing that," Rhodes said.

Seepy ignored him. "It's way back in the back, and on the way I had to pass this shelf."

Seepy hadn't stopped at the figurines. He was a few steps beyond that shelf, standing in front of a tall bookshelf made of some darkly stained wood. It held a jumble of dolls, some of which were missing an arm or a leg; a couple of plastic horses, both of which had all their limbs and one of which even had a saddle; several jigsaw puzzles, which Rhodes suspected might be missing a piece or two; a jar full of marbles; some old vases, one of which had plastic flowers in it; a tangle of electrical extension cords; and three plastic bags filled with remote controls of various sizes.

Stuck behind the plastic bags was a bronze bust of Dale Earnhardt, Junior.

Rhodes knew there could be more than one bust like that in Blacklin County, but the odds were certainly against it.

"You didn't touch it, I hope," Rhodes said.

"I know better than that. It's a clue. I called your office as soon as I saw it."

"Did you mention it to anybody else?"

"No. I didn't even tell your dispatcher." Benton paused and looked thoughtful. "I think he's mad at me about it."

No question about that, Rhodes thought. Hack would get over it, though.

"It is Dale Earnhardt, isn't it?" Seepy said.

"Junior," Rhodes said.

"Right," Seepy said. "How did it get here?"

"That's what I'd like to know," Rhodes said.

Chapter 12

▼

Rhodes and Benton stood in front of the shelf and looked at the bust. Rhodes thought about how it might've gotten there. Eric Stewart came to mind first. He lived there, after all, and he managed the store. If he'd taken the bust from Burt's house, it might have seemed logical to him to hide the bust in plain sight, or in almost plain sight. Rhodes remembered something else from that high school English book where he'd read about the chambered nautilus.

There had been a story by Edgar Allan Poe called "The Purloined Letter." Rhodes had thought that the story was pretty ridiculous, considering that the story's detective, whose name Rhodes had forgotten, would have had to have vision like Superman's to see all he'd seen in the dimly lit room where the letter was hidden. Rhodes couldn't remember whether he'd mentioned that little fact to his English teacher, so he probably hadn't. She would have set him straight if he had, he was sure.

The point of the story wasn't the detective's vision anyway. It was the idea that counted, and that was to hide things in such an obvious place that they'd be overlooked except by someone keener than most persons. Seepy hadn't overlooked the bust, though.

"Did you ever read a story called 'The Purloined Letter'?" Rhodes asked.

"Sure," Seepy said. "In high school. I was nearly as good in English as I was in math. Why?"

"Just wondering."

Rhodes wondered other things, too. He wondered if finding the bust hadn't been just a little too easy. What if someone had put it on the shelf expecting it to be found? What better way to throw suspicion on Stewart?

The problem was that there was no way to know exactly when the bust was placed on the shelf. All Rhodes knew was that no one had pointed it out until now, which was only logical because hardly anyone else knew its significance. Except the killer, of course, and the killer wasn't going to be the one to bring it to anybody's attention.

Rhodes considered his suspects. It would have been difficult for Ella Collins to put the bust there. Highly unlikely, in fact. Manish Patel? He hadn't mentioned dropping by the art gallery that morning, though he could have. Rhodes would have to check on that.

Some of the other suspects were right outside. All Rhodes had to do was ask them. Somehow that seemed a little too convenient, but Rhodes didn't have an objection to anything that might make his job a little easier.

"Ask Eric Stewart to step back here," Rhodes told Seepy.

"All right," Seepy said, and left.

Rhodes contemplated the bust while he waited for Stewart. He found himself thinking of his English class again, and Edgar Allan Poe. All the bust needed was a raven perched on top of it. Not that Poe would have used Dale Earnhardt, Junior in his poem, even if he'd heard of him. It wouldn't have fit the mood.

"What can I do for you, Sheriff?" Eric Stewart asked.

Rhodes hadn't heard him walk up. He was very quiet. Or was "sneaky" the word?

"I was wondering about one of the things here on this shelf," Rhodes said.

"Everything's for sale," Stewart said. "I might even give you a discount. What are you interested in?"

Rhodes pointed. "That bust there. How long has it been here?"

Stewart leaned forward and looked where Rhodes was pointing. "I don't remember seeing that here before." He straightened. "Lots of things were already on the shelves before I got here, though. That could be one of them."

Rhodes couldn't tell if Stewart's forward lean had been calculated to conceal surprise or had been entirely innocent.

"Looks almost new," Rhodes said.

"The fact that I haven't seen it before doesn't mean much," Stewart said. "It could have come in only a day before I got here, or it could've been here for a long time. I haven't taken an inventory of this place." He waved an arm. "It would be impossible."

Rhodes had to agree with him on that point.

"I wonder who it is," Stewart said, peering at the bust. "Doesn't look like anybody famous."

Stewart wasn't a NASCAR fan, or he'd have known who the bust represented. Rhodes didn't think that was a clue, however.

"It might be evidence in a case I'm working on," Rhodes said. "I'll have to confiscate it."

124

Stewart grinned. "I said I'd give you a discount, Sheriff."

"I'm not joking," Rhodes said. "I'm going out to the car to get an evidence bag. Don't touch that bust."

Stewart looked uncertain. "I'll have to tell Lonnie."

"Good idea," Rhodes said. "You can call him while I'm getting the bag."

Rhodes left Stewart standing in front of the shelf and went back through the gallery. Seepy Benton was indulging in the snacks, so Rhodes stopped and grabbed some cheese and crackers. While he was eating, Benton asked him what was going on.

"I'm going for an evidence bag," Rhodes told him.

"You really should make me a deputy," Benton said. "I found an important clue."

"You're a math teacher," Rhodes said, getting himself a cup of punch to wash down the crackers and cheese. "Not a cop. And we don't know how important the clue is just yet."

"I've helped you a lot."

"Stick to the classroom," Rhodes said. He took a drink of the punch. "It pays better."

Benton looked thoughtful. "Probably true. You could make me an honorary deputy, though. Lots of places have them."

"Honorary deputies don't help with investigations. They help support the department by raising money and buying equipment that the county doesn't provide. Things like that."

"I don't like raising money," Benton said. "I'm an introvert."

Rhodes was glad he'd finished the crackers. He might have spewed them all over the place on hearing that statement, which Benton had made with a straight face. Maybe he even believed it.

"I'm going for the evidence bag now," Rhodes said. "I'll be right back."

Benton reached for a cookie, and Rhodes left him there. Marilyn Bradley was still talking to the two women. She was very animated, waving her arms as she talked. The women had backed a few paces away from her.

Don McClaren was gone. Interesting, Rhodes thought. He wondered why McClaren had left. He could have a perfectly good reason, or he might have guessed what Rhodes had been looking at back in the store. Maybe he'd return later.

Rhodes got an evidence bag and some nitrile rubber gloves from the county car and went back inside. Benton had moved over to Marilyn Bradley and the two women and joined in the conversation, or tried to. It appeared that Marilyn was still doing most of the talking, and now she was gesturing at Benton's painting.

Rhodes went on through the gallery and into the store. Stewart was sitting in the old armchair, but he didn't look comfortable.

"Lonnie said it would be all right for you to take the bust," Stewart said, standing up. He did so easily, without having to put his hands on the arms of the chair and push. "I'm sorry if I appeared to be hesitant."

Was he hesitant because he was worried, or because he didn't like the idea of letting store property leave without getting paid? Rhodes couldn't decide. He put on the gloves and put the bust into the bag.

"Hoping to find fingerprints?" Stewart asked.

"It's a possibility," Rhodes said, stripping off the gloves.

"Well, you won't find mine on there. I never saw that thing before."

Was he protesting too much? Again Rhodes couldn't decide.

"If you haven't touched it, you don't have to worry," Rhodes said. "I hope you haven't dusted it."

Stewart smiled. "Does anything in here look as if it's been dusted?"

Rhodes shook his head. "Not in this century."

"That's about right," Stewart said. "Good luck with that bust."

"Thanks. You can go back out and talk to the visitors now."

Rhodes started back toward the gallery, and Stewart followed right behind.

"We haven't had that many visitors," Stewart said. "More than I thought we'd have, though. Jennifer Loam's reports have stirred up some interest. I think it was the riot more than the art."

"It wasn't really a riot," Rhodes said.

"Close enough for Clearview," Stewart said.

Rhodes went outside and locked the bust in the trunk of the county car, then returned to the gallery. Don McClaren was still not there, and the two women who'd been talking to Marilyn Bradley had left as well. Stewart, Bradley, and Benton were the only people left in the big room. Rhodes stopped at the snack table and picked up a cookie before walking over to join them. The cookie was chocolate chip, Rhodes's favorite. He'd have to remember to pick up another one later.

"I wouldn't call my work representational," Benton said as Rhodes walked up.

"Ha," Marilyn said. "I don't know what else you'd call it. It actually looks better with that stripe of paint across it. That old man was right about your painting, at least. It's improved."

Benton looked hurt, but he didn't make any remarks about staircases in the sky. Rhodes thought that Benton showed remarkable restraint.

"As I mentioned yesterday," Benton said in his teacherly way, "all my work is based on the Golden Ratio. The mark on the painting detracts from that. It's almost as if someone had drawn a mark across da Vinci's Vitruvian Man. That image is found all over the place, even on NASA's spacesuits worn during extra-vehicular activity. Would someone draw a mark across an image on one of those suits?"

"It's not the same," Marilyn said. She was even more agitated than before. Her orange hair shook as she jabbed her finger at Benton's chest. "We're not talking about da Vinci's work. We're talking about ours. My painting, now, is different from something like a seashell. Mine had ethereal meaning before that mark was put on it. It wasn't earthbound like yours. Mine suggests regions beyond the world we know and the difficulty of ascending to higher knowledge. Sometimes an ascension isn't even possible."

So that's what the staircases in the clouds meant, Rhodes thought. He was glad she'd explained it. He'd never have guessed it for himself. If he was to judge from the looks on the faces of Benton and Stewart, they wouldn't have guessed it, either.

He looked around the nearly empty gallery. He wondered about Don McClaren, and he also wondered where McClaren was. So he asked.

Marilyn clearly didn't like being interrupted. She started to say something, but Stewart got the first words in.

"Don had to run out to the college," Stewart said. "He didn't say why. Maybe he wanted to pick up something from his office."

"Did he say what it was?" Rhodes asked.

"No. Just that he had to pick something up. Probably something for our final session. Now that the judging's over, we're doing something just for fun. Everyone's out painting now. Don's going to join them and be sure things are going smoothly. He was really upset by what happened yesterday, and he doesn't want anything else to go wrong." Stewart paused and looked at Benton and Marilyn. "What I meant to say is that everyone's painting now except these two. They didn't want to paint the fall colors."

"I prefer flowers," Benton said. "Like sunflowers and daisies. The process of phyllotaxis is easily observed in them."

"Let me guess," Rhodes said. "That big word has something to do with the Golden Ratio."

"Right," Benton said, as pleased as if Rhodes were some apt pupil in one of his classes. "You see—"

"Never mind," Rhodes said. "You should paint an imaginary sunflower or something for the last class. It would do you good to be outside."

"I'll think about it," Benton said.

Marilyn Bradley said nothing. Flowers and trees might not be ethereal enough for her.

"When is the final session?" Rhodes asked.

"It's this evening. We'll meet here and talk about everyone's work. I'll take down these paintings, and we'll hang the new ones when they're brought in."

"That's the problem," Marilyn said. "Creation in a single afternoon? Real art can't be rushed. It takes days, weeks sometimes, to produce real art." She looked at her painting. "The work of weeks can be ruined in seconds, however."

"That's true of a lot of things," Rhodes said, thinking of Burt Collins. "A whole life can end that quickly."

Nobody had anything to say to that, so Rhodes left them there.

He snagged another chocolate chip cookie on the way out to cheer himself up.

When Rhodes arrived at the jail to put the bust in the evidence locker, Hack was on the phone. He was writing something on a note pad, so Rhodes didn't bother him. He logged in the bust and got it put away.

After he'd finished with that, he went to his desk. Hack was ready for him.

"Got a problem for you," Hack said.

"I'm working on a murder investigation," Rhodes told him. "That's a big enough problem right there."

"I know that, but you might want to handle this one that was just called in. Nobody else is close enough. Andy's in Milsby on a domestic spat, and Ruth's in Thurston to check out a break-in at the community center. Somebody's got to take care of this one right now, and you're right here. Ivy might not like for you to do it, though."

"She knows the sheriff has to do the tough jobs. What is it?"

"Naked woman," Hack said.

"You're right," Rhodes said. "Ivy might not like it. What's going on?"

"Don't know for sure. The caller said he didn't know. Just said there was a naked woman at that rest area out on the highway to Railville, just before you get to the county line." Hack looked thoughtful. "Just about fifty yards away from the line, I think. Maybe she's in the other county, but I guess you'll have to check since we got the call. You know where it is?"

Rhodes knew. It wasn't much of a rest area, really, just one old concrete table with cracked concrete benches on either side, looking like an old WPA project from way back in the previous century. There was a trash can made out of a fifty-five-gallon barrel, too, but that was about all.

"What's she doing?" Rhodes asked.

"Runnin' around, the man said. He said he didn't pay her much attention, but he thought he'd better report it."

"That's it?"

"That's all. Except he said she's about thirty, maybe five-seven, red hair, around a hundred and twenty-five pounds."

"Didn't you say he didn't pay her much attention?"

"Yeah, but I was just repeatin' what he said. I didn't say I believed him."

"Is he still at the rest area?"

"Nope. Said he had to leave. He'd done his duty as a citizen, but he couldn't stay. Sounded like he wanted to, though."

"He didn't try to help her?"

"Said he tried, but she just ran off into the bushes."

"I'd better check on it, then," Rhodes said. "Unless you think he was joking."

"He didn't sound like he was joking. Gave his name and address in Railville if you want to get in touch with him. Stanley Eckerd."

"Nobody would make up a name like that, I guess."

"What I thought," Hack said. "You go on out there. I won't tell Ivy about it."

"There's nothing to tell her."

"You ain't got there yet."

"Never mind. When Ruth comes in, tell her to get hold of Judge Fleming and get a subpoena for Burt Collins's phone records."

"It's Saturday. Judge'll be playin' golf."

"Ruth knows where the golf course is. I'd like to see those records. I've been thinking that I pay too much attention to cell phones. Burt didn't even have one of those."

"I'll tell her. May not work. Gettin' the phone folks to cooperate on Saturday's not easy."

"Ruth can do it. That's not all. Have her check the head I just put in the evidence locker for fingerprints."

"Head? What head?"

"It's a bust," Rhodes said. "You know, like a statue, but just the head."

"Oh. The one from Burt's place?"

"I don't know, but the odds are that it is."

"I'll have her check it. I hope I don't have to get that redhead checked for prints."

"You won't find mine on her," Rhodes said.

"That's what I'd say, too, if I was in your place."

"I wouldn't blame you a bit," Rhodes said.

Chapter 13

▼

Rhodes pulled into the rest area behind an old Chevy pickup
with rust spots on the tailgate. He got out of the county car and
looked around. He hadn't been in this rest area in years, but it
looked pretty much the same as ever. It was a pleasant day, plenty
of sunshine, cool but not cold, not much of a breeze to speak of.
Rhodes thought it might not seem so pleasant if he didn't have
any clothes on.

He didn't see a naked woman, but he did see a man sitting at
one of the tables. It was shaded by cedar elms with some green
leaves still on them. Most of the leaves were yellow, and the
ground was littered with them.

The man at the table was eating a sandwich. A brown paper bag
and a can of Dr Pepper sat on the table near him. He took a bite
from the sandwich and laid it down on some waxed paper. He
chewed for a second and then took a swig from the Dr Pepper can.
Rhodes walked over to him, briefly envying him the Dr Pepper.

"Been here long?" Rhodes asked.

The man was about sixty, Rhodes thought. He had a seamed face and close-set eyes. He wore an Astros cap, a floral shirt, and faded jeans. He looked at the badge holder hanging from Rhodes's belt.

"Been here 'bout five minutes. Just got started on my ham and cheese sandwich. That against the law in this county?"

Rhodes eyed the sandwich. It looked pretty good to him. So did the Dr Pepper. "Not in the least."

"If it's not, then you must be looking for the naked woman."

"That's right," Rhodes said. "You seen her?"

"You bet. My name's Gates. Jerry Gates. No relation to Bill, more's the pity. Wouldn't mind having some of that money of his. I'm from Waco. Going to see my cousin over in Palestine. Thought I'd stop here and eat my sandwich." The man shook his head. "Never thought I'd see a naked woman, though, not that I have any objections. Woman wants to go naked, I say let her go. You, now, being a sheriff, you might not feel that way."

"She could be in trouble," Rhodes said.

"Probably is. Probably going to get arrested for public indecency."

"I'm not talking about that kind of trouble. Usually somebody without clothes in a rest area is in some other kind of trouble."

Gates nodded. "I see what you mean. Drugs, assault, that kind of thing."

"Yes," Rhodes said. "That kind of thing."

"Maybe so," Gates said, "but when I asked her if she needed help, she just headed for the bushes. I figured I'd better back off."

Now they were getting somewhere, Rhodes thought. Thick bushes grew at each end of the rest area, and they were even thicker across the barbed wire fence that separated the rest area from privately owned land.

"Which bushes?" Rhodes asked.

Gates pointed. "Across that fence."

Rhodes didn't see how anybody without clothing could cross the fence without some difficulty. Then he saw that someone had built a wooden stile that provided a way over the fence.

"Not any restrooms in this rest area," Gates said. "You can get a little privacy over across the fence."

"You sure she's over there?"

"That's where she went. Can't say if she's still there, but she didn't come back by here."

"I'd better take a look."

"I'm gonna eat my sandwich," Gates said. "If you need any help, you just holler."

"I'll be sure to do that," Rhodes said.

Before he crossed the fence, he went back to the car and looked in the trunk. He had some blankets, but a blanket wasn't really what he needed. He moved the blankets aside and found what he was looking for, a long raincoat with a hood. That would do it. He took out the raincoat, shut the trunk, and headed for the stile.

Gates was finished with his sandwich. He wadded up the wax paper and put it in the paper bag. Picking up the Dr Pepper can, he said, "No place to recycle around here, I guess."

"No," Rhodes said. "Sorry about that."

"Doesn't bother me much." Gates put the can in the bag. He slid off the bench and carried the bag to the trash can. "If you don't think you'll need any help, I'll be going. My cousin's expecting me. We're going fishing this afternoon at some secret place he's got staked out. Never been fished before. Supposed to be some nice fat bass in it."

Rhodes hadn't been fishing in far too long. The thought of an unfished lake with fat bass in it was very appealing, but he knew he'd never get a chance at it.

"You can go on," Rhodes said. "I wouldn't want to keep a man from a fishing spot like that."

"Well, all right, I guess I will, then," Gates said. "I hope you can find that woman. She was kind of pretty. Wouldn't want her to catch a cold, running around out here in the woods without any clothes on."

They weren't exactly in the woods to Rhodes's way of thinking. The bushes were thick around the rest area, but there weren't many trees. Cars passed by on the highway every now and then, their tires droning on the pavement.

"I'll do what I can to help her," Rhodes said.

Gates pitched the bag into the trash and walked to his pickup. Rhodes went on to the fence and climbed the stile. He'd started down the other side when he heard a door slam. Then the pickup started. Rhodes looked back and saw it drive away. He hoped he wouldn't need any help. Then again, Gates might have been as much of a hindrance as a help.

Standing at the bottom of the stile with the raincoat folded over one arm, Rhodes called out, "Ma'am, can you hear me? I'm Dan Rhodes, sheriff of Blacklin County. I have a raincoat here that will cover you, and I can take you home or to a hospital or anywhere you need to go."

No answer.

"Ma'am?" Rhodes said, a little louder. "Can you hear me?"

He thought he saw the bushes move over on his right.

136

"I'm not here to hurt you," he said. "Just to help."

He waited. After about half a minute a woman's voice said, "How do I know you're who you say?"

"I have a badge," Rhodes said.

He unclipped the badge from his belt and held it up. A woman's head peeked over the top of some bushes about ten yards away. She had red hair, just as Hack had said. The bushes were so thick that Rhodes couldn't see the rest of her. Just as well, he thought.

"Are you going to arrest me?" the woman asked.

"Can't say for sure. I don't know what's going on here, so right now I just want to help you."

"You need to arrest Neil, that's who you need to arrest."

Rhodes peered at the bushes. He thought he could see a hint of human flesh through the leaves.

"Who's Neil?" he asked.

"He's the one who took my clothes."

Rhodes thought about the circumstances under which a woman might be naked in a rest area so that someone could take her clothes.

"It's not what you think," the woman said.

Rhodes had to smile. All too often women seemed to know what he was thinking.

"I'll tell you what," he said. "I have a raincoat here. I'm going to walk over there and pitch it over those bushes. You put it on, and then you can come out. We'll talk things over, and you can tell me about Neil."

"He wouldn't like that."

"Do you care?"

The woman didn't say anything for a while. Rhodes waited.

A little breeze had come up. It blew the fallen leaves around the rest area and made even more of them drop off the trees.

After a minute or so the woman said, "All right. You can bring me the coat."

Rhodes walked over to the bushes. "Here it comes," he said, and he tossed the raincoat over the bushes.

The woman didn't try to catch the coat, and it fell out of Rhodes's sight. She rustled around in the bushes while she put it on.

"I'm coming out now," she said.

"I'll just go on back to the table," Rhodes told her. "I'll wait for you there."

He climbed back over the fence and sat on one of the concrete benches. He didn't watch as the woman came over the stile. He wasn't sure how much coverage the raincoat would provide.

As it turned out, it provided plenty. When she neared the table, Rhodes looked up and saw that she'd zipped it all the way up and that it hung down below her calves. She hadn't put the hood on. She was wearing white canvas shoes. Rhodes had wondered how she could traipse around barefooted. Now he knew she hadn't had to.

She sat across from Rhodes at the table, and he decided that the description Hack had been given was accurate. She was no older than thirty, and she definitely had red hair. Her eyes were brown. She had freckles, which the caller hadn't mentioned. Maybe he hadn't gotten close enough to see them.

"I'm Dan Rhodes," Rhodes said. "Sheriff of Blacklin County."

"You already told me that."

"That's right, I did. You haven't told me who you are, though."

"Vicki Patton. Vicki with an *i*, not a *y*." She paused. "I'm not from around here."

"How about Neil?" Rhodes asked. "Is he from around here?"

"Neil Foshee," the woman said. "That's his name."

"I know of some Foshees," Rhodes said. "From out around Milsby."

Milsby had been a town once, but there wasn't much of it left now. There were still houses in the area, however, and people still lived in a lot of them.

"He's one of those Foshees," Vicki said.

That wasn't a recommendation in Rhodes's opinion. The Foshees who lived in the Milsby area weren't the most upstanding citizens in Blacklin County. Rhodes didn't know one named Neil, however.

"He's a cousin," the woman said when he asked about Neil. "I'm not related."

"Congratulations," Rhodes said. "Now about your . . . condition."

"I'd rather not talk about it."

"I don't blame you, but I think you'd better."

It took a few minutes, and there were several stops and starts in the story, but Rhodes finally got it all. Or most of it. Vicki lived in Railville, where Foshee was a mechanic in a little auto repair shop. She'd known him for a while. He'd been an acquaintance of her ex-husband, who'd seemed like a really nice person but who'd turned out to be a no-good who couldn't hold a job and who liked to run around with other women.

Some months after the divorce, Foshee had called Vicki and asked her out. She'd gone to a nightclub with him, and they'd gotten along all right, though she thought he drank too much. He told her he didn't use drugs (not counting alcohol, Rhodes figured), and he was a good dancer. What he didn't tell her was that while he didn't use drugs, a claim Vicki no longer believed, he occasionally sold them.

"He said that he didn't make much money fixing cars," Vicki explained, "so he needed a little extra. He said he just dealt now and then, and he promised me he wouldn't get me mixed up in anything."

Promises, promises, Rhodes thought.

"But he did," Vicki said. "Get me mixed up in something, I mean."

The way it happened was simple enough. Foshee came by her house and asked if she'd like to go for a ride in his convertible. It was a nice day, and Vicki thought it would be fun. It was, too, until Foshee told her what the real purpose of the ride was.

"Drug run," Rhodes said.

"Yeah," Vicki said. "Ice." Then she added, "Crystal meth."

Rhodes nodded. He knew all too well what ice was, and he even knew about the Foshee connection, or the rumors of it. The country around the old Milsby community had plenty of room in it for houses back in the woods, well off even the sandiest and most overgrown county roads, houses where nobody had lived for a generation or two but that could be put back into good enough shape to sleep in and to cook meth in. It didn't take much of a place to cook meth, but the Foshees were supposed to have quality goods. Rhodes hadn't been able to catch them with any-thing, however. Maybe that was about to change.

"He sells it at the clubs," Vicki said. "He was even selling it when I went dancing with him. I didn't know it, or I'd never have dated him. He gets it from his cousins here and sells it around Railville."

Rhodes wondered if the sheriff of the neighboring county

knew about Foshee. Probably not. There were a dozen people like him in every little town in East Texas.

"I told him I wasn't going to have anything to do with drugs," Vicki continued. "We had a big fight about it, and he stopped here and told me to get out of the car. I didn't want to get out. I don't know anybody around here, and I didn't have any way to get home. I told him if he put me out, I'd call the cops." She looked at Rhodes. "I mean the police."

"It's okay to say cops," Rhodes told her.

"I thought it wasn't polite," Vicki said. "Anyway, he stopped here and made me get out of the car. He wouldn't let me take my purse. My cell phone's in it, so I couldn't call anybody."

"What about your clothes?" Rhodes asked.

"Oh, he made me take them off. He said any man who stopped wouldn't listen to anything I had to say, not if I was naked. He said they'd all be afraid of being accused of rape. He said maybe somebody *would* rape me and it would serve me right." She tried to smile but didn't quite succeed. "I sure can pick 'em."

"You'll do better next time," Rhodes said, though he had his doubts. "At least he let you keep your shoes."

"I think he just forgot and drove away before I could take them off."

That was probably it. Judging by what he'd heard so far, Rhodes didn't think Neil was the thoughtful type.

"Come on with me," Rhodes said. "I'll get you fixed up with some clothes and a ride back to Railville."

Rhodes stood up, and after a couple of seconds so did Vicki.

"One other thing," Rhodes said. "Do you know where Neil was going? I don't mean just to see the Foshees. I mean specifically."

"Kind of," Vicki said. "He was trying to find it on his GPS, but he said the road he was looking for wasn't even on there. It's more of a lane than a road."

Rhodes was disappointed. That wasn't much help, and it wasn't even kind of specific. There were probably quite a few old dirt roads that weren't on anyone's GPS device.

"He said he'd have to go by an old school," Vicki said, "and then past what used to be a store. Is that any help?"

"As a matter of fact," Rhodes said, "it is. What kind of car is he driving?"

"It's a Chrysler 300. It's black. Are you going after him?"

"Sure I am," Rhodes said. "I'm the sheriff."

Chapter 14

▼

Rhodes had never taken a naked woman to his house before. He wondered how Ivy would react.

Not that Vicki was really naked. She had on a raincoat, after all, and was modestly covered. A damsel in distress, you might say. Surely Ivy couldn't complain about it.

Rhodes parked the county car in the driveway and told Vicki to wait. He'd explained things to her on the drive to the house, and now he was going to have to explain to Ivy, who he hoped would be at home. Maybe she would, since the insurance office where she worked was closed on the weekends.

"Are you sure this will be okay?" Vicki asked.

"I'm sure," Rhodes said, trying to sound more confident than he felt. "You'll like Ivy. She'll get you fixed up."

Rhodes went to the front door so as not to arouse Speedo, who would want attention that Rhodes didn't have time to give him. As soon as Rhodes opened the front door, Yancey came charging up, his toenails clicking on the hardwood floor, his yips bouncing off the walls. Ivy would know that Rhodes was home or that an intruder had come in through the unlocked door. Yancey would have greeted either one the same way.

Rhodes glanced into the den, where Ivy sat in a chair, reading a book.

"You're home early," she said, closing the book. "Let me guess. You aren't going to be here long."

"Right the first time," Rhodes said. "You're good."

"Just experienced." Ivy stood up, walked over, and kissed him on the cheek. Yancey danced around their feet, as excited as a lottery winner. "You must have a good reason to be here, though. Tell me."

"I have a naked woman in the car," Rhodes said.

"I really should start locking that front door," Ivy said.

"I could have gone around to the back."

"I've always enjoyed your sense of humor," Ivy said.

"It's not exactly a joke, but I'll admit that she's not really naked."

"I didn't think she was."

"She's wearing a raincoat."

"A raincoat."

"Right."

"That's all?"

"Right."

"You're not joking?"

"No. Maybe I'd better tell you the whole thing."

"Yes," Ivy said. "That might be a good idea."

Rhodes did his best. Yancey got bored with the story and left the room. He might go to the kitchen and look at the cats, but looking was all he'd do. He wouldn't dare bother them. More likely he'd get into his doggie bed in the bedroom and take a nap.

When Rhodes had finished telling Ivy Vicki's story, he said, "I thought she could stay here, and you could go out and buy her some clothes. She says she'll pay us back, but she doesn't have her purse."

"Or anything else," Ivy said.

"True. We should help her. When you get the clothes and get her dressed, call Hack and have him send Ruth to take her back to Railville."

"Just leave her here in the house and go looking for clothes?"

Rhodes had to admit that it might not be a good idea to do that. He thought Vicki had been telling him the truth, mostly, but leaving her in the house could be a mistake.

"Take her with you, but leave her in the car. Nobody will notice anything."

Ivy gave in, but Rhodes could tell she wasn't happy about it.

"What could possibly go wrong?" he asked.

Ivy laughed. "More than you could imagine, but maybe it will work out. Bring in your friend and we'll see."

"Friend" wasn't the right word, but Rhodes wasn't going to argue. He went to the car to get Vicki, who was sitting right where he'd left her. He hadn't been a hundred percent sure that she would be.

"Is it okay?" Vicki asked.

"It's fine. She'll get you some clothes and a ride home. Come on. I'll introduce you."

Yancey was back, bouncing and yipping as soon as Rhodes opened the front door again.

"What a darling little dog," Vicki said, crouching down to pet him.

Yancey stopped his bouncing and stood still. He loved attention, and it didn't matter to him where it came from. He never met a stranger.

Ivy came in from the den, looked at Rhodes, and nodded. Anybody who liked Yancey was all right.

Vicki stood up, and Rhodes introduced her. "I'll have to leave now. I need to see what I can do about Neil Foshee."

"I thought you were working on Burt Collins's death," Ivy said.

"I am, but this has just come up, and it's urgent."

"It's always something," Ivy said.

"You got that right," Rhodes said.

As soon as he was back in the county car, Rhodes got Hack on the radio and asked if Andy had settled the domestic dispute.

"Wouldn't say he settled it," Hack said. "Got 'em calmed down, though. He's on his way back to town now."

"Tell him to turn around and meet me at the old school building there in Milsby," Rhodes said.

"What's going on?"

"I'll tell you later," Rhodes said, happy to keep Hack in the dark.

"What about that naked woman?"

"You can ask Ivy about that," Rhodes said, grinning as he broke the connection.

The school building was made of red brick, and it had been deserted for years. Rhodes thought it should have been torn down years ago, but no one would claim it, much less take responsibility for it. In a few more years it was going to fall into ruin on its own. The windows were gone already, and someone had even taken the doors. The weather would do the rest.

Andy's county car was parked in the shade on the east side of the building. Rhodes parked beside him and put down the window so they could talk.

"What's happening, Sheriff?" Andy asked.

"I hear there's some kind of drug transaction going on out here. I thought we ought to look into it."

"All right! A little action!"

"We need to be careful. You know about the Foshees?"

"I've heard about them. Sort of outlaws. Live in the country, poach deer, fish in people's stock tanks, make a little meth."

"All true, or supposed to be," Rhodes said. "We'll need to be careful."

"They'll be armed," Andy said.

"And dangerous," Rhodes said. He was a little worried about Andy's excitable nature. "We don't want to start anything we can't finish."

"Right. Shotguns?"

"Good idea," Rhodes said.

They both got out of their cars and got their shotguns and extra shells from the trunks.

"How many of them are there?" Andy asked, thumbing shells into his shotgun.

"No idea," Rhodes said. "I know of one, a cousin of theirs named Neil. He's from Railville, and he's supposed to have come to buy some meth. I figure at least four or five of his cousins will be at the meth house."

"Where's the house?"

"You can follow me," Rhodes said. "We'll go in slow. No sirens. We want to sneak up on them."

"Got it," Andy said.

"And no shooting until I say so. Or until somebody starts shooting at us."

"Got it."

"Good. Let's go."

They got in their cars, and Rhodes led the way, driving past the school and down the dusty country road until he came to what had once been Barton's Grocery. Once it had done a fairly good business with the people who lived in the area nearby. Now no one lived nearby and it was nothing but a collection of planks fallen together and mostly covered by trees and vines that had grown up around and over it. The roof of the porch had fallen down over the front of the remains of the building, and the flooring of the porch had disappeared. Nothing was left but the concrete blocks that had supported it.

Rhodes had been driving slowly, but now he went even slower as he looked at both sides of the road for any signs of a lane that might lead off to an old house. Off to the right about half a chimney stuck up among the mesquite trees that had taken most of a field. The chimney was all that remained of a farmhouse that had once been there. Rhodes wondered if the former residents had bought their groceries at Barton's store.

About a quarter of a mile past the chimney, Rhodes spotted what he'd been looking for, a narrow lane, nothing more than a couple of ruts with weeds and grass growing between them. Rhodes saw tire tracks in the lane, so he knew it had been used recently. The lane was lined with trees that grew close to the ruts.

Rhodes pulled into the lane and drove about twenty yards, with tree branches skreeking on the side of the car all the way. He stopped and got out of the car to wait until Andy pulled in behind him and parked.

"We're going to walk from here," Rhodes said when Andy rolled down his window.

"How far is it?" Andy asked.

"I don't have any idea," Rhodes told him. "They might hear us coming if we take the cars, and we want to surprise them. We'll leave the cars here to block the lane. They won't be able to get out unless they're on foot."

"Sounds like a plan," Andy said.

He got out of his car, then reached back in and got his shotgun. Rhodes got his pistol from the ankle holster and then got his own shotgun. Andy checked his sidearm, a 9 mm Glock, and pushed shells into the shotgun.

Rhodes loaded his shotgun as well. He was sure the Foshees would be armed, though he didn't know what kind of weaponry they had.

The shotgun shells were loaded with double-aught buckshot, but Rhodes was alternating them with slugs. He knew that Andy would be doing the same.

Both men got their Kevlar vests from the car trunks and slipped into them. They were heavy and hot, but it was a cool day. Besides, Rhodes didn't worry much about the heat or the weight of the vest. He wasn't wearing it for comfort.

"The county should buy us some AR-15s," Andy said when Rhodes was ready.

"Maybe next year," Rhodes said. "They cost a couple of thousand dollars, and things are tight right now."

He thought about the time Mikey Burns, one of the commissioners, had wanted to buy an M-16 with some of the Homeland Security funding. Rhodes had thought at the time that buying a gun like that was a foolish idea. Now he was having second thoughts.

"Time to go," Rhodes said.

They started walking, Rhodes in the right-hand rut and Andy in the left. The sunlight came through the trees and made patterns on the ruts and weeds.

After they'd walked for a couple of minutes, Rhodes heard a noise. He stopped.

"Gasoline generator," Andy said. "Not a very big one."

"Big enough for some lights and fans," Rhodes said. "They're probably cooking the meth with a propane stove."

"That generator's so loud, they won't hear us coming," Andy said. "I guess they'll have somebody watching, though. Even out here, they'd need to be careful."

"I don't think they'll have anybody watching," Rhodes said. "If they have any security, it'll be dogs."

"I'd hate to shoot a dog."

"We won't shoot anything or anybody unless we have to. Maybe we'll get lucky."

"You ever shot anybody, Sheriff?"

Rhodes nodded. "Once or twice."

"Kill 'em?"

"Never had to kill anybody. Hope I never will. I might not sleep as well at night if I did. I'd do it if I had to, though, but let's hope today's not the day I have to."

"Or me," Andy said. "I'd hate to do it. I would, but I wouldn't like it. You ever been shot?"

"Yes," Rhodes said. "Nothing serious, though. Just a scratch."

"You think these vests we have are really bulletproof?"

"That's what they tell me."

"You don't know for sure, though."

Rhodes could understand why Andy might be a bit worried. Anybody would be. Including Rhodes.

"They're guaranteed," Rhodes said, "so they must work. If they don't, you can sue the manufacturer."

"I might not be around to sue."

"Then I'll do it for you," Rhodes said. "Give you a big send-off. The whole town will turn out."

"You really know how to make a guy feel good about things," Andy said.

Rhodes nodded. He knew Andy would be fine. "Just part of the job. We'd better stop talking now. Wouldn't want to make it too easy for the dogs or the sentries."

Andy put a finger to his lips and nodded, making Rhodes grin.

The lane made a slight curve about fifty yards ahead, and Rhodes thought the meth house wouldn't be much farther. In fact, he could smell it already. It smelled like ammonia mixed with cat urine. The Foshees must be cooking up a batch. That was all right with Rhodes. He doubted the dogs would smell him and Andy, thanks to the stink coming from the house.

Just before Rhodes got to the curve, he motioned for Andy to take to the trees. Rhodes did the same. They could still see each other if they looked, but now they wouldn't be out in the open for the Foshees or their dogs to see them. Rhodes hoped there wouldn't be dogs, but he was expecting them.

When he rounded the bend, Rhodes caught sight of the house through the trees. Parked in the sandy lot in front of it were two pickups, both nearly new and both black, along with a black

Chrysler 300 that dust from the road had settled on. So Neil was likely to be there. To one side of the house were a couple of ugly brown patches where waste chemicals had been dumped.

The house was an old one, looking as if it were about to fall off the brick and concrete blocks it sat on, and badly weathered. No one had lived there for a very long time. The tin roof was rusty and peeled back in a couple of places. The top bricks were missing from the chimney, as was all the window glass. The missing window glass was a bonus for the meth cookers because the toxic fumes could escape more easily. If the Foshees were being careful, they had a few big fans blowing in the house to further help with the ventilation.

Rhodes looked all around, but he didn't see anyone watching. He looked over at Andy, who shook his head, so he didn't see anyone, either. There was no sign of any dogs so far, which Rhodes thought was a good sign. He'd expected the Foshees to be care-less, and they were. They didn't have much of a reason for caution, being well off the road, and being well away from anywhere that someone would pass by and notice them, so they didn't bother with security.

One of the many problems with meth was how easy it was to make, and people like the Foshees could set up just about any-where, including the trunk of a car. Making meth was dangerous, though, and it polluted the workspace so badly that any house where it was made usually had to be condemned. The best thing to do was to find some old place well away from anywhere and use that. They'd be less likely to be caught, and once they'd pol-luted that place so much that even they couldn't stand it, they could leave and find another old house that was equally deserted and equally well hidden.

The good news was that there wasn't a big meth problem in Blacklin County, not like some other counties in East Texas, where it was like a plague, involving whole generations of families. Rhodes didn't know how many generations of Foshees were mixed up in this operation, but he had a feeling he was about to find out.

He wasn't looking forward to it.

The circular clearing was about thirty yards in diameter, with the house in the middle. Stumps stuck up here and there in the clearing, none of them very big, and brush was stacked in a big pile off to one side. Rhodes didn't think the trees had been cut down too long ago, maybe a month at most. He figured the Foshees would be moving on to somewhere else soon. Or they would be if Rhodes and Andy didn't put a stop to their business.

Rhodes neared the edge of the trees. If there were dogs around, they'd be coming out soon. They might not smell anybody, but they'd sense the presence of strangers somehow. Dogs had a way of doing that, especially dogs in the employ of meth cookers.

When he'd gotten as close to the clearing as he thought he could without being seen, Rhodes crouched down. He looked over at Andy, who did the same. There was movement in the house, but no indication that whoever was inside knew that any-one was watching.

Rhodes waited until his knees started to bother him. He'd still seen no sign of any dogs. Maybe there weren't any. He stood up and took a step forward.

As soon as he did, three dogs surged from beneath the house, barking, showing their fangs, and running as fast as they could, straight toward him.

Chapter 15

▼

The dogs were the kind called leopard hounds, though Rhodes knew they weren't really hounds. They were often trained to hunt feral hogs, which meant they were a popular breed in Blacklin County, one of many in the state being overrun by the wild porkers. It also meant that they could be trained to be very unfriendly to strangers, which Rhodes was. He didn't think they were inclined to make friends.

Halfway across the clearing, one of the dogs swerved off in Andy's direction. Andy glanced at Rhodes, who aimed his shotgun high above the dogs and pulled the trigger.

The buckshot didn't have much of a spread, and it wasn't much use beyond twenty yards. It rattled against the tin roof of the house.

Andy fired, too, and the noise of both guns was enough to give the dogs a reason to stop and look around. While they were stopped, Rhodes fired a slug into the ground in front of the two nearest him. Dirt flew up into their faces. The dogs didn't like that at all. They turned and ran. The third one turned and followed them. They scuttled back beneath the house.

Just as the dogs managed to hide themselves, two men burst out of the doorway. Both of them were armed with AR-15s with thirty-round magazines. Selling meth was quite profitable, so they could afford more firepower than the county. Rhodes had hoped they'd be armed with something small, like pistols. He'd also hoped they wouldn't be quite so prepared to start shooting. So much for hope.

Both men started bump-firing the rifles toward the trees. Rhodes was already on his stomach, and he hoped Andy was, too. He squirmed behind the thickest nearby tree and tried to make himself invisible. Bullets whizzed above him, clipping off tree branches right and left and filling the air with flying leaves.

It took only a second or two for thirty rounds to go through an AR-15 the way the Foshees were firing. They had to change magazines, and even though they could do that quickly, it gave Rhodes a chance to jump to his feet and run forward.

He fired a blast of buckshot in the direction of the porch. He didn't think it would disable anybody, but it would sting. He fired a slug that barely missed one of the men on the porch just before he slid down behind the Chrysler.

The AR-15s chattered again. Rhodes looked around as he slid shells into his shotgun. Andy was on the ground behind one of the pickups. Bullets clanged into the metal of the trucks and the car for a couple of seconds. Then it was quiet.

"This is Sheriff Dan Rhodes," Rhodes called out. "Put down your weapons and give it up."

The men answered with another volley.

Andy responded by hammering away with his Glock. Rhodes

waited until the firing stopped. When it did, in the brief and total silence that followed, Rhodes heard something hit the wooden porch. That sound was followed by cursing. Either they were trying to fool Rhodes or they'd dropped one of the magazines. Rhodes bet on the drop, jumped up, and ran forward, firing the shotgun low, aiming for the men's legs.

One of the men fell off the porch. The other ducked back into the house.

Rhodes didn't think the man would be stupid enough to fire a gun inside an enclosed space where meth was being cooked. No matter how well ventilated the place was, an explosion was too great a risk.

"Cuff him, Andy," Rhodes yelled as he passed the man on the ground.

Rhodes stopped when he reached the porch. He was in a bad position. If the man did risk firing, the bullets would rip right through the walls of the old house. If the house blew up, it wouldn't matter whether Rhodes was inside or standing where he was. He'd be in big trouble either way. So would the Foshees.

Rhodes thought about it for a second, and then he heard a squeal like unoiled hinges.

"Got the prisoner secured," Andy said, coming up to stand beside Rhodes. He'd holstered the Glock and held the shotgun ready. "He's not going anywhere. How many more do you think there are?"

"Two, at least. Let's find out."

"How will we do that?"

"Go around back," Rhodes said, "and be careful. I have a feeling they're slipping out that way. You take the left side."

Rhodes ran around the right side of the house. Sure enough,

as he neared the back he saw two men running into the trees. Both had pistols, but neither was carrying an AR-15, so Rhodes figured they were out of magazines. That suited him just fine.

The old "stop or I'll shoot" trick most likely wouldn't stop them, so Rhodes blasted a slug over their heads. Andy did the same. Both of them pumped a fresh shell into the chambers of their shotguns as the spent ones were expelled.

The men ducked behind trees and hunkered down, ready to return fire, but the trees didn't conceal them very well. One of them fired a shot that went right over Rhodes's head. Rhodes thought he was close enough to hurt them with the double-aught buck, but not too badly, so he fired back at them. So did Andy.

Both men yelled. They were hit for sure, and Rhodes said, "Next shots are slugs. Anybody want to feel them?"

"Not me," one of the men yelled. "I'm putting down my gun."

"Let me see it," Rhodes said.

The man held a revolver up, then put it on the ground.

"Earl's hit pretty bad," the man said. "I'll get his gun, too."

"Careful how you do it," Rhodes told him.

The man moved to the tree where Earl was slumped and held up a pistol, which he then laid on the ground.

"That's all we got," he said.

"It better be," Rhodes said. "Are you Neil?"

"How'd you know that?"

"Lucky guess. Lie facedown. Tell Earl to do the same."

"He's hurt pretty bad."

Rhodes didn't believe it. "Just tell him. I'd hate to have to hurt him any worse."

Neil said something to Earl and lay down. Earl rolled over on his side, then over on his stomach.

"Hands behind your backs," Rhodes said, and Earl and Neil complied.

Rhodes and Andy walked forward with their shotguns aimed at the prisoners.

"You have enough cuffs?" Rhodes asked.

"Always carry four," Andy said.

"Good. Neil and Earl, my deputy's going to cuff you. Hold still."

The two men held still. Rhodes saw that Earl's right arm had taken a pretty good hit, but the bleeding had about stopped.

"I hope you two turned off your cooker before you left the house," Rhodes said.

"Didn't have time," Neil said as Andy cuffed him.

"You think it'll blow?" Andy asked as he cuffed Earl, who was moaning as if he'd been gutted.

"Could," Rhodes said.

"You want me to go in and turn it off?"

"Good idea. You sure you want to risk it?"

"It's my job," Andy said.

Rhodes thought the risk was small enough, so he said, "Bring out those rifles when you come back."

"No problem," Andy said.

"I hope not," Rhodes said. "Let's stand these two lunkheads up and get them moving."

They helped Earl and Neil to their feet. Earl was still taking on, but Rhodes ignored him and gave him a little push to get him started.

When they got around to the front of the house, they saw that the third man had managed to squirm a few feet in the direction of the pickups, but his legs were bloody, and he hadn't tried to stand.

"You think he can walk to the cars?" Andy asked.

"We'll find out," Rhodes said.

"Don't leave without me," Andy said, and he headed for the house to turn off the propane stove.

"We don't mind waiting," Rhodes said. "Do we, fellas?"

Earl and Neil didn't say anything, so Rhodes asked them the third man's name.

"That's Louie," Neil said.

"All of you Foshees?"

Neil nodded. "How'd you find us? It was that bitch Vicki, wasn't it? I knew I should've shot her."

"Good thing you didn't," Rhodes said. "You're in enough trouble without that."

Neil just looked at him. Earl had stopped whining and stood staring at the ground. Louie wasn't talking, either. Rhodes nudged him with the toe of his shoe.

"Hop up, Louie. Time to go."

"Get bent," Louie said.

Andy came out of the house. He had the AR-15s with him. "All taken care of, Sheriff. What about the dogs?"

Rhodes had forgotten about the dogs. They were still under the house. All the shooting had discouraged them.

"You planning to adopt them?" Andy asked when Rhodes told him where they were.

"Ivy would kill me," Rhodes said, "but we'll find a place for them. Get old Louie there up on his feet."

"I can't get up," Louie said. "I'm wounded."

"You can manage," Rhodes said, and he grabbed hold of the cuffs with a jerk that encouraged Louie to discover that he could indeed get up.

"Read them their rights, Andy," Rhodes said.

Andy proceeded to rattle off the Miranda warning, supposedly reading from a little laminated card he pulled from his shirt pocket, though Rhodes knew he'd memorized it.

"Nothing at all in there about not having to walk," Rhodes said after he'd asked them if they understood their rights. "So here we go."

They started off, but Rhodes stopped them. "Hold on. I forgot something."

While they waited, Rhodes went to the Chrysler and looked inside. He saw a woman's purse sitting on the front seat. He checked the car door and found it unlocked. He opened the door and got out the purse. It had a strap, so he hung it off his shoulder.

Rhodes and Andy marched the prisoners down the lane to the county cars. It was a bit awkward because Andy had the two AR-15s in addition to his shotgun, and Rhodes had Vicki's purse.

The prisoners might have considered making a run for it, given the circumstances, but Rhodes assured them that the purse wouldn't hinder his shooting.

"First one to run gets a slug. Next gets buckshot. Sure would hurt in the backside."

The prisoners grumbled a little, but nobody tried to make a break, and Rhodes and Andy didn't have to prod them more than a couple of times. It didn't take long to reach the county cars.

Rhodes put the AR-15s in the trunk of his car, along with Vicki's purse and his vest. He and Andy got the prisoners safely in the backseats, Earl and Louie with Andy, Neil with Rhodes. After the shotguns were stowed, Rhodes told Andy to take his two men by the hospital to get them checked out.

"Will do," Andy said, and while he backed down the lane,

Rhodes called Hack and told him to send the fire department's hazmat team.

"You know we ain't got one of those," Hack said. "I'll send the fire department men that's trained for it. You want to tell me what's goin' on?"

"Nope," Rhodes said. "Send Alton Boyd, too. We have three dogs that need taking care of."

"You want to tell me just exactly where you are?"

Rhodes gave him specific directions and said, "Get Cal Autry and tell him there are three shot-up vehicles here that need to be impounded."

"Shot-up? You gonna tell me about that?"

"Maybe," Rhodes said. "Later. You know what to do?"

"You know I do. You comin' here now?"

"With one prisoner," Rhodes said. "Andy's taking the other two to the hospital."

"Hospital? What happened?"

"Later," Rhodes said, forking the mic and hoping that Hack didn't explode from curiosity. It felt good to be one up on him for a change.

Come to think of it, Rhodes still hadn't told him about the naked woman. He was two up.

"What're you so happy about?" Neil said from the backseat.

Rhodes looked at him through the grille.

"Nothing you'd understand," he said.

After getting Neil booked and printed, Rhodes asked Hack if he'd had Ruth drive Vicki back to Railville.

"Yeah," Hack said. "Who's this Vicki, anyway?"

"The naked woman," Rhodes said.

"You had Ruth take a naked woman home?"

"She wasn't naked anymore, I hope. Ivy was supposed to help her get some clothes."

"What was she naked for?"

Rhodes gave in and told Hack and Lawton all about what had happened. He didn't do it in a straightforward way, however. He used their own technique and made them draw it out of him little by little while he was writing up his report.

"Low T," Lawton said when Rhodes was finished. "He wouldn't treat us this way if he didn't have the low T."

"Gotta be it," Hack said. "Otherwise, he'd have asked us what'd been goin' on here while he was out shootin' up the countryside."

Here we go, Rhodes thought.

"Maybe you'd better tell me," he said.

"Ruth checked the head for fingerprints," Hack said. "Guess what."

"No prints," Rhodes said.

"Right, mostly. She got some smudges to come out, but nothing you could call a real print."

Too bad they couldn't use smudges to get a conviction, Rhodes thought. They still might be able to prove the bust was the murder weapon, however. It was possible that some traces of blood could be found on it at the state lab. Rhodes would send it off if it came to that.

"What about the phone records?" he asked.

"She found the judge and got the subpoena. She'll bring the records by later, she said."

"Good," Rhodes said, thinking that it had been too easy to get the information. That meant there was something more.

"Is that all?" he asked.

"Got a phone call," Hack said.

"We get calls all the time," Rhodes said.

"Yeah, but this one wasn't from just any old body."

"What old body was it from?"

"Better not let him catch you callin' him old," Lawton said.

"That's right," Hack said. "He wouldn't like it."

"I wouldn't know," Rhodes said, "since I don't know who we're talking about."

"The mayor," Hack said. "Mr. Clifford Clement, that's who."

Rhodes wondered what had taken Clement so long.

Chapter 16

▼

Clifford Clement had been the mayor of Clearview for several years. The city didn't have any term limits in its charter. While there had been a few rumblings among the citizens who wanted to change that, nothing had been done, and Clement kept on winning elections.

The mayor didn't much care for Rhodes, and Rhodes didn't blame him. When a man's been a suspect in a murder investigation, it's not surprising that he might not be too fond of the investigator, even if he knows the investigator is just doing his job. It only made things worse if the investigator uncovered some unsavory facts about the suspect's private life in the process of looking under various rocks. Even knowing that Rhodes would never tell anyone about those facts, Clement was bound to be a little resentful.

It being Saturday, the mayor wasn't in his office. The mayorship of Clearview wasn't a full-time job anyway, and Clement had a business to run, not that he ran it on Saturdays. He was an investment counselor, and he liked to say his job was to make money for other people. Rhodes didn't know if he actually did make money for other people, but he must have known something about investing because he made plenty for himself if his house was any indication. It was in a part of the town that was more or less untouched by time, where the houses of the wealthy from another era were now owned and cared for by people who had the money to afford them. Clement had the money.

The house sat on about three lots, and the lawn was perfect. So were the flower beds, which looked like a magazine illustration. Rhodes thought about his own shaggy lawn and weedy beds. He was glad it was October. He wouldn't have to mow but a couple more times that year, and the weeds would die during the winter.

Walking up to the front door of the house, Rhodes felt a little like Dorothy must have felt on the Yellow Brick Road, as if he were headed to the Emerald City. It had been years since Rhodes had seen the movie with Judy Garland, but he remembered the scene well. Clement wasn't that much different from the great and powerful Oz, though Rhodes could never say that to Clement.

It wasn't Clement who came to the door when Rhodes rang the bell. It was Clement's wife, Fran, a short woman with very black short hair, who'd had occasion to flirt with Rhodes in the past. She wasn't in a flirty mood today, however, which meant that her husband was at home.

"Hello, Sheriff," Fran said. She wore a blue blouse and dark pants that hadn't come from Walmart and probably not from any shop in the county. "You look like someone who's had a bad day."

"Sometimes busting crime is dirty work," Rhodes said.

"I can see that. Well, come on in."

Rhodes could tell she'd rather he stay outside. He'd tried to wash off most of the dirt at the jail, but his clothes still showed the signs of the dirt and dust he'd picked up at the meth house.

"Clifford's in his office, waiting for you," Fran said. "I'm sure he'll be glad to see you."

Rhodes had his doubts about that, but the mayor had made it clear when Rhodes called him from the jail that he wanted to see Rhodes immediately if not sooner. He was one of Rhodes's bosses, since the city of Clearview, not having a police department, contracted with the county for its law enforcement, and Rhodes didn't have much choice other than to show up and see what Clement wanted, even though he thought he already knew the answer.

Rhodes followed Fran down the hallway and into the den. The last time Rhodes had been there, Fran had been drinking a little. Not this time. She was all business. Maybe she didn't indulge in either drinking or flirting when her husband was at home. That was just fine with Rhodes.

"Clifford's right in here," Fran said, leading Rhodes into a room just off the den. "I'll leave you two to have your little talk."

Fran went out and closed the door behind her. Rhodes glanced around the office. It was bigger and nicer than the one downtown that Clement got from the city. The desk was big and black, with a slick glass top, the two chairs for visitors were covered with smooth leather, and the carpet looked brand-new.

Clement got up from the ergonomic chair behind the desk, came around it, and shook Rhodes's hand.

"Have a seat, Sheriff," he said, "and tell me when you're going to find out who killed Burt Collins."

He went back behind his desk, and Rhodes sat down, thinking that it was just as well that Clement had come right to the point. He figured he'd do the same.

"I don't know," he said. "There are a lot of other things going on right now."

Clement didn't ask for an example. He said, "Do any of those things involve murder?"

"No, but—"

"Do any of those things involve a video of a riot at an art show?"

"No, but—"

"And have any of those things pretty much destroyed the town's reputation with all the people at that art thing?"

"No, but—"

"I'm supposed to be at the art thing tonight," Clement said. "The closing party or whatever it is. I'm supposed to make some kind of short speech about how happy we are to have the artists in our little town. I'm supposed to tell them I hope they'll be back next year, when the whole shebang will be even bigger and better. How many of them do you think will come back if they start thinking about some unsolved murder that went on right under their noses and got started because somebody defaced their paintings?"

Rhodes didn't bother to try to answer.

"Well?" Clement said.

"You didn't seem interested in listening to me," Rhodes said. "I thought I'd wait for you to run down."

Clement's face twitched. "You don't have to take that tone with me."

"You didn't have to take that tone with me, either," Rhodes

said. "Do you want to listen to me now or keep on asking me questions?"

Clement stared at him. The stare didn't bother Rhodes. He waited it out.

"All right," Clement said after a while. "Go ahead. You talk. I'll listen."

"Okay. As I was trying to tell you, there are a lot of other things going on. We have a small department, and we can't drop everything to investigate one thing, even if it is a murder."

"If you're looking for more money," Clement said, "you'd be better off talking to the county commissioners. The city makes its deal with them."

"I'm not looking for money," Rhodes told him. "I'm trying to explain something. Last night we had an armed robbery. Today we shut down a meth lab. Yesterday it was donkeys gone wild. Maybe tomorrow we'll find out who killed Burt Collins. Right now, we're doing what we can."

"Do you have any leads?"

"A few," Rhodes said, thinking of the bronze bust. "So far they haven't taken us anywhere."

The mention of the bust triggered a thought, something that Rhodes hadn't considered before. He'd have to try to remember it later.

"So, then," Clement said, "tonight can I say something like, 'The sheriff tells me he has some solid leads in the case'?"

"Sure. Tell them that if you think it'll make them feel better. You can tell them to keep looking at Jennifer Loam's Web site for updates, too. Maybe they'll see the meth lab story. They'll see what a fine department we have."

"Are you sure it'll be there?"

168

Rhodes thought about Andy Shelby's relationship with Jennifer Loam. He was surprised that Jennifer hadn't come to the jail while he was telling Hack and Lawton about the meth bust. She must have been working on something else, but by now she'd have talked to Andy and visited the jail to see Rhodes's report.

"The story will be on the Web site before long, if it's not already," Rhodes said. "I'm about a hundred percent certain of that."

"Well, that might help," Clement said. He stood up. "I'm sorry if I seemed a little overwrought. It's just that I hate to see the town getting a bad reputation. You can understand."

Rhodes stood, too. "I can, and I'll be doing all I can to find the killer."

"All right, then. Thanks for coming by."

"My pleasure," Rhodes said, trying not to sound sarcastic. He thought he did a good job of it, but he didn't really care.

As Rhodes was starting the county car, Hack came on the radio.

"You got a lot of fans today," Hack said. "Somebody else wants to see you."

"Who?" Rhodes asked.

"Mr. Mikey Burns, your favorite county commissioner. He's at the county barn, provin' to the citizens that he even works on a Saturday."

Rhodes didn't think any citizens would be impressed, because they wouldn't know. Hardly anybody ever dropped by the county barn even during the week, and Burns would be the only one there on Saturday. Even Mrs. Wilkie, his secretary, wouldn't be there.

"Are you sure he wants to see me today?"

"That's what he said."

"Then I'll drive out there and see what he wants."

"I bet you already know."

"Yeah, I do," Rhodes said. "He wants me to have Burt Collins's killer behind bars."

"Nope," Hack said.

"What, then?"

"You'll find out," Hack said.

The door between Burns's office and the reception desk was open, so Rhodes walked right in. Burns sat behind his desk, but he wasn't wearing his usual brightly colored aloha shirt. The background of this one was dark blue, and it was covered with ukuleles of various sizes.

Burns didn't bother to stand up. He just motioned Rhodes to a chair and asked him how the investigation into Collins's death was coming.

"I've been busy," Rhodes said, "but I have a few ideas."

"Good," Burns said. "That's good. Glad to hear it, but that's not really what I want to talk about. You know I wouldn't call you in on a Saturday afternoon unless it was about something big, I hope."

"I know," Rhodes said, though he didn't really know. He had no idea what Burns was talking about.

"You remember when I wanted to get us that M-16?" Burns asked.

"I was just thinking about that today, as a matter of fact," Rhodes said.

"Good. That's good thinking, but this is even bigger than that." Burns smiled. "Much bigger."

Rhodes still didn't know what was going on. Burns must have noticed his puzzlement. He leaned forward and said, "Drones."

"Drones?" Rhodes said.

Burns looked around. "Is there an echo in here?" He laughed at his own joke and said, "Not drones. I shouldn't have said that. I meant one drone."

"Like a spy plane?"

"Exactly. I read about a sheriff's department in California that's going to get a government grant to get one. We wouldn't need one of the kind that can kill people, just something to watch them with. Not much bigger than the model planes I used to build when I was a kid. Weighs about four pounds, has a four-foot wingspan. You get somebody on a computer and fly it all over the county. Right over that meth house you busted a couple of hours ago, for instance."

"You know about that?" Rhodes asked.

"Hack told me. Anyway, if we had one of those drones cruising the county airspace, we could find places like that before they got started good. Then you could swoop in and shut them down."

"If you had an armed one, you could just bomb the place."

"Man, wouldn't that be a sight? Might be dangerous, though, blowing up a meth house. The explosion might kill whoever was inside, and we wouldn't want that. We couldn't handle all the lawsuits."

"What about the lawsuits from people who think we're spying on them?"

"Nothing wrong with a little spying," Burns said. "We have every right to do that." He paused. "Don't we?"

"Some people think so," Rhodes said. "Others, well, they wouldn't agree at all."

"You mean they'd actually sue? Who'd do a thing like that?"

Rhodes thought about Able Terrell in his compound down in the south part of the county.

"Able Terrell," Rhodes said. "He wouldn't sue, though. He'd just shoot down the drone."

"Wouldn't that be illegal?"

"I don't know," Rhodes said. "He could tie the county up in court for a long time if we tried to arrest him for it."

Burns frowned. "Maybe we'd better hold off on the drone."

"Not only that," Rhodes said, "but you'd have to find someone qualified to pilot the drone from a computer console. Probably two people at least so they could work in shifts. That would be quite an expense, even if you could find someone with the expertise to do it."

"What about that Benton fella? He did a good job helping with the county Web site."

"As good as he thinks he is, I'm not sure he could handle something like a drone. Besides, he has a job already."

"Yeah, I guess he does. I might better give this some more thought."

"Probably a good idea," Rhodes said.

"Drones are the coming thing, though," Burns said. "People can fight it all they want to, but in ten years, every law enforcement group in the state will have drones. I don't want to be the last county to get one."

"You could bring it up with some of the other commissioners, see what they think about it. Maybe start working on a grant proposal. Mrs. Wilkie would probably enjoy that."

172

Rhodes had no idea if Mrs. Wilkie would enjoy it, but it would give her something to work on.

"That might be best," Burns said. "It sure would be great to be able to watch what was going on all over the county, though, like they do in the big cities. Cameras on every corner."

"The drone would be watching you, too," Rhodes told him.

"I don't have anything to hide. I'm a law-abiding citizen."

"That's good to know," Rhodes said.

Chapter 17

▼

Rhodes didn't bother to go by the jail again. It was late afternoon and time to go home. He parked in his driveway and went around back to see Speedo, the border collie, who had his own private Styrofoam igloo to live in. Speedo came bounding up to greet him. The collie was always glad to see Rhodes, any time of the day or night, which was more than Rhodes could say for most humans he knew, especially humans like Clifford Clement.

Speedo was eager to play, but Rhodes knew that he couldn't neglect Yancey, who was barking at the screen door and asking to be let outside. Rhodes started for the door, but he'd only taken a couple of steps before Ivy opened it. Yancey hopped down the two concrete steps and out into the yard, where he proceeded to harass Speedo, circling him and yipping.

Ivy followed Yancey outside and sat on the top step. "Those two have more energy than I do," she said.

"More than I do, too," Rhodes said, looking around for the rubber squeaky toy the dogs liked to play with.

174

"You look a little raggedy," Ivy said. "Rough afternoon?"

Rhodes had known Ivy would notice his clothes.

"Just the usual gun battle with meth cookers," he said. "The good guys won."

"You know I worry about you, don't you? All the time?"

"Comes with the territory."

"The gun battles or the worry?"

"Both," Rhodes said. "It wasn't much of a battle. Three of them and two of us. They didn't stand a chance."

Ivy sighed. "If you say so."

"I do. Did you get Vicki taken care of?"

"Yes, Ruth took her home. She's coming back on Monday to file charges against Neil Foshee."

"Good," Rhodes said. "I have her purse at the jail. She'll need it."

"She's had a bad time since her divorce," Ivy said. "She made a big mistake with that Neil."

"Her husband was no prize, either, not if she was telling the truth about him."

"I heard that story, too," Ivy said. "I believe it. Vicki needs someone to keep her on the straight and narrow."

"Are you volunteering?"

"I'm thinking it over," Ivy said.

Rhodes found the squeaky toy, a green and yellow frog, lying in the grass near the steps. He picked it up and mashed it, making it squeal. Yancey and Speedo bounded over and stood a couple of feet away from Rhodes, watching him with wary anticipation.

With a flick of his wrist Rhodes sent the frog spinning across the yard a few feet above Speedo's head. The dogs turned and went after it. It wasn't possible for Yancey to keep up with Speedo, but Yancey never seemed to catch on to that fact. He always charged headlong toward the frog as if he knew, just *knew,* that this time it was going to be different. This time for sure, somehow or other, he was going to get to the frog first.

He didn't, but as Speedo scooped it up in his mouth and turned back to Rhodes, Yancey made his play, leaping up and grabbing one of the frog's legs in his mouth. Speedo shook his head, and Yancey fell to the grass. Speedo didn't even look at him but instead ran back to Rhodes. He didn't give up the frog at first. He made Rhodes work for it, and when Rhodes had it in his hand, Speedo waited for the next toss.

Yancey, meanwhile, was lying low in the grass back where the frog had hit the ground the first time. He couldn't outrun Speedo, but he could outsmart him if only Rhodes would cooperate.

Rhodes did. He spun the frog in Yancey's direction, and the little Pomeranian pounced on it with doggish glee as soon as it hit the grass. Instead of bringing it back to Rhodes for another round, he took off around the yard with Speedo tearing after him.

When Speedo caught up, Yancey hunkered down and growled at him through teeth clenched on the frog.

"It takes so little to keep them happy," Ivy said.

"You say the same thing about me," Rhodes told her.

"Only because it's true. Except I can tell that you're worried today."

"Worried about Burt Collins," Rhodes admitted. "His killer, that is. I think I may have missed something."

"Do you know what?"

"I have an idea or two. I need to make a phone call. You keep the dogs entertained."

"They don't like the way I throw the frog."

176

"You may never have to throw it," Rhodes said. "I don't think Yancey's going to give it up. I'll be right back."

He went past Ivy and into the house. He could've called from his cell phone, but he didn't like cell phones. He preferred a landline when he could get to one.

The two cats were sleeping peacefully in the kitchen. They didn't need entertainment as long as they had a good place to sleep. They were even easier to keep happy than the dogs. Sam opened one eye and looked at Rhodes. When he saw who it was, he closed the eye.

Rhodes sneezed as he picked up the phone.

Seepy Benton answered Rhodes's call on the first ring.

"What's up, Sheriff?" he asked. "Any crimes you want solved? Any rowdies you want me to subdue?"

"Nothing that hard," Rhodes said.

"Subduing the rowdies wasn't hard. You just have to know how to use the pressure points. It's not tricky. I could show you how it's done if you want me to. I was Professor Lansdale's star pupil."

"Never mind that. What I want to know is the time of the closing ceremonies for the art conference tonight."

"Seven o'clock. Why?"

"I'm invited, I suppose."

"It's open to the public, so that would include you. It won't be as good as it could be because of the damage to some of the work, but we hope a few people show up. We might have a good crowd because of the extra added attraction."

Rhodes didn't like the way that sounded.

"We're going to have live entertainment," Benton said. "People like live entertainment while they're looking at art."

"I wouldn't know about that." Rhodes almost hated to ask his next question. "What kind of entertainment will there be?"

"I'm going to sing."

Worst fears realized. Benton had been singing his own compositions and accompanying himself on guitar at a barbecue restaurant on Saturday evenings, but the owner, Max Schwartz, had decided to try something new, or that was the way Benton had explained it to Rhodes. Schwartz had replaced Benton with a barbershop quartet called the Next Edition. Rhodes had seen one of their videos on YouTube, a barbershop version of "The Lion Sleeps Tonight" that he thought was a bit better than Benton's warblings.

Benton had been somewhat less impressed than Rhodes, or so he'd said. "The tenor's okay," he'd told Rhodes. "Not a bad falsetto, but I can't say much for that lead singer."

Rhodes thought Benton was just upset because he'd been replaced, but Benton claimed that wasn't the case. Rhodes supposed it didn't matter so much now that Benton had an opportunity to perform again, even if it was just a one-shot. Since it was an audience that for the most part hadn't heard him before, maybe it would go all right.

"You'll be there, won't you?" Benton asked.

"Is there going to be food?"

"Major snacks," Benton said. "Not a meal, though. Isn't the entertainment enough of a draw? I have some new numbers. You'll like them."

Rhodes doubted it, and he wondered what a major snack was. Whatever it was, it would be better than nothing at all. He hoped.

"I'll be there," he said. "Ivy, too."

"Good. She loves my work."

Rhodes knew better, but he didn't say so.

"Ruth's coming," Benton said. "Practically the whole department will be there."

"Are you counting yourself?" Rhodes asked.

"Well, I'm not officially part of the department, as you keep reminding me, but I do feel as if I'm an informal helper."

"Don't be saying that to anybody," Rhodes told him.

"The secret is safe with me," Benton said. "Working undercover is just my speed. I'll see you this evening."

"I'm looking forward to it," Rhodes said, wondering if Benton could tell he was lying.

When Rhodes went back outside, it was getting close to sundown, and the air was cool. Speedo was still trying to get the frog from Yancey. Every time the collie made a move toward the frog, Yancey would jerk backward, keeping just out of his reach.

"They could keep that up all day," Ivy said. "Why doesn't Speedo just jump on Yancey and take the stupid frog?"

"That would spoil their fun," Rhodes said, sitting beside her on the step. "It's such a nice night, why don't we go out for dinner?"

Ivy gave him a suspicious glance. "What's going on?"

"Nothing," Rhodes said, trying to look innocent. It wasn't easy to do, as he'd learned from hundreds of interviews with guilty parties over the years, but he thought he pulled it off. "I just thought it would be fun."

"I was planning to fix chicken meat loaf," Ivy said.

While Rhodes thought that sounded better than vegetarian meat loaf, it wasn't exactly enticing.

"You could have that some other time. What about going out?"

"I'd like that. Where will we go?"

"I thought the closing event for the art conference might be fun," Rhodes said. "They're having major snacks."

He thought it might be best not to mention the extra added attraction.

"This is work, isn't it," Ivy said.

"But fun, too. Business and pleasure."

"They don't mix, I've heard."

"This time they do. Trust me."

"You're going to shower and put on fresh clothes, I hope."

"Naturally." Rhodes stood up and put down a hand. Ivy took his hand and pulled herself up beside him.

"There's still something you're not telling me," Ivy said.

"It's a surprise," Rhodes said. "An extra added attraction."

He went down the steps and across the yard, where he grabbed the frog away from Yancey.

"Go on inside," Rhodes said to Yancey. "I have to feed Speedo."

Yancey pranced across the yard, looking back at Speedo a couple of times on the way as if to say, "You didn't get the frog, nyah, nyah, nyah."

"He's a real caution, isn't he?" Rhodes said, watching Yancey go.

Speedo barked twice.

Rhodes took that for a yes.

Chapter 18

▼

There had been a time that still remained in the memory of a lot of people living in Clearview when the downtown area on Saturday night was the place to be if you wanted to see people you knew. The stores were open late, and the streets were crowded. The cotton farmers all came to town on Saturday, and it wasn't easy to find a parking place on the streets in front of the stores.

That had all changed now. The streetlights still came on when the sun went down, but the streets were deserted. The old buildings were dark, and it was impossible to tell now what kind of businesses had been in them. Even the movie theater facades were anonymous, and most of the older residents had forgotten exactly where the Saturday matinees had been shown.

Tonight, however, there was one exception to the darkness. The lights were on in the art gallery, and their glow spilled out onto the sidewalk. Cars lined the street in front of the building.

Although the senior center was closed, the outside was lighted. It was almost as if the town had come alive again.

By the time Rhodes and Ivy arrived at the art gallery, the festivities had already begun. The crowd was bigger than Rhodes had expected. Seepy Benton sat on a stool at one end of the gallery, strumming his guitar softly. When Rhodes and Ivy walked in, he was explaining that his next number was called "The Medical Marijuana Song."

"It's available on my YouTube channel," he said. "Seepybenton's channel. Seepybenton is one word. You can watch me anytime."

Rhodes looked around the gallery. People were moving around and chatting. Some of them were picking up food from the long table in the middle of the room. Very few of them seemed to be listening to Seepy.

The lack of interest in what Seepy had to say didn't prove to be a deterrent, however. Seepy launched right into his big number, which sounded vaguely familiar to Rhodes, especially the chorus, during which Seepy sang, "All we are saying . . . is give weed a chance."

"What are the chances of that happening?" Ivy asked.

"You mean giving weed a chance?"

Ivy nodded.

"This is Texas," Rhodes said. "So I'd have to guess the chances are zero."

"That's what I think, too," Ivy said. "It might be just as well that nobody's really listening. They might get the wrong idea about Seepy."

"We wouldn't want that," Rhodes said.

Ivy laughed. "Let's look at some of the paintings."

They strolled around, and Rhodes noted some of the works that he hadn't seen before. One of them was of a group of people with umbrellas walking along what appeared to be Clearview's main street. The old buildings looked familiar, but the scene didn't. It wasn't raining rain. Or violets or pennies from heaven, for that matter. It was raining feathers that swirled in the air and pooled in the street.

"I wonder if whoever painted that was giving weed a chance," Ivy said.

"You have to understand the symbolism," Rhodes told her.

"Why don't you explain it to me?"

"The local pillow factory exploded."

"There's no pillow factory here."

"You have to use your imagination."

"I see," Ivy said. "Or maybe not. What about that one?"

Ivy pointed to a painting that looked to Rhodes as if it might just be a solid red square, but when he squinted he saw that there was a fine white diagonal line across it. He wondered if that was one of the defaced paintings, but Ivy said it wasn't.

"It's supposed to be like that. It makes you wonder whether it's two red triangles or a red square divided into two triangles."

"I see," Rhodes said, though he didn't.

"I read something about a painting like that not long ago," she said. "Except that it was solid blue and had a wider white line that was painted down the middle. It was also a lot bigger than that one."

"I didn't know you read articles about art," Rhodes said.

"I don't, usually. This one caught my eye because of the picture and because of the price it brought at auction."

Rhodes looked at the red painting again. He didn't think he'd pay much for anything like that, but maybe someone would.

"How much?" he asked.

"I can't remember exactly," Ivy said, "but it was more than forty million dollars."

Rhodes thought he might not have heard her correctly. "Forty dollars?"

"Forty *million*."

"That settles it," Rhodes said. "I went into the wrong profession."

Ivy laughed. "Maybe not. It takes a lot of talent to sell something for forty million dollars. There's Ruth Grady. I'm going to talk to her while you do whatever it is that you came here for."

"Eating," Rhodes said, though he was still thinking about the forty million dollars.

"You don't really expect me to believe that."

"Watch and see," Rhodes said. He was never going to make forty million dollars, so he might as well eat. He headed for the buffet table.

While the food was an attraction, it wasn't the main one. What interested Rhodes even more was that three of his suspects were standing near one end of the table, talking in low voices. Don McClaren gripped Eric Stewart by his upper arm and leaned in close, saying something Rhodes couldn't hear. McClaren's hand was so big that it easily encircled Stewart's arm. Both men's faces were red. Marilyn Bradley stood beside McClaren as if she were taking his side in whatever discussion was going on. They paid no attention at all to Seepy's singing or to Rhodes's approach.

Rhodes thought that as long as he was by the table, he might as well see what the major snacks were, proving to Ivy, if she was watching, that he'd been telling the truth.

After he'd gotten some major snacks, he could interrupt the discussion. He saw sliced cheese with several kinds of crackers nearby, sliced ham rolled up and secured with toothpicks, little quesadillas, pizza rolls, chicken wings, deviled eggs, celery stuffed with pimiento cheese, and some kind of dip surrounded by raw broccoli, cauliflower, and carrots. There were other things, too, but that would do for a start. Major snacks, indeed. There were also cookies.

Rhodes got himself a napkin and a plate. He filled the plate and looked to see if the three suspects were still engaged in conversation. They were. He drifted in that direction. McClaren and Stewart paid no attention to him, so he stopped nearby, hoping to listen in.

He didn't get to hear much, but maybe it was enough. He was sure he heard McClaren whisper something about a head on a shelf. Then Marilyn Bradley saw Rhodes and poked McClaren in the ribs.

McClaren's head jerked, and he saw Rhodes standing close by. Stewart took advantage of McClaren's lapse of attention to free his arm.

"Good to see you, Sheriff," Stewart said, sounding as if he meant it. "We were just talking about the success of the art conference. The mayor made a wonderful little speech."

Rhodes looked around and saw Clifford Clement, who was wearing a suit that cost more than Rhodes's monthly salary. The mayor was talking to Ruth and Ivy. Jennifer Loam had joined them. Rhodes wondered if he was charming them. Not a chance, he thought.

"Dr. Benton's quite a singer, too," Stewart went on.

"I can see you're listening closely."

Stewart ignored that. "He writes his own songs, you know. A very talented guy."

"So he keeps telling me," Rhodes said. He bit into a piece of quesadilla and got a taste of grilled chicken and cheese. "Food's good, too."

"I have to go now," McClaren said. His voice was strained. "I need to make sure the guests are all taken care of."

He walked away. Rhodes didn't see any reason not to let him go. He'd catch up with him later. It was Stewart that he wanted to have a few words with at the moment. Marilyn Bradley, too.

He didn't get the chance to talk to either of them, however, because Lonnie Wallace walked up. Lonnie was wearing Western garb, as usual, but tonight he had on a dark suit with Western-cut jacket and a string tie.

Rhodes bit into a pizza roll. It didn't really taste much like pizza.

"I've been wanting to talk to you, Sheriff," Lonnie said. "How's the food?"

"Fine," Rhodes said.

Seepy Benton had begun another song that sounded familiar to Rhodes, like an old Gene Autry song from some movie Rhodes had seen on TV years ago. The chorus was something about being back in the classroom again. Rhodes wondered if it was on You-Tube.

Lonnie wasn't interested in the song. Rhodes didn't think Lonnie even heard it.

"Eric told me about the bust you found in the antiques shop," Lonnie said. "He says you think it's a clue."

"Could be," Rhodes said. "It's being checked for fingerprints."

No need to tell them that it had already been checked and found wanting. That was the kind of information Rhodes didn't like to have floating around.

"It was in my store," Lonnie said, "but I don't know how it could've gotten there."

Rhodes waited a few beats to see if Stewart would have anything to say. When he didn't, Rhodes said, "I don't know, either. I was hoping you might have some idea."

Lonnie took a step backward. "Me? How would I know?" He paused. "You don't think I put it there, do you?"

"I hope you didn't," Rhodes said, "but you still do consignment sales, don't you? I thought maybe somebody gave it to you and asked you to sell it for them."

"We don't do many consignments now," Stewart said. "Too much paperwork."

"That's right," Lonnie said. "Someone else put the bust there. I had nothing to do with it. Neither did Eric."

Rhodes wondered if they thought the bust had simply materialized in the store, but he remembered what McClaren had said the previous morning about locking the place up.

"Did you lock the gallery after yesterday's little episode?" Rhodes asked.

"No," Stewart said. "Not today, either. We didn't think Burt would come back and spray anything, what with him being dead."

Sarcasm didn't really become Stewart, Rhodes thought.

"What about stealing from the antiques store? Did you lock the door between here and there?"

"No," Stewart said, with a glance at Lonnie.

"Who'd want to steal anything from there?" Marilyn asked. "It's not really valuable."

"Nobody, maybe," Rhodes said, "but somebody must have put something there today."

"Not necessarily," Lonnie said. "We have some artsy stuff

back there. Maybe the bust had been there for a while and nobody noticed."

"A bust of a NASCAR driver isn't art," Marilyn said as if insulted by the very idea. "There must be hundreds of them. Thousands, maybe. Art is unique and irreplaceable, the single product of the creative mind."

"That's right," Stewart said. He gave Marilyn a glance. "About how easy it would be to put it there or how long it could've been there, I mean. We discussed that this morning, Sheriff. Remember?"

"I remember," Rhodes said. "By the way, what was Don McClaren so upset about?"

"Upset?" Stewart said. "Don?"

"I thought he was going to pull your arm off a minute ago," Rhodes said.

"Oh, that," Stewart said. "I'd just told him and Marilyn about the bust being in the back, and Don was upset, all right. He said that if word got out that there was a clue to the murder hidden here, people would all walk out of the party and go home. The conference would be ruined and we'd never have another one. He said that the college would be the one to suffer because it was helping to sponsor this, and that might affect his job. I can sympathize. Jobs teaching art are hard to find."

"I can vouch for that," Marilyn said. "Even a part-time job is hard to find. I know. I've tried. I thought winning a ribbon here might help my chances, but now that's not going to happen, thanks to the terrible Collins man."

"I don't like to have my store associated with a murder," Lonnie said. "It's bad enough at the Beauty Shack."

"It hasn't hurt your business there," Rhodes said.

"People like to look good," Lonnie said, "no matter what they have to go through. Sitting in a place where someone died won't stop them, maybe, but buying antiques is different."

Seepy Benton was now singing something about opening up your heart. Nobody much cared. Rhodes wished that the people he was talking to would open up their hearts and tell him something helpful. Maybe they already had and he just didn't know it yet.

Clifford Clement walked up before Rhodes could ask anything else. Rhodes didn't mind. He couldn't think of anything else to ask anyway.

"You were right about the meth bust, Sheriff," Clement said. "Everybody's talking about it. Good work."

"He's right," Lonnie said. "I saw it on Jennifer Loam's Web site before I came tonight. She says that you took on three armed meth cookers and a pack of dogs, single-handedly."

It took a second for that to sink in.

"That's not anywhere near the truth," Rhodes said when it did.

"Well, your deputy was there, too," Clement said. "She mentioned that, but you're the one who led the charge. Dogs barking, bullets flying, the meth house about to explode . . ."

"Just like a chapter in a Sage Barton thriller," Lonnie said.

Rhodes suppressed a groan.

"Those are wonderful books," Marilyn said. "Everyone knows you're the model for Sage Barton, Sheriff."

"Any resemblance to actual persons, living or dead, is purely coincidental," Rhodes said. "It says that in every book."

"They have to say that," Clement said. "Lawyers can cause all kinds of trouble if you use real people. But we all know the truth."

"Isn't there going to be a Sage Barton movie?" Lonnie asked. "I think I heard that there was."

"I heard that, too," Clement said. "I hope it's true. It would really put our little town on the map. Maybe they'd even film it here, put Sheriff Rhodes in a small role."

"Why not have him play himself?" Stewart asked.

"They'd need a big-name star to carry the picture," Clement said. "George Clooney, maybe."

"Did you ever wonder about Sage Barton's initials?" Rhodes was desperate to change the subject.

"No," Lonnie said. "Why should we?"

"I know the answer," Marilyn said. "Shall I tell them, Sheriff?"

"Please do," Rhodes said.

"His initials are S. B.," Marilyn said. She looked around, saw Seepy, and pointed discreetly. "Just like his. He says he's the model for Sage Barton."

That wasn't exactly what Benton had said, as Rhodes recalled, but he didn't see any reason to correct things. The conversation was going in a much better direction now.

"Seepy Benton as Sage Barton?" Lonnie said. "You must be joking."

Marilyn shrugged. "I'm not the one who said it. You could ask him about it."

"I don't think so," Lonnie said as Ivy, Ruth, and Jennifer walked up.

"How's the food?" Ivy asked Rhodes, who wondered why people kept asking him that.

"My plate's empty, so I must like it," he said.

"You deserve some good food," Ruth said. "I've just been hearing about how you took on a big gang of meth cookers all by yourself."

Rhodes looked at Jennifer. "You didn't really tell her that, did you?"

Jennifer smiled. "Not exactly. I showed her the Web site, and she read it." Jennifer took a smart phone out of her purse, punched a few buttons, and handed the phone to Rhodes. "Here, you can see for yourself."

Rhodes took the phone. Jennifer had called up *A Clear View for Clearview* on the phone's Web browser, and the headline at the top said, "Sheriff Shuts Down Meth Lab, Battles Miscreants."

That was all Rhodes needed to see. He handed the phone back to Jennifer.

"Miscreants?" he said.

"You could look it up."

"I know what it means. I just thought it was a fancy word for those knotheads."

"Just good journalism."

Rhodes wasn't convinced. "Besides, I didn't battle anybody, and if I did, I had help. Did you read my report?"

"Yes, and I talked to your deputy, so the article is accurate. He's mentioned in it. I just shortened the headline so it would sound good. The facts are all there in my story."

"Possibly a little slanted, though."

Jennifer looked around at everyone. "Do I seem like the kind of person who'd slant the facts?"

Everyone except Rhodes agreed that she didn't.

"You can't slant facts, anyway," Jennifer said. "They're the facts. They speak for themselves."

"Sometimes the way you present them can slant them," Rhodes said.

"I'd never do that. I leave that kind of thing to unprofessional Web sites."

Rhodes knew when to quit arguing. Besides, how many people

outside the county even looked at *A Clear View for Clearview*? There couldn't be many, and everybody in the county already seemed convinced that he was the model for Sage Barton. Some of them, Mikey Burns being at the top of the list, wished that Rhodes would try to live up to the character of Barton, who'd never have hesitated to wipe out a few meth dealers with an M-16 or to bomb their meth house with a drone and leave a crater the size of an oil storage tank.

Rhodes was trying to think of a good way to end the conversation with Jennifer when he heard raised voices at one end of the gallery. He looked in that direction and saw that Don McClaren was having some kind of discussion with Dr. King, the dean of the community college. Marilyn Bradley was standing near them, looking as if she wished she were somewhere else.

Rhodes, on the other hand, wanted to be right there, listening in, so he excused himself to Ivy and the others, put his plate on the buffet table, and walked over.

Rhodes had seen Dr. King in stressful situations before, but he'd never see her lose her composure. Even when one of her faculty members had been killed on the college campus not so long ago, she'd remained in control of herself and the situation. Now, however, she was so upset that a strand of her black hair was out of place, something else Rhodes had never seen.

Rhodes couldn't hear all of what was being said because Seepy Benton had begun a particularly loud version of "Gandhi Wore a Loincloth," a number that Rhodes had heard him sing before. Maybe he thought it was appropriate to the situation and would calm things down, and maybe it would have if anybody had been listening. Nobody was, however, least of all Don McClaren and Dr. King.

The gist of what Rhodes heard led him to believe that Dr. King had mentioned to McClaren that the college was in enough trouble already, what with that recent murder of a faculty member, and that another murder connected with that school, especially one that involved out-of-town guests, was the kind of thing that was likely to bring down the wrath of the board. The wrath, Dr. King had made clear, wasn't going to fall on her, or if it did, it wasn't going to remain there for long.

"I was trying to save the college," McClaren said as Rhodes got closer, "not to cause it any more trouble."

Rhodes was quite interested to hear that sentence. It sounded almost like a confession, but McClaren immediately qualified it. He hadn't been talking about killing Collins.

"Several of us tried to have Collins arrested. If the sheriff had just followed through, Collins would be alive now, and everything would be fine."

Rhodes didn't feel a bit guilty for not having arrested Collins. Nobody had yet proved to Rhodes that Collins had vandalized the paintings. He was, no question, the most obvious suspect, but that didn't mean he'd done it.

Rhodes stepped up to McClaren and said, "Are you claiming I didn't do my job?"

"I'm sure he doesn't mean that, Sheriff," Dr. King said. "He's upset because of the whole situation. You can hardly blame him. Some of the people whose paintings were damaged have complained to me about the art conference, and I've passed on that information to Mr. McClaren. It was his idea to get the college to help sponsor it, and he's a bit upset, as you may have noticed."

"Damn right I'm upset," McClaren said. "I think you're blaming me. None of this is my fault. I couldn't have done a thing to prevent any of it. I can't believe I've been singled out."

"So you singled me out instead," Rhodes said.

"No, I—" McClaren paused. "Okay, maybe I did single you out, but you have to admit that if you'd just arrested Collins, he'd be alive now."

"Maybe," Rhodes said. "Maybe not. He'd have been released as soon as he made bond, and that wouldn't have taken long. He'd have been back at home last night, no matter what I did or didn't do."

"Also no matter what I did or didn't do, then," McClaren said.

"True enough," Rhodes said. "Dr. King, who were the people who complained?"

Dr. King looked around. "I'd rather not mention any names. I don't believe they have anything to do with your investigation."

She didn't have to name any names. Rhodes thought he knew who at least one of the complainers was without having to be told. Marilyn Bradley had disappeared.

Chapter 19

▼

Rhodes thought it was possible that Marilyn was one of those people who disliked being caught in an awkward situation, standing beside two people who were arguing and maybe being a little embarrassed by what was happening. What seemed more likely, however, was that she'd been one of the complainers that Dean King was talking about.

The crowd had thinned considerably, and it was easy enough to spot Marilyn. Her orange hair would have made it easy even if the place had been packed. She was standing near Seepy Benton, who'd set his guitar down by his stool. She was talking to him about something, so Rhodes decided he'd join the conversation. McClaren and King didn't seem sorry to see him go.

Rhodes passed by the buffet table on his way, so he picked up a clean plate, snagged a napkin, and loaded the plate with major snacks and a couple of cookies before walking over to Seepy and Marilyn.

Benton was explaining to her that while he knew far more than three chords on the guitar, most of his songs did happen to employ about that number.

"It makes them easy to sing along with."

Rhodes was tempted to say that he hadn't noticed anybody singing along, but he refrained. Instead, he ate a quesadilla and listened to Marilyn tell Seepy what a nice voice he had.

"You don't think it's too low for a lead singer?" he asked. "I'm normally a bass, but when you're doing a solo act, you can't sing everything in the low ranges."

"Your voice is fine," Marilyn said. "It's . . . rough-hewn, that's what it is. It's what you need more of in your art. What you did was all right, but it was too obvious and polished. You need to put more feeling into it."

Rhodes ate a deviled egg and pondered what she'd said. It didn't take him long to conclude that he had no idea what she was talking about. To him there was just as much feeling in Seepy's cross-sectioned seashell as there was in some upside-down stairs. It was clear that he wasn't cut out to be an art critic. He knew his deviled eggs, though, and the one he'd just finished was a good one.

"Sorry to interrupt," he said, "but I need to ask Marilyn a couple of questions."

"Oh," she said. "What about?"

"Art," Rhodes said. "We can move over there so Seepy can sing another number."

"I think it's time to close the show," Seepy said. "I have a new love song I'm going to try out for the first time tonight. I think it's great."

Seepy thought everything he sang was great. Rhodes said, "I'll be right over here, listening."

He had no intention of listening, but it wouldn't hurt to let Seepy think he was. He planned to be too busy talking to Marilyn to hear the song.

Marilyn had already moved over near the door into the antiques shop. The door was closed, and Rhodes suspected that it was also locked. He hoped that Lonnie and Eric had learned their lesson about that.

"What questions did you have about art?" Marilyn asked when Rhodes joined her.

"They're not so much about art as about whether you're one of the people who complained to Dean King about the problems with the conference," Rhodes said.

Marilyn didn't answer. She looked toward Seepy, who was now doing his tender love ballad. Rhodes looked for Ruth Grady and saw her still standing near Ivy. She was the only one who appeared to be listening.

Rhodes ate a cookie while he waited for Marilyn to respond. Chocolate chip. When he'd eaten it, he said, "Well?"

"I don't see what complaints have to do with anything," she said.

"You never know," Rhodes said. "I need all the information I can get."

"All right, then, yes. I complained. This was a very important event for me. I've told you that already. I needed to win, and that man ruined my chances."

"Burt Collins," Rhodes said. Even someone like Burt deserved a little bit of respect after his death.

"Whoever," Marilyn said. "He cost me a prize."

Seepy Benton finished his song to light applause and thanked everyone for their kind attention. Rhodes didn't applaud, but he had a good excuse since he was holding his plate from the buffet table.

"I thought the judges disregarded the marks on the paintings," Rhodes said to Marilyn.

"Oh, sure, that's what they'd like us to believe. They had to say that. They weren't fooling me, though. I knew better. And if you want to know the truth, I think the whole thing was rigged. There's just no way some of the paintings were better than mine."

Rhodes wondered if she had any specific painting in mind.

"Seepy Benton's, for example?"

"Maybe." Marilyn started to walk away. She'd gone only a step before she turned back. "His voice isn't rough-hewn, either. It's just scratchy."

Rhodes couldn't argue with that. He ate another deviled egg and was considering a return to the buffet table when Don Mc-Claren approached him.

"I hope you didn't get the wrong idea from my discussion with Dr. King," McClaren said. "I was a little upset, sure, but I didn't really mean that you were in any way to blame for that man's death."

"Burt Collins," Rhodes said.

"Right. Mr. Collins. He made a mess of things, but it's nothing that can't be worked out. We'll do this again next year, and it'll be bigger and better."

"An event like this could be good for the town if it became an annual thing," Rhodes said. "It would get more people downtown and make it look a little livelier."

McClaren nodded. "Exactly, and that's why we need to keep it going. I hope you catch whoever was responsible for Mr. Collins's death."

"I will," Rhodes said. "Sooner or later. While I'm figuring that out, maybe you can answer a couple of questions for me."

McClaren looked doubtful. "You can ask. I can't promise I can answer."

"I think you can. It's about the judging of the paintings. You were one of the judges, weren't you?"

McClaren looked relieved. "That's an easy one. Yes, I was one of the judges, and Eric was the other one." McClaren rubbed his forehead. "Next year, if there is a next year, we're going to bring in outside judges. We would've done it this year, but we didn't have the money."

"Where will you get the money next year?"

"The college is going to pitch in some more. The dean and I were just talking about it. I've promised her that things will go smoothly, and she really doesn't blame me for this year's problems. At least I think I've talked her out of that, and I've convinced her that it's a good thing for the town and the college, too. By the way, let me repeat that I'm sorry I said what I did about you. That was wrong, and I know it."

"I've already forgotten about it," Rhodes said. "Now about the judging. You and the dean were talking for a while before I came over. Did she mention any complaints about the judging?"

"Yes, and that's why we're bringing in outside judges when we do this again. Some people complained that Eric and I showed favoritism."

"Did you?"

"Of course not. We were strictly impartial." McClaren rubbed his forehead again. "Okay, let me rephrase that. I'm not sure any judge can be strictly impartial. Most people, even judges in art shows, have their own ideas about what's good and what's not good."

Rhodes knew he had his own ideas, all right. He thought about Marilyn Bradley. She certainly had her own opinions as well.

"It's hard not to let your own ideas influence you," McClaren said. "Even when you're trying not to. Sometimes you even bend over backwards not to be prejudiced, and that can work against you just as much as the other can."

"You want to explain that?" Rhodes asked.

"Let's say you like representational art," McClaren said.

"I do. I like things that make sense to me."

"There's not a thing wrong with that. So you like representational art, but you're a judge and you want to be fair."

"No chance of me ever being a judge of an art contest," Rhodes said.

"Never say never. So you're a judge, and you see something you really like, and you ask yourself, 'Do I like that because it's good or because it's just the kind of thing I like?' You might wind up excluding it when really it was one of the best things in the show."

"I get it," Rhodes said. "From what you're telling me, I'd have to say that you and Eric were as fair as it's possible to be."

"That's what we tried for. We discussed everything before making our final decisions. I resent the fact that someone claimed we weren't impartial. We were, or at least we were as impartial as it's possible for two people to be."

"Here's where it gets even more personal," Rhodes said. "Why didn't Marilyn Bradley's painting win?"

McClaren smiled. "You're kidding me, right?"

"Nope," Rhodes said. "I know you might not want to discuss it. Judge's ethics, maybe, but I'd like to know."

"You're right about the ethics, but in this case it doesn't really apply. Eric and I said we'd be happy to give a private critique to anybody who wanted one."

200

"Did anybody ask?"

"Several people did. Your friend Dr. Benton was one of them."

"What about Marilyn Bradley?"

"She didn't ask."

"Too bad, but now's your chance, I'm asking for her. For me, too. It could be important."

McClaren thought it over. "This won't go any further?"

"Not an inch."

McClaren looked around to see if anyone was listening. Nobody was. The only people left in the building were Seepy Benton, Ivy, Ruth, and Eric.

"The coast is clear," Rhodes said.

"Yeah, I guess I was being a little obvious," McClaren said. "Anyway, Marilyn's painting didn't win because it isn't very good. It wasn't even considered."

"What about the deep hidden meaning?"

"Do you see it?"

"No, it's too well hidden for me," Rhodes told him, "but I don't know much about art."

"You wouldn't have to. There isn't much technique on display, either. Sloppy work, if you ask me, but she didn't, which was just as well. She wouldn't have been happy about it. I'll tell you something else, too."

Rhodes waited while McClaren looked around again, maybe just to be sure nobody had wandered back into the gallery.

"That man who was killed? Mr. Collins?"

Rhodes nodded.

"He did Marilyn a favor. She probably knows it. Because of what he did, she has a good reason to complain about not winning. Even though we told everybody we disregarded the markings because we'd seen all the paintings before he defaced them, she doesn't believe it. She can always tell herself that it was the marks and the prejudiced judges that cost her an award."

The catering crew from the college came into the gallery then to clear away the food and plates and trash. Rhodes thanked McClaren for answering his questions and ate his last cookie before returning his empty plate to the table so the crew could pick it up. He put the plate down and went over to see if Ivy was ready to go home.

Seepy Benton was with her and Ruth, telling them how great the crowd had been and how well everyone had responded to his songs. It was true, Rhodes thought, that people saw things differently, whether it was art or music or audience response.

"Things went really well," Benton said. "I should've tried a sing-along. I'll bet that would've been fun."

"I'd have given it a try," Ruth said.

Ivy and Eric kept quiet.

"How about you, Sheriff?" Benton said. "Would you have joined me in a rousing audience participation number?"

"I may have mentioned before that I'm not a singer," Rhodes told him.

"Everybody's a singer. You have to forget your inhibitions and sing right out. It's good for you."

"You haven't heard me sing," Rhodes said, "and you should hope you never will." He turned to Ivy. "Are you ready to go home?"

"Anytime," Ivy said.

* * *

Before going home, Rhodes made the short drive around what was left of downtown. It was just as depressing as usual, and maybe even more depressing because things looked worse after dark. Even though Rhodes knew that the Walmart parking lot was full and that people were visiting other places of business out on the highway, it still bothered him that the downtown looked for the most part like a deserted city in some postapocalyptic movie.

"It's not just Clearview," Ivy said, reading Rhodes's mind. "It's like this in a lot of small towns. Things aren't like they used to be."

"I know," Rhodes said, "and they never were."

"Who said that?"

"I did. Just then."

Ivy poked him in the arm. "I know you said it, but you stole it. Who did you steal it from?"

"I'm not sure," Rhodes said, and he wasn't. "Will Rogers, maybe."

Ivy grinned. "I wonder if anybody younger than you even knows who Will Rogers was."

"You're younger than I am, and you remember who he was."

"He died a long time before either one of us was born, but I did hear about him when I was younger. Not so much now, though." Ivy was quiet for a moment. "Another thing he's supposed to have said is that he never met a man he didn't like."

"He never met Burt Collins," Rhodes said.

"Was Burt really that bad?"

Rhodes thought about what Ella's sister had told him. "Bad enough. We never got a domestic violence call from Ella, but Bonnie Crowley said we should have. There was some hitting. And other things."

"Bonnie is Ella's sister?"

"Right. She lives down in Thurston."

"You think Ella killed Burt?"

"She could have," Rhodes said. "Bonnie thinks she *should* have."

"What do you think?"

"I think she could've killed him and gotten rid of the thing she hit him with before I got there."

"You're not sure, though."

"I'm not sure about anything right now," Rhodes said.

After Ivy and Rhodes got home, it took Rhodes a few minutes to get Yancey settled down. The cats, of course, were already settled down and didn't bother to get up.

"Did you get enough to eat at the gallery?" Ivy asked Rhodes.

"Yes, but if there's any dessert around, I could use some."

"I saw you eating those cookies. Do you really want dessert?"

"Just kidding. I was checking to see if you knew I ate the cookies."

Ivy gave him a skeptical look. "Really?"

"Really. Let's watch the rest of that DVD we started the other night."

"*Justified*?"

"That's the one. I like that hat Raylan Givens wears. Maybe I'll get me one like it."

"You? In a hat?"

"I was kidding again. Where's the DVD?"

Ivy located the DVD, and Rhodes put it into the player. They'd watched almost five minutes of the show before the telephone rang.

"Are you going to answer that?" Ivy asked.

"I'm the sheriff. I have to answer it."

"You'll be sorry."

"You're probably right," Rhodes said, and she was.

Chapter 20

▼

"Robbery in progress," Hack said as soon as Rhodes answered the phone.

Rhodes knew it was serious because Hack didn't try to prolong things.

"Oscar Henderson's place," Hack said. "Shots fired. Oscar's in hot pursuit."

"Hot pursuit?" Rhodes said. Hack had been listening to Buddy too much.

"That's right, hot pursuit."

"What was Oscar doing at his store?"

"He was watchin' the place, I guess. You can ask him when you get there. You better get a move on."

Rhodes knew it was urgent, but he needed more information. "Which direction is the pursuit headed?"

"It's on foot, in the trees back of the store. It was Chris that called it in. He sounded shook up. Second night in a row and all."

206

"What about Duke and Buddy?"

"You're a lot closer than they are. You goin' or not?"

"I'm on the way."

Rhodes hung up, got his pistol from the gun safe in the closet of an unused bedroom, and told Ivy not to worry about him.

"I always worry."

"I always come back, too. Maybe a little beat up, maybe a little dirty, but at least I make it home."

Ivy kissed him on the cheek. "Get home early. I'll make it worth your while."

"I'll do my best," Rhodes said.

He was at the convenience store within five minutes of Hack's call, and maybe within ten minutes of when things had started, but ten minutes can be a long time when guns are involved. That didn't mean Rhodes could rush into things. He parked in front of the store, got his sidearm in his hand, and went inside to talk to Chris, who was shaken up even more than he'd been the previous night. The sight of Rhodes's pistol didn't calm him down.

"What happened?" Rhodes asked, slipping the pistol into his back pocket.

"Man came in with a gun, said give him the money."

"Same man?"

"Same one, stocking over his head, same funny-looking gun."

"Where was Oscar?"

"He was lurking around behind the chips counter. He came running out while I was giving the guy the money. The man grabbed the money and took off."

"Does Oscar have a gun?"

"Yeah. It's a big one, but it's legal. He has a concealed-carry license." Chris looked thoughful. "Maybe I oughta get a license, too. Get me a big gun like Oscar's."

Rhodes thought Chris would be a menace with a handgun, so he didn't encourage him. Instead he asked what happened next.

"Oscar ran out after the robber," Chris said, "and I heard a shot."

"I'll go check on Oscar," Rhodes said. "You stay here."

"I can't go home?"

"Better not. We might need you later."

"What if I get killed?" Chris's voice was shaky.

"I'll try not to let that happen," Rhodes told him.

Rhodes left Chris there, not looking very happy, and went outside. He took his pistol out of his back pocket. The parking lot was well lit, but it was very dark in the trees in back of the store. Rhodes got his flashlight, a big Maglite, from the trunk of the county car. He also slipped into his Kevlar vest.

Rhodes wished that Oscar hadn't gone running out after the robber. He wished that Oscar hadn't been lurking around the store, and he wished that Oscar hadn't brought his gun with him. He wished that once in a while his wishes would come true.

When he got to the rear of the store, he called out, "Oscar, you all right?"

He didn't get an answer. He didn't like the idea of going to look for Oscar, considering the fact that Oscar might think he was the robber and shoot him. Sure, he had on the vest, but Oscar would probably shoot for his chest and hit him in the head. You just couldn't trust an amateur in this kind of situation. Rhodes could see Jennifer Loam's headline now: "Sheriff Shot by Panicked Store Owner." Things like this never happened to Sage

Barton, but then Sage Barton would probably have had a flamethrower and burned down any trees that got in his way. Any humans, too. Nobody messed with Sage Barton.

Unfortunately, as Rhodes kept telling anybody who'd listen,
he wasn't Sage Barton, and he didn't have a flamethrower. He
could ask Mikey Burns to buy one for the county. Burns would
probably go for it.

"Oscar?" Rhodes called again. "You hear me?"

If Oscar heard, he wasn't answering. Rhodes didn't have much
choice other than to go after him.

Rhodes turned on the flashlight, holding it at arm's length from
his body, and entered the trees. He didn't call out again and made
as little noise as possible, not knowing who might be in there.

The night was overcast, and though the trees had lost a lot of
their leaves, hardly any light filtered through them. Rhodes walked
a few yards, stopped, and shined the light around. Not seeing
anything other than trees, he went a bit farther and stopped again.
This time he stayed put. He turned off the flashlight and listened
for a couple of minutes. There was never complete silence in a
copse of trees even on a windless night. Small animals moved
around; birds rustled the leaves in the trees. Cars passed on the
nearby roads. Rhodes had thought he might hear some other sound
among those, some indication that Oscar was chasing the robber.
He didn't hear anything like that.

Rhodes's eyes had adjusted somewhat to the darkness, so he
left the flashlight off and moved on into the trees and brush. He
wasn't sure exactly how much area the trees covered, but it was
several square blocks. Plenty of room for someone to hide in.

Rhodes had thought he might hear Oscar thrashing around,
but maybe the chase was over. If that was the case, where was

Oscar? Had he gone after the robber on foot? Had the robber kidnapped him?

There were a couple of other possibilities, neither of them pleasant. Rhodes would rather think that Oscar had caught the robber on the other side of the trees and was even now frog-marching him down the street and back to the store. It wasn't likely that things had happened that way, however.

Rhodes walked right into a low-hanging tree branch. It scraped across his forehead, and he could feel the blood pop out. Just a scratch, but he'd have to be more careful. He wiped his forehead with the back of his hand, held the flashlight away from his body, and turned it on again.

The beam landed right on Oscar Henderson, who was lying near a tree. His pistol, a Glock 9 mm, lay not far away. Oscar's legs were spread, his head turned to the side. Rhodes turned off the flashlight and ducked behind a tree, just in case the robber was hanging around waiting to take a shot at him.

"Oscar," Rhodes said.

Oscar didn't answer, and Rhodes took a quick look around the trunk of the tree. He thought he saw a foot twitch. He called Oscar's name again, louder. Oscar still didn't answer.

Rhodes turned on the flashlight, stuck it out beside the tree and started reciting some lines from a poem his father had often quoted when Rhodes was a boy. Rhodes couldn't remember much of it, but he did his best and used his loudest voice:

The boy stood on the burning deck,
his feet were full of blisters,
he didn't have any underpants,
and so he wore his sister's.

Rhodes's father hadn't had much better taste in poetry than Rhodes did, but that wasn't the point. The point was that the robber would surely have taken a shot at the light if for no better reason than to shut Rhodes up. It didn't happen, so Rhodes concluded that the robber had fled the scene, as Buddy would have said.

Rhodes hoped that was what had happened. He left the shelter of the tree trunk and picked up the Glock, which he stuck in his waistband. Then he went to kneel beside Oscar. He put his flashlight on the ground and touched Oscar's neck. He was glad to feel a strong pulse. He picked up the light and played it over Oscar. He didn't see any blood on the clothing, but he did see a large knot on Oscar's forehead.

Rhodes looked around. He saw no flashlight on the ground, so Oscar had been running through the trees practically blind.

Leaving Oscar where he was, Rhodes stood up. Sure enough, a thick branch stuck out from a tree at just about the level of Oscar's forehead. Rhodes thought about his own little scratch. Oscar hadn't been quite so lucky.

On the other hand, Oscar hadn't been shot, which was good news for everybody, including the robber.

Rhodes knelt back down and shook Oscar's shoulder. "Oscar, wake up."

Oscar stirred but didn't come to life. Rhodes put the flashlight down again and got out his cell phone. He had to admit that sometimes it did come in handy.

The paramedics had gotten Oscar out of the trees and into the ambulance. They assured Rhodes that he'd be all right, though he most likely had a concussion. It was a small price to pay for what Rhodes hoped was a valuable lesson to Oscar. Maybe next time he'd leave the law enforcement up to the law.

Oscar had regained consciousness as they were putting him in the ambulance. He was groggy, but he managed to say, "Did I get him?"

"I don't know," Rhodes said, "but at least he didn't get you."

"He didn't even try. I shot at him, but he didn't shoot back."

"Just as well," Rhodes said, and the paramedics pushed the gurney into the back of the ambulance and closed the doors.

When the ambulance pulled out of the parking lot, Rhodes went into the convenience store and told Chris that Oscar was going to be fine.

"He wasn't shot," Rhodes said. "He just bumped into a tree."

"I'm glad he's okay," Chris said. "You think I can go home now?"

Rhodes knew that the store was supposed to stay open until eleven, and it was only ten thirty now. On the other hand, Oscar was never going to know that Chris had left a half hour early unless someone told him. Rhodes wasn't going to, and he figured Chris wasn't, either.

"You ever have many customers after ten?" Rhodes asked.

"One or two. Not enough to make it worth the time to keep the store open. Mr. Henderson says we should, though. He doesn't want to lose any trade."

"You do what you think is best," Rhodes said. "I have to go check on some other things. Will you be all right here by yourself?"

"I think so."

"How much money did the robber get?"

"I didn't count it," Chris said, "but it wasn't much."

"You said he had a funny-looking gun. What did you mean by that?"

"Nothing. It was just funny-looking. I never saw one like it. I mean, it looked like a gun, and it looked real, but then again, it didn't. You know?"

Rhodes didn't know, but it was something to think about. He left Chris there to close down the store and went outside. While he was there, he might as well take a look around the perimeter of the trees and see if he could pick up any clues.

He drove along the side of the trees on a seldom-used street that didn't really go anywhere other than to a county road that wound around through the country. Other roads branched off of that one, and the robber could have taken any of them. Some would have brought him back to town. Others would have taken him out of the county.

Rhodes parked on the county road and got out of the car. It was too dark to see much outside the span of his headlights. He walked a few yards down the road and thought maybe he saw where a vehicle had pulled off to the side and mashed down the grass. There wasn't much of a clue in that.

Rhodes decided that he wasn't going to find anything helpful. He went back to his car and checked the clip from Oscar's pistol. Looked as if only one shot had been fired. Rhodes put the pistol away. He could send Ruth out in the morning and have her check around to see if he'd missed anything. He'd write up his report then, too. Right now, it was time to go home.

When he got home, Rhodes had to calm down Yancey, as usual. This time it wasn't hard to do. Yancey was sleepy at that time of night and hardly bounced around at all. He yipped a few times and went to his doggie bed for a long nap.

Rhodes went into the kitchen and found Ivy sitting at the table. The cats were asleep, as usual, in the same spots they'd been in the last time Rhodes had seen them. Ivy was reading a book about Mr. Monk, an obsessive-compulsive detective who'd had his own TV show for a while. Or rather some actor had been on the TV show portraying a character named Monk. Monk wasn't real. Or at least Rhodes didn't think he was.

The book was by someone named Goldberg. When Rhodes asked, Ivy said that, as far as she knew, Goldberg the author was not related to Rube Goldberg the famous cartoonist. She also said that the book was related to the TV show only by the characters. The stories were different from the ones on TV.

"If you were like Monk," she said, "I don't think I could put up with you."

"I probably am like Monk," Rhodes said. "I'll bet he always gets his man."

"Well," Ivy said, "there's that, but he's so compulsive that it would be impossible to stay around him."

"He can solve crimes, though, I take it."

"He can, and he's very good at it," Ivy said, "but he doesn't go about it the same way you do."

"Sure he does. We great detectives are all alike."

"No, you aren't. Monk doesn't just see. He observes. He sees the things that nobody else sees, and that's how he solves the crimes."

"Like Sherlock Holmes, then."

"No," Ivy said, "not like Sherlock Holmes." She put a bookmark in the book and closed it. "Or maybe he is. I hadn't thought about it, but you have a point."

"All us great detectives are observers," Rhodes said. "Me, Sherlock Holmes, Mr. Monk. I'll probably solve two or three cases this week, thanks to my superior powers of observation."

"What about the robbery of Oscar Henderson's store?"

"Okay, maybe not that one." Rhodes told her about what had happened.

"The robber must think he's found a soft touch," Ivy said when he'd finished.

"Could be. I'll have to tell Duke to keep a close eye on the place from now on."

"You mean you're not going to solve the crime with your keen powers of observation?"

"I didn't observe the robbery, and I haven't run across any clues. I'll figure it out, though. Maybe with my keen powers of observation, maybe not. Maybe someone will confess. Whatever happens, I'll get whoever did it."

"I'm sure you will." Ivy stood up and looked at the kitchen clock. "Would you consider this early?"

It was a few minutes before eleven.

"I will if you'll make it worth my while," Rhodes said.

"I'll see what I can do," Ivy told him.

Chapter 21

▼

The next morning Rhodes was up early, a little before six. He'd had a strange dream that involved Godzilla, a singing group that Rhodes thought might have been the Bee Gees, and a rodeo. Other than that, the details were blessedly vague, and Rhodes knew even those would be gone within an hour or two. He'd be glad when they were.

Rhodes went outside to feed Speedo, and Yancey followed him. The morning was dry and crisp. The sun was coloring the clouds a little, but it wouldn't be up for a few minutes yet. The dogs liked the cool air, and they chased each other around the yard while Rhodes got out the food. As soon as Rhodes began to scoop the food into Speedo's bowl, the dogs heard it and came running over.

Yancey tried to nudge his nose into Speedo's food. Rhodes told him to wait his turn, but Yancey was too impatient. Speedo snapped at him, and though it had happened dozens of times before, Yancey acted surprised and hurt. He let out a sad little yip and moved over to his own bowl, where he sat looking at Speedo as if he'd just been betrayed by his best friend.

Rhodes put some food in Yancey's bowl, and after a few seconds Yancey decided to stop feeling sorry for himself and eat. When they'd both eaten and drunk some water, they ran around the yard for a while, and then Rhodes called Yancey to the door. They went inside, where Ivy had fed the cats and was cooking some of the turkey bacon. Rhodes told himself again that, while it didn't smell like real bacon, it wasn't too bad.

"I thought you'd sleep in today," he said.

"So did I," Ivy said, "but you woke me up with all your thrashing around."

"I had a bad dream," Rhodes said.

"I don't want to hear about it. Do you want eggs with your bacon?"

"Don't have time," Rhodes said. "Crimes to solve and killers to catch."

"Did you dream a clue?"

Rhodes thought about the dream, and suddenly he remembered that the Bee Gees had been riding goats in the rodeo arena.

"If it's a clue," he said, "it'll be the strangest crime I've ever solved."

When Rhodes got to the jail, the first thing he did was check on the prisoners that Andy had brought in from the meth house. They'd been treated at the hospital, but neither of them had a serious wound, so they were now guests of the county. They weren't happy about it, but that didn't bother Rhodes. He'd rarely had a jail inmate who was happy about his circumstances.

"They think the bunks are too hard," Lawton said as he and Rhodes stood outside the cells and looked in on the prisoners. "I told 'em we were all out of those memory-foam mattresses. You reckon we'll be gettin' any more of 'em?"

"Nope," Rhodes said. "We never had any in the first place."

"Oh, yeah," Lawton said. "I shoulda mentioned that to 'em."

"We want our guests to be happy, though," Rhodes said, "so I'll put in a requisition."

"Ha ha ha," Neil Foshee said. The other two said nothing.

"No sense of humor," Lawton said. "Can't take a joke."

"Well, it wasn't a very good joke," Rhodes said.

He left the cellblock and went to his desk to do his report on the convenience store robbery. Hack hadn't asked him about it, which was a bad sign. It meant that Hack had something to tell him, and that meant that Rhodes would have to draw him out. In a few minutes, Lawton came out of the cellblock into the office. This was another bad sign. It meant that they were going to double-team him.

"You catch anybody last night?" Hack asked.

"Nope. Sent somebody to the hospital, though."

Rhodes thought that at least he could have his own fun with Hack, but it didn't work out like that.

"Yeah," Hack said. "I know all about it."

Rhodes sighed. It was hard to get ahead of Hack. "How'd you find out?"

"Jennifer Loam heard the call for the ambulance on her police scanner. She was at the hospital when they brought Oscar in. They kept him overnight for observation, so she visited with him and got the whole story. It's up on her Web site this morning."

Rhodes wasn't tempted to look at it.

"Made Oscar sound like the new Sage Barton," Lawton said.

"Sure did," Hack said. "Went after that robber with nothin' but a pistol. Shot at him, too."

"Didn't hit him, though," Lawton said. "Oscar's not much of a shot."

"It was dark," Rhodes said, "and there were trees. Besides, Oscar was running. Even a good shot wouldn't be likely to hit anybody under those circumstances."

"You could," Hack said. "You and Sage Barton."

Rhodes didn't want to hear any more about Sage Barton. "We don't need citizens going after robbers and shooting at them. It's dangerous, and Oscar probably knows that now. Besides, if he'd hit the robber, he'd be in real trouble."

"Yep," Lawton said. "Robber'd get himself a good lawyer and sue Oscar's pants off. Robber'd wind up owning the store."

"I think Oscar's learned a good lesson," Rhodes said.

"Took a hard hit to the head to teach him," Hack said. "We can't go hittin' all the citizens in the head just to teach 'em a lesson, can we?"

"Maybe we could start with just a few of 'em," Lawton said.

"I can think of some that could use it," Hack said. "I'd like to be the one to make the list of who gets hit."

"Like that woman last night," Lawton said. "She'd be on it."

Rhodes knew they were about to get to it. Not that they'd get there directly, but the journey of a thousand miles had at least begun with the first step.

"She didn't need a knock on the head," Hack said. "She just needed some help from the law. That's what she said, anyway. Said it was an emergency."

Rhodes knew it was his turn, so he said, "Help for what?"

"Car trouble," Hack said.

"We don't usually call that an emergency," Rhodes said.

"This kind of car trouble is," Lawton said.

"What kind was it?"

"The kind where she said somebody'd broke into her car," Hack said.

"Cleaned it out," Lawton said. "Took ever'thing."

"Sure did," Hack said. "She told me the stereo was gone, the radio was gone, the steering wheel was gone, and even the accelerator and brake were gone."

"That's some serious trouble, all right," Rhodes said, wondering how anybody could make off with all that. Why would anybody even try? Who would want a steering wheel?

"Who'd you send to investigate?" he asked.

"Sent Ruth. She was on patrol down around Thurston, and that's where this happened."

"It must have taken more than one person to dismantle a car like that," Rhodes said.

"Maybe not," Lawton said, and Hack favored him with a hard look.

"What makes you say that?" Rhodes asked.

"Might not have taken even one person, that's why," Lawton said before Hack could cut him off.

Rhodes didn't get it. He knew there was a catch. There was always a catch, but he couldn't figure out what it was. He told himself he wouldn't ask, but he knew he would, eventually, so why not get it out of the way?

"What did Ruth find?" he asked.

"She didn't find anything," Hack said.

"Surely she found the car and investigated the complaint."

"Well, she found the car. Found the woman, too. Turned out

there wasn't any complaint. Woman apologized, and Ruth gave her a ride home."

Rhodes was getting more confused than ever, but he tried not to show it. "I can see why she needed a ride. Hard to drive without a steering wheel or a brake. I don't see why there wasn't a complaint, though."

"'Cause none of that stuff was missing," Hack said. "It was all there."

"Then why did the woman call us?"

"It looked like it was all gone to her," Lawton said. "See—"

"I'm the one got the call," Hack said. "Seems like when Ruth got there, she found out what the trouble was. Hadn't been anything taken after all. It was just a mistake."

"How could anybody think all that was missing if it wasn't?" Rhodes asked.

"Easy," Hack said. "She was in the backseat instead of the front."

Rhodes finally caught on. "Alcohol was involved."

"Right. I'm surprised she could even use a cell phone, bein' that impaired. That's why Ruth took her home. She'd been drinkin' at her boyfriend's house, and when it came time to go home, he wasn't in any shape to drive her. So she was goin' to drive herself."

"Couldn't, though," Lawton said, "not havin' a steerin' wheel and all."

"Just as well she got in the backseat," Rhodes said. "I don't like to think about what might've happened if she'd gotten on the road."

"Maybe not much," Hack said. "Hardly anybody out on the roads down in Thurston after dark."

"Mighta been somebody, though," Lawton said, "and she couldn't see 'em if they were there."

"Sure couldn't," Hack said. "Couldn't even see she was in the backseat 'stead of the front."

Rhodes was reminded of what he and Ivy had been talking about the previous night, about the difference between seeing and observing. The woman in Thurston couldn't see where she was, much less observe anything. He thought about some of the things he'd seen during the past couple of days. Doris Clements had told him he was pretty observant when he'd talked to her on the phone at Frances Bennett's house. Rhodes wondered if he really was. He'd seen some things that he hadn't observed carefully enough. As he thought back on them now, some of them started to mean a lot more to him than they had at first.

"I have to go see Ella Collins," he said.

"Her sister's from Thurston, ain't she?" Hack asked.

"She is, but she wasn't the woman in the car last night."

"Nope. That was Liz Corley in the car. That's what she told me, anyway. What you want to see Miz Collins about?"

"I'll tell you later," Rhodes said, and he scooted out the door before Hack could say anything more.

It was still early, but Rhodes thought that Ella Collins would be up and about. He didn't think her sister would be there. She would've gone back to Thurston, having helped Ella make the funeral arrangements. The funeral would most likely be on Monday, and Ella would have a lot of last-minute things to take care of.

Rhodes went up on the porch and knocked on the door. Ella came quickly and opened it. She seemed a little surprised to see him.

"I thought you might be somebody bringing food," she said.

"I hope you didn't bring anything. I already have a kitchen full. Casseroles and vegetables and all like that. Lots of desserts, too. You know how it is."

Rhodes knew how it was. When someone in Clearview died, people wanted to help somehow or other, and everyone seemed to believe that the best way to do that was to bring food.

"I didn't bring anything to eat," he said, "but I'd like to come in if that's all right."

Ella pulled the door all the way open. "Did you find out who killed Burt?"

"Not yet," Rhodes said. "I have an idea or two about that, but I can't say for sure. Do you feel like answering a few questions?"

"I guess so," Ella said. "Come on back to the kitchen."

Rhodes followed her to the kitchen. Ruth had removed the crime-scene tape from the living room, but Rhodes could understand why Ella might not want to go in there to talk. Or to do anything. She might not want to go in there for a long time, or ever again.

When they walked into the kitchen, Rhodes saw that the counters were lined with pies and cakes, along with bowls and casserole dishes covered with foil or plastic wrap. He smelled coffee.

"You want something to eat?" Ella said. "I got plenty."

Rhodes wasn't sure if she was making a joke, so he said, "No, thanks. Just some talk."

"Cup of coffee?"

"I don't drink it," Rhodes said.

"You one of them Mormons?"

"No," Rhodes said. "I just never learned to like it."

"You mind if I have some, then?"

"Not a bit. You go right ahead."

"You just sit at the table there, and I'll pour myself a cup," Ella said.

Rhodes sat down and waited while she poured a cup of coffee from the carafe in the Mr. Coffee. She put sugar in the cup, stirred it with a tablespoon, and sat across from Rhodes.

"You said you wanted to ask me something?"

"It's about Frances Bennett. Did you stay with her last night?"

Ella took a sip of the coffee. "No, I didn't. She's got other friends, and I didn't feel like it, not with Burt and all."

"You were with her the night Burt was killed, though."

"Yes, I was helping her that night. I thought I already told you that."

"You did, and I called her, just to be sure."

"I don't blame you. You're the sheriff. It's your job to do things like that."

"Sometimes I don't like the things I have to do," Rhodes said. "Like now."

Ella drank some more coffee, then said, "You don't like talking to me?"

"It's not the talking I don't like," Rhodes said. "It's the questions I have to ask."

"I don't mind," Ella said.

Rhodes thought she was going to mind a lot when he got started on the really important ones.

"Before I say any more, I'd better tell you what your rights are," he said. "I want to be sure you understand them."

"I don't know what you're saying."

"I'm saying you have the right to remain silent," Rhodes told her, and then he went through the rest of the Miranda warning. "Do you understand all that?"

"I understand it, but I don't know why you're telling me. I hope you don't think I killed Burt."

"I don't think that. This is about something else."

"I don't know what it could be."

"Maybe it's nothing at all," Rhodes said. "Just let me ask the questions, and you can answer them. If we don't get anywhere, we'll just forget I ever started."

"That sounds all right to me."

"You left Frances's house a little early the night Burt was killed, didn't you," Rhodes said.

Ella's eyes narrowed just a little. Rhodes had questioned a lot of people. The eyes nearly always told him as much as their words.

"I don't think so. I came home about the usual time, and Burt . . . Burt was dead when I got here."

"You got home about the usual time," Rhodes said, "but you left Frances's early. I think you gave her the pain pills a little before the usual time, and when she went to sleep, you left. You didn't come home, though. You went somewhere else. You want to tell me about that?"

"I came home," Ella said. "That's all."

"You came home, all right, but first you went somewhere else. You went to Oscar Henderson's store."

"I never."

"I should've thought of it before," Rhodes said, paying no attention to her denial. "You had red lines on your face, but I thought they came from crying. They didn't. They came from the stocking you had pulled over your head."

Keen powers of observation, just like Sherlock Holmes and Monk. Ivy would be proud of him.

Ella set her coffee cup on the table and pushed it away from her. She didn't meet Rhodes's eyes.

"I don't think you can even buy stockings anymore," she said.

"You can cut the leg out of a pair of pantyhose," Rhodes said. "You were wearing jeans and a shirt, and you disguised your voice. Chris never considered that a woman might be robbing him, so he thought you were a man."

"Wasn't me," Ella said, without conviction.

"What really gave it away, though," Rhodes said, "was the pistol. I knew Burt used to coach track, and I should've thought more about that. You know you could've been killed last night when Oscar got after you and started shooting? He thought you had a real gun, but what you had was Burt's old starter pistol. Isn't that right?"

"Starter pistol just shoots blanks," Ella said. "Not even a real pistol."

"That's right, but it looks enough like one to scare somebody like Chris."

Rhodes looked around the kitchen. All that food, and Ella wasn't going to be there to eat it. Maybe she'd like to donate it to the jail to feed the prisoners.

"I know you needed money," he said. "You couldn't even pay Abby at the Beauty Shack. It wasn't the first time. You paid her eventually, though. After you robbed Oscar's store."

"Burt was a tightwad. He never let me have any money. You heard what Bonnie said."

"I did. It was a shame he treated you like that."

"He was a good man in some ways," Ella said. She paused. "Sometimes it's hard to remember what they were, but we had food on the table. Sometimes not much of it, but we always had something. We paid all our bills on time, too, mostly. Burt's retirement wasn't all that good, and he was always looking for ways to get more money. Never found any, and he wouldn't ever let me get a job. He didn't like spending on what he called frivolous things, like my hair appointments. You ever wonder why our house is painted different colors?"

"I thought maybe Burt had an artistic side."

"He never did, but he did paint the house himself. Couldn't afford to hire anybody. It's different colors because he couldn't afford to buy all the paint at once, and he just got what was cheapest."

That was as good an explanation as any for the paint job, Rhodes thought. Kind of a sad one, too.

"He wouldn't let you have any money at all?"

Ella shook her head. "He said taking care of money was the man's job because he was head of the house. My mama always told me that was the way it was supposed to be. The man was the boss, so I just did what he said. I thought it was the right thing."

"Bonnie doesn't seem to think that way," Rhodes said.

Ella half-smiled. "Bonnie never did listen to Mama. She never did like Burt, either. Maybe I should've been more like her."

Rhodes thought the same thing.

"You going to take me to the jail now?" Ella asked.

"That's my job," Rhodes said.

"I guess you'll make me give Oscar his money back."

"Yes, you'll have to do that."

"Sure do hate to cheat Abby. She does a nice job on my hair." Ella touched her head. "That stocking really did mess it up, though."

"I think it looks fine."

"You do? Really?"

"Really," Rhodes said.

"Will I be able to go to Burt's funeral? It wouldn't be right if I wasn't there."

"You'll be there," Rhodes said. "I'll see to it."

He would, too. She could go with one of the deputies as an escort. Ruth, most likely.

"You think I could call Frances Bennett?" Ella asked. "I need to let her know I can't be helping her out anymore."

"Sure, you can do that."

Ella stood up, went over to the phone, and made her call. Rhodes noticed that she didn't explain why she couldn't help out any longer.

When Ella hung up, she said, "I guess we might as well go, then. You going to put handcuffs on me?"

Rhodes knew that he should, but he said, "No, I don't think that's necessary."

"I appreciate it," Ella said, and Rhodes thought she really meant it.

When he'd booked Ella into the jail, Rhodes sat down to write yet another report. Hack wasn't going to stop pestering him, however.

"You never told me that you thought Ella was the robber," he said. "You coulda told me that before you left."

"I didn't want to jinx it," Rhodes said.

"Jinx it? You don't believe in jinxes or haints or any of that stuff."

"Maybe not, but it's better not to take chances. Anyway, now you know."

"You say she confessed?"

"I don't remember saying that."

"Well, did she?"

"More or less. She'll tell us more, I'm sure. She showed me Burt's starter pistol, and I brought that with me."

He'd already logged it in and put it in the evidence room. If Chris could identify it, that would help things along.

"She never hurt anybody," Hack said. "Couldn't have, not with that starter pistol. I bet she didn't even load it with blanks."

"Probably not."

It hadn't been loaded when she showed it to Rhodes, and it didn't appear to have been fired in years.

"You oughta just let her go," Hack said.

"Can't do it. Have to do the job, even if things don't always work out like we want them to."

"I know that. Just seems like a shame, considerin' the circumstances."

"The judge and the jury will have to do that for us. Not our job."

"I know that, too. What I think is, you oughta be doin' somethin' about Burt's murder 'stead of arrestin' his poor old widow."

"That reminds me," Rhodes said. "What about that paperwork Ruth was going to get for me?"

"What paperwork?"

"Burt's phone records. Did she get them?"

"Hard to get that stuff on the weekends," Hack said. "It used to be a whole lot easier before we got all these cell phones and different carriers."

"Sure. In the old days you could just ring up the exchange and ask for Myrt."

"You been listenin' to Fibber McGee again," Hack said.

He was right. Rhodes had subscribed to satellite radio, and he enjoyed listening to the channel that played old-time radio shows when he had the chance. He no longer had much access to the kind of bad old movies he enjoyed, but the radio shows were on twenty-four hours a day.

"You think the phone records would help?" Hack asked.

"Yes, mainly because they'd give me a motive. Or at least point me to something I think could be a motive."

"You gotta know who did it before you need a motive."

"Oh, I already know that," Rhodes said.

Chapter 22

▼

Rhodes hadn't been entirely truthful with Hack. He didn't really know who'd killed Burt Collins, not in the sense that he was a hundred percent certain, but he thought he was on the right track. He even thought he knew what the motive was, but he needed to clear that up. The phone records would've helped, but he probably wouldn't be getting those until the next day at the earliest. While he wanted to make an arrest before then, he didn't want to rush into anything. There was no rush. He didn't think the killer was going to do away with anyone else, just as he didn't think that Burt's death had been premeditated.

Hack tried to pry the name of the suspect out of Rhodes, but it didn't work. Rhodes wasn't going to spill anything prematurely.

"You'll just have to wait," he told Hack. "You'll find out soon enough."

"I want to know before that Jennifer Loam does," Hack said. "It's gettin' to where the news is out on that Web site of hers before I even find out what's goin' on."

"She's a good reporter," Rhodes said.

"She's wormin' things out of Andy, is what she's doin'."

"I wouldn't be surprised," Rhodes said.

The phone rang, and Hack answered. He talked a couple of seconds and then said, "I'll see what he thinks. Hold on."

Hack muted the phone and turned to Rhodes. "This here's Oscar Henderson. He says they're kickin' him out of the hospital and he needs a ride to his store. He says you're the one put him in the ambulance, so you owe him the ride back to his car."

If Oscar was doing well enough to be discharged from the hospital, he'd probably be able to answer a few questions, so Rhodes said, "Tell him I'll see him in five minutes."

Oscar was sitting in a wheelchair in the hospital lobby when Rhodes came in. He had a bandage on his forehead and a grumpy look on his face.

"They say I have to stay in this thing until I'm out of the hospital," Oscar said, patting the arm of the wheelchair. "I can walk just fine, but they're scared I'll fall on my butt and sue 'em for a million dollars."

"You know that's not true," a nurse said as she came up behind Oscar. "I'll wheel you out, and then the sheriff can be responsible for you."

"He owes me money," Oscar said, "so he better treat me right."

"I don't owe you a thing," Rhodes said. "The money's in the evidence locker at the jail."

"My money," Oscar said. "You got it. You owe me."

The nurse gave Rhodes a look that said Oscar was probably crazy, and Rhodes nodded. The nurse grinned and pushed the chair outside with Rhodes trailing along behind her. Oscar complained all the way about how he was perfectly able to walk out on his own two feet, but he seemed happy enough to have Rhodes and the nurse help him out of the chair when they got to the curb. The county car was parked only inches away, and while Oscar was steady enough to get inside by himself, Rhodes kept a hand on his arm anyway, just in case. He made sure that Oscar got in the car safely and fastened his seat belt.

"I feel like a ten-year-old kid," Oscar said.

"Must be nice," Rhodes said. "I feel like I'm about a hundred."

He shut the door and went around to the driver's side to get in. When he was seated and belted, Oscar said, "You really feel like you're a hundred?"

"No," Rhodes said. He started the car and pulled away from the hospital. "I was just kidding. I don't feel like a ten-year-old kid, though. More like about twenty-seven. Old enough to have more sense than to go chasing somebody with a gun through a dark woods at night. Now that's something a ten-year-old might do."

Oscar touched the bandage on his forehead. "I can't argue with that one."

"I didn't think you could. Next time you get the idea to hang around your store with a loaded pistol, do me a favor. Go home. Better yet, leave the pistol at home to start with and don't try catching robbers on your own."

"I got a license," Oscar said.

"You have a license to carry, not to go around playing Dirty Harry."

"Yeah, I know," Oscar said. "It was a dumb thing to do, but I had a feeling the robber might come back to get the money he dropped. I know you can't have a deputy there all the time, so I thought I'd see what I could do."

"What you did was get hurt," Rhodes said, "and it could've been a lot worse. You could've shot somebody. Even a ten-year-old would have better sense than to run through the trees and fire a pistol at somebody."

"Well, that's the thing," Oscar said. "You got me all wrong on that. I didn't fire at anybody."

"The pistol had been fired," Rhodes said. "I checked."

"I didn't say it hadn't been fired. I just don't remember being the one who fired it. I think it must've gone off when I hit my head."

Rhodes could see how that could've happened. He decided to believe it, which would save him from having to charge Oscar with something like discharging a firearm in the city limits. It was a good thing that stupidity wasn't a crime, since Oscar wasn't the only one in town who was guilty of it. Plenty of people were. The jail wouldn't hold all the guilty parties if a law was ever passed against it. Rhodes was afraid he might even get tossed in there himself.

"I'm glad you didn't get hurt any worse than you did," Rhodes said.

"So am I, and I'm glad I didn't hurt anybody. I wouldn't want to have that on my conscience. I hope he doesn't come back again, though. I'm tired of being robbed, and I think Chris likes it even less than I do."

"It's not going to happen again," Rhodes said. "We have somebody in custody."

Oscar looked surprised. "You do?"

"We do. It wasn't a man who robbed you, by the way. It was a woman."

"You mean I might've killed a woman?"

Rhodes didn't think it was likely that Oscar would kill any-body except by accident. The problem was that accidents hap-pened, which is why he'd given Oscar the little lecture.

"Would killing a woman be any worse than killing a man?" Rhodes asked.

Oscar thought about it. "I guess not. Seems worse, somehow, but it's all the same. Somebody dies."

"That's right," Rhodes said. "Somebody dies."

"Sure looked like a man to me," Oscar said after a while.

"It was the disguise. It fooled Chris, too."

"It was a pretty good disguise. Who was it?"

"Ella Collins. You know her?"

"I know Burt. *Knew* Burt, I mean. I hope she wasn't robbing me to pay for his funeral."

"You don't have to worry about that," Rhodes said. "That wasn't it. Not even close."

"What did she rob me for, then?"

"To pay for a haircut," Rhodes said.

Rhodes let Oscar out at the convenience store and stayed there while Oscar went inside to see if his day manager was taking care of things. Oscar seemed to be getting around just fine. Just leaving the hospital had been good for him.

While Oscar was checking on his business, Rhodes thought things over. He still wished he had the phone records, but he could always just ask the person he suspected of getting the call, whether he had the records or not. In fact, just talking to him might be the best approach, and if he got the answer he expected, he wouldn't really need the records.

Oscar wasn't in the store for long, and when he came out, he asked Rhodes what he was still hanging around for. "You told me there wasn't any danger of me getting robbed again, at least not by the same person. Nobody robs me in the daylight anyway. You don't have to stand guard over the place."

"I was waiting for you," Rhodes said. "You didn't think I was going to let you drive home and be a menace to the citizens of Clearview, did you?"

Oscar stiffened. "I can drive just fine."

"Maybe. I'm not offering to chauffeur you anymore. I'm just going to follow you home, so if you run over a fireplug, I'll be there to help you out of the car before you drown."

Oscar didn't smile. "You aren't half as funny as you think you are, you know that?"

"I've had that feeling for a while, but I keep trying."

This time Oscar grinned. "You might as well give it up."

"Can't do it," Rhodes said.

"Too bad," Oscar said.

He got in his car, started it, and drove out of the parking lot, with Rhodes close behind.

Oscar didn't run over a fire hydrant or anything on the way to his house, so Rhodes figured he could get inside and lie down or watch TV or do whatever it was that he did without any help. Rhodes left him there and drove around for a few minutes. He went by a few of the churches, where the parking lots were starting to fill up. Sunday school would be over in a little while, and the main services would be starting. The Methodists always started a half hour earlier than everybody else so they could get out and get to the restaurants before the Baptists did.

Rhodes drove downtown, where it was as quiet as a cemetery.

The only cars he saw were parked in front of the art gallery. Seepy Benton and Eric Stewart were inside, so he parked the car and got out.

"What's up, Sheriff?" Seepy said when Rhodes came into the building.

"I was going to ask you the same thing," Rhodes said.

Neither man was dressed for church. Benton had on jeans and a rumpled white shirt, along with a black fedora that looked as if a horse had sat on it. Stewart wore a pair of khaki pants and a blue work shirt with a button-down collar.

"We're working on art, of course," Benton said. "You tell him, Eric."

"Good morning, Sheriff," Eric said. "Part of the idea of the art conference was that we'd keep some of the work here in the gallery and try to sell it for the artists. Lonnie and I would get a commission, of course, but only a very small one, and it would go to help pay for the next conference."

"So we're choosing which pieces to keep," Seepy said. "Naturally mine will be one of them, but it probably won't be here long. Somebody will snap it up the first day. Maybe the first hour. You could get ahead of them, though. We haven't put prices on the pictures yet, so I can make you a really good deal."

"I'll think about it," Rhodes said. He did, and an excuse came to him. "Too bad it has that streak of paint across it."

"We might be able to clean it off," Eric said. "I'm going to see what I can do."

"What about the others?" Rhodes asked to change the subject.

"I'll have to start with just one. I'll try cleaning a small spot and move on from there. Or not, if it can't be done. I'm not a professional restorer, and to be honest about it, these paintings might not be worth the trouble."

"Except for mine," Seepy said.

"Naturally," Eric said, rolling his eyes. "That's probably not why the sheriff stopped by, though. Is it, Sheriff?"

"No, but it's interesting. When I saw you in here, I thought it might be a good time to ask a couple of questions about yesterday."

"What about yesterday?"

"The morning event, where you were giving out the awards. Did everybody come at once, or was it a come-and-go affair?"

"There were a few people waiting outside when I opened the doors," Eric said, "but it was come-and-go."

"You happen to remember who they were?"

"No. I just came out of my apartment and opened the door from inside. The ones who were waiting came in. I wasn't taking names or anything like that."

"And after that people were drifting in and out all morning," Rhodes said.

"That's right. Why?"

"I'm still thinking about how that bust might have gotten into the other part of the building. You didn't see anybody go back there, did you?"

"No, but it would've been easy for someone to put it there, if that's what you mean. There were quite a few people milling around in here, and it wouldn't have taken long for somebody to walk into the other room, stash the bust, and come back out here. We've talked about that, and I still think that thing could've been back there for a while. Maybe it came in with some other things and got shelved. It's obviously mass-produced, though why anybody would want to produce it is beyond me."

Rhodes saw that he wasn't going to get anywhere with that line of talk, so he asked Seepy if he'd been waiting outside when the doors opened.

Seepy laughed. "I don't get up that early. I came in about half an hour after things got started."

"Was it crowded?"

"Sort of. Not wall to wall, but there must have been fifteen or twenty people."

"Look," Eric said, breaking in. "You have to realize that everybody was interested in the paintings and who got ribbons. They were especially interested in how their own paintings had done. Nobody was watching anybody else to see if they left the room."

That was about what Rhodes had expected. It would've been too much to hope that either Seepy or Eric had noticed someone going into the other part of the building. Of course, there was one person who definitely could've put the bust on the shelf without anyone knowing, and that was Eric. He lived there, after all. Rhodes, however, had decided that Eric wasn't the guilty party. He just wanted to be sure that everyone else had access.

"Did anybody besides the artists come to see the exhibit?" Rhodes asked.

"Sure," Seepy said. "People around here aren't as uncultured as you think. We had a good many visitors who didn't have any connection to the conference or the show. Did you have anybody in mind?"

"No," Rhodes said. "I was just wondering. Where's Don Mc-Claren, by the way? I thought he was one of the judges."

"He was," Eric said, "but he's in church this morning. Me, I'm pretty much home-churched, so I had time to do this."

"You might have noticed that there aren't any synagogues in Clearview," Seepy said. "I study the Torah on my own. I've even written articles on it. Right now, though, I'm writing a little textbook on group theory, symmetry, permutations, and Rubik's Cube."

Rhodes could tell that he'd lost control of the conversation, if he'd ever had it. He said, "Hack told me the other day that he saw something about a man who could solve three Rubik's Cubes while he was juggling them."

"That's nothing," Benton said. "I can swallow a Rubik's Cube, and when it comes out the other end, it's solved."

"Too much information," Rhodes said.

"Performance art," Eric said. "I wonder if we could figure out some way to have you do it here at the gallery."

"YouTube," Benton said. "It would be viral within minutes."

Rhodes held up a hand before things could go any further. "Somebody told me this morning that I wasn't nearly as funny as I thought I was, but you two make me seem like a professional comedian."

"That wasn't my best stuff," Seepy said. "I'm saving that for my singing act."

Rhodes thought it wouldn't be kind to mention that Seepy no longer had a regular gig, so he just thanked both men for their help and started to leave.

Seepy stopped him. "Have you given any thought to making me an honorary deputy? On a permanent basis?"

"No," Rhodes said. "I forgot all about it."

"Now that you remember, what do you think about the idea?"

"What do you think about raising money for the department?"

"I think I can do it," Seepy said. "I told you that I don't like doing it, but now that I've thought about it, I have something that will work."

Rhodes was curious. "What would that be? And don't tell me it's a video of your Rubik's Cube act."

"That would do it, but I'm too modest for that. I was thinking that instead of that, I could donate the profits from the sale of my artwork and my textbook to the department."

"And how much do you think that might come to?"

"It could be thousands."

"Or not," Rhodes said.

"Yeah," Seepy said, "there's that."

The drive to the Patel hotel didn't take long. Rhodes spent the brief time wondering about the color of so many of the new hotels that had sprung up. It wasn't exactly yellow, but it wasn't gold, either. Rhodes couldn't think of anything to call it. Whatever it was, it went well with the red tile roofs, and it was distinctive enough so that a traveler could spot the hotel easily from the highway. Not that spotting a three-story building in Clearview would've been difficult in any event, since there weren't any others.

This time when Rhodes entered the lobby he saw Manish's wife, Sunny, at the reception desk. He'd known one of the family would be there. The Patels didn't know about taking a day off from work. He had no idea what their religious affiliations were, if any, but he knew that any day of the week he could find some or all of the family members keeping busy around the hotel. It took a lot of keeping busy to take care of a hotel, and the Patels were willing to do whatever it took.

Sunny had black hair, brown skin, and very white teeth. She

wore a dark blue blouse with her name tag pinned on it. She gave Rhodes a smile and asked if he wanted a bagel.

"We have not quite cleaned up our continental breakfast yet," she said, "and I'm sure there are some bagels and cream cheese left."

A bagel spread with cream cheese was quite a temptation, but Rhodes didn't think it would be a good idea. He said, "Thanks. That's the best offer I've had all day, but I'd better not. I'd like to speak to your husband if he's around."

Sunny gave Rhodes another bright smile. "Oh, yes. He is around. He is always around. There is a small problem with the air conditioner in two-thirty-three. I will show you where it is."

"That's all right," Rhodes said. "I can find it."

"It will be to the left when you get off the elevator," Sunny said.

Rhodes thanked her and rode the elevator to the second floor. He knew it would've been better for him to take the stairs. He probably needed the exercise, but the elevator was right there, too handy to pass up.

The second-floor hallway was well lit, and Rhodes had no trouble finding the room. The door was open, so Rhodes looked inside. Patel wore a leather tool belt, and he had the cover off the air conditioner. He had a screwdriver in one hand and was leaning over to look at something that Rhodes couldn't see.

Rhodes tapped on the door with his knuckles. Patel straightened and turned around.

"Good morning," Rhodes said. "Need any help fixing that thing?"

It was just something to say. Rhodes had no more idea of how to repair an air conditioner than he did about how to solve Rubik's

Cube the conventional way, much less while juggling it or by some even more bizarre Seepy Benton method that didn't bear thinking about.

"A loose connection," Patel said. "Nothing more. Easy to fix." He stuck the screwdriver in the tool belt and put the cover back on the air conditioner. "Did you see Sunny when you came in?"

"Yes," Rhodes said. "She offered me a bagel."

"I hope you accepted."

"No," Rhodes said. "I've already eaten. I didn't come to bum a free meal anyway. I came to talk to you."

"Then I am honored. What did you want to talk about?"

"Burt Collins," Rhodes said.

Chapter 23

▼

Patel and Rhodes went down to the office where they'd talked before. Patel removed the tool belt and put it on the floor by his desk while Rhodes looked at the framed pictures of Gujarat and thought about how far away he was from the colorful world. It seemed a shame to have to bring up the subject of murder in these surroundings, but that was what Rhodes had come to discuss.

After they'd taken seats, Patel asked if Rhodes was sure he didn't want a bagel.

"They get stale," Patel said. "We like to get fresh ones every day."

Rhodes had a hard time imagining people in Clearview eating bagels, except for Seepy Benton. He wondered where Patel even found fresh bagels in Clearview.

"Thanks," Rhodes said, "but I'd better skip it. I'm trying not to gain any weight."

"We have low-fat cream cheese."

Rhodes grinned. "I appreciate the offer, but I'm not here to eat."

"I know," Patel said. "It is just that when the sheriff comes to call and says he needs to talk, I get nervous."

"No need to be nervous," Rhodes said.

"Burt Collins makes me nervous, or he did. Now, talking about him does the same thing. I thought we covered that subject the last time you were here."

"We did, but now we need to cover a little more of it."

Patel shifted in his chair and looked uncomfortable, and while he didn't object, it was clear that Burt Collins wasn't his favorite topic.

"This won't take long," Rhodes said. "You told me yesterday you didn't wish Burt any harm, even though you hadn't forgotten what he'd done to your building."

"That is true," Patel said. "The words he wrote were impossible for me to forget, but they are no longer there. So I have put them out of my mind."

"No need to think about them now, either. This is about Burt, not what he wrote. Did he call here on Friday night?"

"Why would he call here?"

"I think I know why, but first I have to be sure that he called."

"I was not answering calls on Friday night, and I never check to see who called. We do not keep a record of that. We keep a record of outgoing calls, however."

"Those aren't the ones I'm interested in," Rhodes said. "I wouldn't need the records if you'd recognized Burt's voice."

"It is possible that I might have," Patel said, "had I been taking the calls. I do not wish to speak ill of the dead, but he was a gruff, abrupt man, and speaking to him was never pleasant. Not under the circumstances in which I encountered him."

"Who was taking calls Friday night?"

"I believe Sunny was on the desk."

"Then she's the one I need to talk to. Would it be all right if she came in here?"

Patel frowned. "Is that really necessary?"

Rhodes didn't even have to think about it. "No, not really, but she might tell me something I want to know. You might say that it's not necessary, but important."

Patel nodded. "If it is important to you, I will call Sunny."

Like the sheriff's department and the Beauty Shack, the hotel also had old-fashioned landline phones. Patel picked up the receiver and punched a button. When his wife answered, he asked her to get Jack to take over at the desk and come to the office. Rhodes and Patel passed an uncomfortable five minutes while they waited. Rhodes wished he'd accepted the bagel.

Sunny came in with a smile, and Patel told her that Rhodes had a question for her about a call she might have gotten on Friday night.

"I don't know if you can answer," Rhodes said, "but I thought I'd give it a try."

"I will help you if I can," Sunny said.

"Do you get many calls?" Rhodes asked.

"Not many," Sunny said. "Maybe two or three in the evenings. I think we had at least that many on Friday. That was easy to answer. Was that your question?"

"Not the main one. You remember Burt Collins?"

Sunny looked at her husband, who gave a slight nod.

"I remember him," Sunny said. "I would rather that I didn't, but I do."

"Then here's my question," Rhodes said. "Did he call here Friday afternoon or evening?"

Again Patel gave Sunny a slight nod. She said, "I could not be certain that he did."

"But you think so?"

"One of the callers sounded like him, but if I were asked to swear in court, that would not be possible."

"It won't go to court," Rhodes said. "This is just for my ears only."

"Then I would say that yes, he called."

"I underestimated the number of questions I have," Rhodes said. "Here's one more. I believe some of the artists in town for the conference are staying here. Did he call one of them?"

"I would just be relying on my memory," Sunny said.

"I'm sure you have a good memory," Rhodes told her.

Sunny smiled. "Thank you. He did ask for one of our guests by name."

"You remember the name, too, I'll bet."

"Yes," Sunny said.

This was turning out to be like a conversation with Hack and Lawton, and Rhodes thought that Sunny was enjoying the game as much as they did. It was time to bring it to an end, however.

"Marilyn Bradley," Rhodes said.

"Yes," Sunny said. "That is the one."

Marilyn Bradley had made a mistake. Rhodes hadn't spotted it at first, but he'd caught it later on. It wasn't enough of a mistake to convict her of Burt Collins's murder, but it had given Rhodes a place to start, and he'd worked backward to find a motive. He'd found that, too, or so he thought, but he needed the phone call to confirm it.

Rhodes stood up and thanked the Patels for their help.

"Is Marilyn Bradley still here?" he asked.

"She has not checked out," Sunny said. She looked at a clock sitting on the desk. "It is an hour until checkout time."

"I'd better talk to her, then," Rhodes said. "What room is she in?"

"I believe three-fifteen," Sunny said.

"Is there going to be trouble?" Manish asked. "I would not like for there to be trouble. I would not like for my guests to be disturbed."

"I'll try not to disturb them," Rhodes said.

"This is about Burt Collins, obviously. Did she kill him?"

"I think she might have," Rhodes said.

Manish sighed. "Very well. Do you wish me to go with you to the room?"

"No, that won't be necessary. I do need to make a call first, though. If she tries to check out before I get back, don't let her leave."

"She can check out on the TV," Manish said. "We would not see her. I would not like to confront her, in any case. What would I say?"

"You don't have to confront her," Rhodes said. "Just watch the back door. If she leaves, let me know. I'll be right back."

Rhodes left the office and went out to the county car. He had a good view of the entrance to the hotel, and if Marilyn came out that way, he'd see her.

He got on the radio, called Hack, and asked which deputy was closest to the hotel.

"Buddy's on the way back from Obert. Had a little fracas over there between a couple of neighbors, but it's all settled now."

Rhodes didn't bother to ask what kind of fracas. It would take forty minutes to draw the story out of Hack.

"You want him to stop at the hotel?" Hack asked.

"I do," Rhodes said.

"I'll tell him," Hack said.

Rhodes racked the mic and waited. Nobody left the hotel, and in a couple of minutes Buddy came into the parking lot and parked beside Rhodes.

"Hack said you needed me," Buddy said when he got out of the car. "What's the beef?"

The phrase sounded like something out of the previous century, and Rhodes wondered, as he occasionally did, where Buddy picked up his cop slang.

"First, tell me what happened in Obert," Rhodes said. He could get the story from Buddy in a lot less time than he'd ever worm it out of Hack.

"It was a backyard chicken thing," Buddy said.

Rhodes nodded. They'd had some of those before, not to mention the big stink with the chicken farms at Mount Enterprise. There was still an occasional complaint about the smell out that way, but for the most part the new owner had taken care of things.

Buddy rested his rump against the side of Rhodes's county car. "This wasn't the usual complaint about a loud rooster early in the morning. Some fella named Roger Belvin claimed that his neighbor's dog was sneaking into his backyard chicken run at night and killing his hens. Neighbor's name was Claude Washburn, and he said it wasn't his dog doing it but a coyote. Said he heard coyotes howling every night, and besides, his dog's in a fenced yard. Belvin said the dog jumped the fence, and they got into it. Washburn's wife called it in, and I got there before there was any damage done."

"Did you manage to settle it?"

"Sure," Buddy said. "I told 'em to show me the tracks if there were any, which there were, right there in the chicken run. They were coyote tracks."

"Hard to tell the difference between a dog's track and a coyote's track," Rhodes said.

"Takes an expert," Buddy said. "I'm one of 'em." He grinned. "Not really. It's easy to tell if you know what you're looking for. It's all in the shape of the paw. We went and looked in Washburn's yard and found some tracks his dog made, and I showed Washburn and Belvin the difference between them and the coyote tracks. Problem solved. Except now Washburn's got to watch out for coyotes at night. Now, what's the beef here?"

"I'm going to see a suspect, maybe make an arrest," Rhodes said. "You can back me up."

Buddy hitched up his utility belt. "I'm ready for that. Who's the perp?"

"A woman named Marilyn Bradley. I think she might've killed Burt Collins."

Buddy fingered the butt of his service weapon. "Will we be doing this the easy way or the hard way?"

"You never know," Rhodes said, "but let's hope for the easy way. She doesn't know I suspect her."

"Okay," Buddy said, pushing himself away from the car. "Let's do it."

They went into the hotel. Sunny and Manish were both at the desk, and Rhodes stopped to ask if anything had happened with Marilyn while he was outside.

"She has not checked out on the TV," Manish said, "and she has not left the hotel."

"Good," Rhodes said. "Room three-fifteen, right?"

"That is correct. I checked to be sure. Do you want a key?"

Rhodes didn't think he'd need a key, but as he'd told Buddy, you never know.

"Might be a good idea," he said, and Patel handed him a thin piece of plastic. Rhodes slipped it into his shirt pocket and joined Buddy, who was waiting at the elevator. Rhodes didn't want to take any chances on Marilyn getting past them, so he told Buddy to take the stairs to the third floor.

"You can use the exercise," Rhodes said, though it plainly wasn't true. Buddy was stick thin. "I'll take the elevator."

Buddy didn't argue. He just asked what the suspect looked like.

"You can't miss her," Rhodes said. "She has orange hair."

"Orange?"

"Very."

Buddy grinned, nodded, and went through the doorway that led to the stairs. Rhodes punched the elevator button. He expected the doors to open, but they didn't. He glanced up at the lights above the door. The elevator was in use on the second floor, but it wasn't long before he heard it start to descend. The doors opened, and Rhodes saw a man, a woman, three children all under the age of ten, and several suitcases. He stood aside and held the door while they got organized and got out of the elevator. The children gave the badge holder on his belt some curious looks, but the adults didn't notice. When they cleared the door, Rhodes got in and punched the button for three. He figured Buddy was nearly at the top of the stairs.

When the elevator passed the second floor, Rhodes heard a metallic clanging, and he put a hand out to touch the side of the elevator to make sure it wasn't about to fall apart.

It wasn't, and in a couple of seconds the doors opened onto the third floor. Rhodes looked around for Buddy, but the hallway was empty.

Room three-fifteen was just past the door to the stairway. The door to the room was closed, and Rhodes had a bad feeling about that. He bent down and got his pistol from the ankle holster, then walked to the room and knocked.

He got no answer to his knock, so he used the key, standing to the side as he pushed the door open. The room was empty. He did a quick check of the bathroom to be sure. Nobody there. He noticed that the curtain was drawn back on the big window that looked out into the parking lot. He could look right out and see the two county cars, which is what Marilyn Bradley must have done. She'd seen Rhodes and Buddy jawing away and decided it was time to get out of town.

Thinking of Buddy, Rhodes remembered the metallic noise. He left the room and went to the stairs. He pushed the metal door open, but he didn't see Buddy at first. He looked down and saw the deputy lying on the landing at the foot of the first short flight of stairs.

Rhodes stuck his pistol in his back pocket before he went down and knelt by Buddy, who looked up at him and said, "She hit me with the door."

That must have been the noise Rhodes had heard.

"It was an accident," Buddy said. He had a kind of a horizontal dent just about in the middle of his forehead where the edge of the door had hit him. "Wrong place, wrong time."

Same result as if it had been deliberate, Rhodes thought.

"You stay put," he said. "I'll get an ambulance here."

"I'm okay," Buddy said. "Just bunged up some. Help me get up."

252

"Stay right there. That's an order. You might be hurt worse than you know."

Buddy didn't argue about it. Rhodes grabbed a pair of his handcuffs, jammed them in a front pocket, and ran on down the stairs. When he came out into the hall by the elevator, he looked toward the lobby. Manish Patel pointed to the back door, and Rhodes went outside. He saw a black Toyota Prius pulling out of a parking space. The driver had orange hair.

Rhodes had three choices. He could let the car go, he could throw himself in front of it and hope Marilyn would stop, or he could shoot.

His life wasn't in any danger, so he didn't like the idea of shooting.

He didn't care for the idea of throwing himself in front of the car, either. He didn't think Marilyn would stop.

So he let her go.

Chapter 24

▼

Rhodes ran back through the hotel to the county car. As he passed the desk, he called out to the Patels.

"Call 911. My deputy's on the stairs, third floor."

Rhodes rushed out the front door and jumped into the county car. Marilyn was just pulling out onto the highway. Instead of heading back into town, she turned toward Obert. Rhodes was glad of that because it meant he wouldn't be chasing her through the after-church traffic.

He started the car and rolled out of the lot after Marilyn. He gave Hack a call on the radio to give him his location and to let him know he was chasing a suspect.

"Ruth's been in Milsby," Hack said. "She's on the way back. Want me to send her?"

"Yes," Rhodes said. "I'll try to make the stop, but I might need some backup."

He didn't give Hack a chance to ask anything more. He had

other things to do. Marilyn was a quarter of a mile ahead of him, driving a little over the speed limit. Rhodes didn't think he'd have any trouble overtaking her. The Prius was great for gas mileage, but it couldn't match the Dodge for speed and power.

Marilyn passed one of the old oil fields from which the forest of derricks had long since disappeared but where some of the wells were still producing even after a hundred years. Not much, but a little, and a little oil was better than none.

Rhodes caught up with her just past the oil field. He turned on his flashers, but Marilyn didn't stop. Instead, she increased her speed.

Rhodes knew she'd seen him, so he turned on the siren to give her another chance to stop. She paid no attention. He hadn't really expected her to.

Since they were on a long, straight stretch of road with no cars headed in their direction, Rhodes pulled into the left lane and mashed down the accelerator. In a couple of seconds he was right alongside Marilyn. He looked over at her and motioned for her to pull over on the shoulder. She ignored him and drove faster.

Rhodes let her pull ahead of him. When he'd dropped back behind her, he considered his options. He knew Marilyn couldn't outrun him, but he couldn't just chase her until she ran out of gas. Considering the difference in the gas mileage of a Prius and a big-engine Dodge, Rhodes was a lot more likely to run out of gas than Marilyn was. And even though the towns ahead of them were small, she was still likely to be a danger to herself and others if she kept going.

Rhodes decided that his best bet was a PIT stop, which was how he referred to the Pursuit Intervention Technique. The highway was clear, the road was level, and there was plenty of room on both sides.

It should be simple enough to perform the maneuver, but it might not work, considering the fact that the Prius was a front-wheel-drive vehicle. A really good driver could regain control of the car and start back in the opposite direction. Rhodes hoped Marilyn wasn't a really good driver.

He pulled into the left lane again and glanced at the speedometer. Almost sixty-five. He started to pull alongside Marilyn again. He got as close to her car as he dared, and as soon as the nose of the county car was even with the Prius's front door, Rhodes applied the brake.

The big Dodge didn't slow much, and Rhodes pulled the steering wheel hard to the right, slamming the front part of the Dodge against the rear quarter of the Prius.

Metal crashed and squealed, Rhodes braked the Dodge, and the Prius spun down the road. Marilyn couldn't regain control, and the Prius spun around three times before it left the road and slid into the ditch on the left-hand side. Rhodes drove off the road, stopped, and jumped out of his car. He ran to the Prius.

Marilyn sat behind the wheel, looking dazed. The car's air bag had deployed. Rhodes stuck the pistol back in his pocket and opened the door. Marilyn turned her head toward him but didn't speak. Rhodes pulled her from the car and got the cuffs from his front pocket. She didn't resist when he cuffed her arms behind her.

Just as he got that done, Ruth Grady drove up. She stopped near Rhodes's car and got out.

"Need any help?" she asked.

"I think everything's under control," Rhodes told her. "I need to give her the Miranda warning."

He recited the warning to Marilyn and asked if she understood it. She nodded.

"I'd like to hear you say it," he told her. "Did you understand?"

"Yes," she said. Her face was powdered and red from the air bag. "I understand."

Rhodes turned to Ruth. "I'll let you transport the prisoner to the jail, though. I'm going to check on Buddy. He might be hurt."

"Where is he?"

"He's at the hotel back near town. Fell down some stairs. He'll be okay."

"You think your car is driveable?"

"The fender's a little crushed, but that's all. The commissioners are going to be upset, though. I seem to have banged up a lot of cars lately."

"They'll get over it," Ruth said. "They always do. What are the charges against the prisoner?"

"We can start with theft of services," Rhodes said. "I don't think Ms. Bradley paid her hotel bill."

Manish Patel was apologetic. "I am sorry I allowed her to escape, but I didn't know if she was armed." He smiled. "Besides, she had paid her bill."

"You're joking," Rhodes said.

"No, I am not. She checked out on the TV in her room. The bill is charged to her credit card."

"I have a feeling she won't be paying off her card this month," Rhodes said, thinking that he'd have to come up with a different charge to hold Marilyn on. Assaulting an officer would do for a start. "I guess the card company will make good on the charges."

He and Patel were in the office again, talking over what had just happened. The paramedics had taken Buddy to the hospital for observation. He didn't seem to have any broken bones, but he probably had a mild concussion, along with a few bruises and contusions, so they'd keep him for several hours if not overnight. Buddy had protested the whole time they were putting him into the ambulance, but it didn't do him any good.

"If she is a killer who has been brought to justice," Patel said, "then I suppose I can forgo collecting a few dollars. I hope she will be punished."

"She will be," Rhodes said. "Or I hope she will. There's one little problem."

"And what is that?"

"We have to prove she did it," Rhodes said.

Ruth Grady put Marilyn Bradley in the interview room. Rhodes watched through the two-way mirror as Marilyn sat at the old wooden table with the scarred top. Ruth left the room and joined Rhodes.

Marilyn didn't look much the worse for her encounter with the Prius's air bag, Rhodes thought, but she didn't seem a bit happy about being where she was. Rhodes didn't blame her. In her place, he'd have been unhappy, too.

"You going to let her wait a while?" Ruth asked.

"Just a couple of minutes," Rhodes said. "I think she'll tell me what I want to know."

"What if she asks for a lawyer?"

Rhodes shrugged. "Then we'll have to stop talking."

"What if she doesn't ask for a lawyer but doesn't confess?"

"You're just a little ray of sunshine," Rhodes said, and Ruth grinned.

In the interview room, Marilyn looked at the mirror, looked at the other walls, looked at the ceiling. She didn't seem nervous, just unhappy.

"You think she will?" Ruth asked. "Ask for a lawyer, I mean."

"We'll see," Rhodes said. "Wish me luck."

"Luck," Ruth said, and Rhodes went into the room.

He sat in the chair opposite Marilyn and said, "You almost got away from me."

"You wrecked my car," she said. "Sage Barton couldn't have done it better."

Rhodes wished she hadn't brought up Sage Barton. He didn't want to talk about that.

"I hope the county plans to pay for the car," Marilyn continued. "It's a very nice one."

"We can talk about that if you want to," Rhodes said. He took a small digital recorder from his pocket and set it on the table. "Before we get started, though, you should know that I'm going to record our conversation."

"Go ahead," Marilyn said. "I don't care."

Rhodes turned on the recorder, said a few words, and played them back to be sure the recorder was working. He didn't trust technology to work more than half the time, but the recorder was fine.

"Now that I know the recorder's doing its job," he said, "I should tell you that you have a right to have a lawyer present if you want one."

Marilyn gave a wry grin. "I have a right to remain silent, too. You told me that. It seems as if I have a lot of rights."

"That's what the justice system is all about," Rhodes said. "Fairness."

"Fairness? You want to tell that to all those innocent people who spend years on Death Row? How many have been freed in Texas now?"

"Quite a few," Rhodes said, "but not a one from this county."

"That's not going to help me, though, is it."

"Probably not, but you won't get the death penalty. What you did wasn't premeditated, was it?"

"How do you know what I did? I might not have done anything. I didn't skip on my hotel bill, you know."

"I know, but you did assault an officer."

"That was an accident," Marilyn said. "He was in the way. They need a better door-closer, or whatever those things are called. That door shouldn't have opened that fast."

Rhodes had gone by the hospital after leaving the hotel. Buddy was sitting up in bed and ready to leave. He'd told Rhodes what had happened. Just as he'd pulled on the door to open it, Marilyn had pushed it from the other side. His pulling along with her pushing had caused the door to crack him a good one in the forehead.

"My deputy would agree with you," Rhodes said, "but you hurt him because you were running. You'd seen us in the parking lot, and since you knew what we were there for, you thought you'd better leave town fast."

"I wanted to get home in time for lunch," Marilyn said.

"Nice try," Rhodes told her. "It won't work, though. I know you killed Burt Collins, and I can prove it."

"How?" Marilyn asked. She looked genuinely curious.

Rhodes decided he'd tell her. It wouldn't do any harm.

"You made a big mistake the other night at the reception when we were talking about the bust that the killer used to hit Burt.

You said that a bust of a NASCAR driver wasn't art. Nobody knew that a bust of a NASCAR driver was the murder weapon. Some people knew it was a bust, but nobody knew who it was."

Actually, Seepy Benton had known, but he was the only person outside the department who did. Rhodes trusted him not to talk, just as he trusted his deputies. Even Eric Stewart hadn't known, and he'd seen the bust. Rhodes hadn't enlightened him.

"I didn't say that."

"You did, and there are witnesses. That's not all, though. Burt was blackmailing you."

"He . . . how do you know that?"

Rhodes hadn't known it, but he'd suspected it. He said, "You weren't going to win any awards, and you knew it. You were upset and jealous. It wasn't the first time you hadn't won, or even the second or third. Maybe you thought the judges weren't fair to you."

"They weren't. My art is beautiful. So much of what was in the gallery was just . . . trash."

That was one way to look at it. Eye of the beholder, Rhodes supposed.

"Anyway," he said, "you're the one who defaced the paintings. You got back early and didn't think anyone would see you. Nobody would have if Burt hadn't happened by. He told us he didn't do it, but nobody believed him. You tossed the spray-paint can in the trash and let him take the blame. Were you wearing gloves?"

Marilyn leaned back from the table and slumped in her chair. "I keep disposable gloves in my purse. I need them sometimes when I'm painting."

Rhodes nodded. "You saw people coming back, and you hid in the antiques store. All you had to do was wait until people were in the room. Then you could come back out and mingle.

Nobody would notice where you came from. Maybe you hoped Burt would get away before he got caught, but he didn't. He was happy to take the blame for defacing the art because he thought he might be able to get some money from you. He called the hotel later and asked for your room. The desk clerk told me that this morning."

Rhodes didn't know how well Sunny Patel's testimony about that would hold up, but he wouldn't have to worry about it if Marilyn would give him a confession.

"He told you to come to his house," Rhodes said. "To talk. He didn't want to be seen at the hotel. When he asked you for money to keep quiet, you got upset. That's when you hit him with the bust."

"He was a terrible man," Marilyn said, "but at least his house was a minor work of art. Or so I thought."

"He didn't think it was art," Rhodes said. "He just used the cheapest paint he could get."

"He told me that and said his house was ugly. He hated it. That's why I hit him, you know. Not because he asked me for money. He asked for money, all right, and he said if I didn't give it to him, he'd tell everybody what I'd done. He said I was crazy, too. Not because of spraying the paintings but because I didn't know anything about what was pretty and what wasn't. He said that the paintings in the gallery were awful, especially the one with the crazy stairs. He said he didn't blame me for trying to paint over it. He laughed about that, and I got upset. I grabbed that bust, and it scared him. He turned to run, and I hit him. I didn't mean to kill him."

Rhodes believed her. Maybe the district attorney would, too, but Rhodes doubted it.

"Death shouldn't be like that," Marilyn said. "So quick and ugly. It should be beautiful, a work of art, like life. Do you know John Keats?"

Rhodes was tempted to say that nobody by that name lived in Clearview, but he didn't see any need to play dumb. Keats was another poet he remembered from high school.

"He wrote a poem about a bird," Rhodes said.

Marilyn seemed surprised that he knew. "That's right. There's a line in that poem about being 'half in love with easeful death.' I've always thought that death could be easeful and artful, not painful and messy. I made a mess of things, though, didn't I. With my life and with Mr. Collins's, too."

"That sounds about right," Rhodes said.

"Not entirely, though," Marilyn said. "He didn't look dead, lying there. He looked like an artful arrangement, like something I'd created, and I had, but I knew I couldn't take credit for it."

"So you left," Rhodes said.

"I took the bust with me. I don't know why, because then I had to get rid of it. I cleaned it up and put it in the antiques shop before the awards."

"Not a bad idea, sticking it there," Rhodes said. "If Seepy Benton hadn't spotted it, it might have sat there for years."

The mention of Seepy Benton's name caused Marilyn to sit up straighter in the chair.

"He's the one who found it? The man knows nothing about art. A cross-section of a seashell? Give me a break."

She wasn't likely to get a break, Rhodes thought. Not for a long time.

*   *   *

Ruth took Marilyn back to her cell, and Rhodes went back to the office area to put away the recorder until someone could transcribe the interview and get Marilyn to sign it. Hack and Lawton were waiting for him.

"Looks like you've solved another big case," Hack said. "Some real crime-bustin' goin' on around here."

"I try," Rhodes said.

"Yeah, well, about that," Hack said.

"About trying?"

"About crime-bustin'," Lawton said, then shut up when Hack looked at him.

"Sometime I wonder who's the dispatcher around here," Hack said. "Me or him."

Rhodes kept quiet. He wasn't going to take sides.

"It ain't really a crime," Lawton said, proving that he wasn't to be intimidated.

"Could be," Hack said. "Loose donkeys could be a crime."

"Loose donkeys?" Rhodes said. "Again?"

"That's right, down toward Able Terrell's compound. Maybe they're Able's mules. You could ask."

"Me?" Rhodes said. "What about Alton Boyd?"

"He's already on the way. He needs some help."

"What about Ruth?"

"What about me?" Ruth asked, coming from the cellblock.

"You need to get down to Thurston," Hack said. "Miz Annie Galloway says there's a stranger been hanging around her house. She wants somebody to take a look. Said she didn't want me sending any man 'cause the prowler might try to trick her into thinkin' he's the law. Miz Galloway lives right on the main street, down past Barrett's store."

"I'll get right on it," Ruth said, and she headed on out the door.

"This isn't going to be like Mrs. Harbison's peephole again, is it?" Rhodes asked.

Hack wouldn't commit himself. "Can't say. Could be, but maybe not."

Rhodes wished he was the one checking on it, but he had another assignment.

"Donkeys," he said.

"That's right," Hack said. "Donkeys. Better take your lariat rope with you."

"Watch out and don't let one of 'em kick you," Lawton said.

"Donkeys," Rhodes said, and he followed Ruth out the door.